Determined Hearts

Diana Stout

Cover design Cover Bistro
Formatting by Sharpened Pencils Productions LLC

Originally published as *The Man on the Romance Cover*
a Moonlight Romance by Starlog Press
Copyright © 1993 Diana Fox

Reprinted as *Determined Hearts*, a Smashwords Edition
Copyright © 2014 Diana Fox

Reprinted as Determined Hearts, a Kindle Edition
Copyright © 2016 Diana Stout
AISN: B01D3UMAT2

ISBN-13: 978-0-9974223-1-3 (Paperback)

DEDICATION

To Milburn Smith, my first editor, whose praise still resonates, even after all these years..

CONTENTS

ACKNOWLEDGMENTS

I want to give a special thank you to writer, Maris Soule, who was my first mentor, and who has been one of my strongest cheerleaders throughout the years. I want to thank Anne Stone, as well, for the fine catches she made; you have quite the skill, my friend. And, I wish to thank all my writing sisters in the Mid-Michigan chapter of Romance Writers of America – you weren't there when I published my first book, but you've certainly been there for my recent books.

CHAPTER 1

High in the Salmon River Mountains of Idaho, Jennifer Frost squinted her eyes against flying dust the helicopter blades stirred up and shouted to the pilot, handing him a fat, white envelope. "Here's your payment. No matter what happens you don't come back for me until the two weeks are up. You got that?"

Smitty nodded once and shouted back, "I hear you loud and clear." Pulling his headset back over his ears, he gave her the thumbs-up signal and she backed away.

In no time, the helicopter disappeared beyond the forest of lodgepole pines. Seconds later, the peaceful sounds of the forest returned.

Her only link to civilization was gone.

She grinned. It'd been three months since her last wilderness excursion, and it had been a disappointment. She'd accompanied a recording star to a dude ranch and found it had more modern trappings than a plush hotel. This place, however, suited her.

Turning around, she faced the rustic log cabin that had been built by Hawk Hunter, former romance cover model, now recluse, and wondered how long she'd have to wait before meeting him. Smitty had told her it wouldn't be any longer than an hour.

Sitting down on her luggage, facing the mountains, she decided to wait for him there. She didn't want to trespass into the cabin uninvited; the last thing she wanted to do was have him distrusting her.

Jennifer watched squirrels chase one another in the tall poplar trees. Beyond the trees stretched a panoramic view of the mountains, which she'd photograph later when the sun wasn't straight overhead.

Dusk and dawn provided the perfect light for outdoor pictures as the noon sun washed colors together. As a photographer, she'd seen a variety of settings, but few could compare to the landscape before her. Although it was late August, snow already dusted the upper peaks of the distant mountain range. The valley below was a sea of green forest, with a few pockets of yellow and red, hinting at the riot of color that would arrive in another few weeks. Except for the cabin behind her, the area was remote, without a trace of civilization—just the way she liked it.

Two blissful weeks. She almost regretted she'd be spending the time with someone else. Needing some time alone, she would have enjoyed the solitude. Nevertheless, she was going to enjoy herself totally despite the fact her boss, Bob Edwards, editor of *Personality*, wanted this to be the most thorough interview she'd ever conducted.

There was no question in her mind—she had to do well on this assignment. All she'd ever wanted to do was be a wildlife photographer. Unfortunately, early on, she had learned she couldn't just step into a job like that. She had to work her way up and prove that she was good at it. But, then she'd been caught in the proverbial circle; she couldn't prove she was good until she got assignments, and she couldn't get assignments because she hadn't proven her ability.

Now, this was her opportunity—probably the only one she'd have in a long time to come—to do just that. When Edwards told her Hawk was working here, saving eagles, and that he would be their next feature in the "Where Are They Now? " celebrity series column, she'd seen this as her chance to do a wildlife assignment. She'd gone to *Wildlife and Wilderness* and received the go-ahead to do a feature on the eagles and the work Hawk was doing.

Later when Edwards found out about the second assignment she'd arranged, he made it clear to her that *Personality* came first. If she returned to New York without the piece he wanted, her career in the publishing industry—in any aspect—would be over, and her wildlife feature would never appear. He'd not only fire her, but make sure no one else hired her either.

She'd succeed, despite Edwards and any other obstacle in her path. Her chance to get away from the sleazy style of *Personality*—and Edwards—was finally going to happen, no matter what. She was on her way to being an honest-to-goodness full-time, wildlife photographer.

She wondered if Edwards had bothered trying to notifying Hawk that she'd be coming. Edwards told her he would, but she didn't trust him. In either event, she wasn't worried. She'd never had any problems in the past with getting permission, and she didn't expect to have a problem now. Most celebrities talked about maintaining their privacy, but she'd learned these people were in the public eye because they enjoyed being there. She had no doubt Hawk would be just like the rest of them—once he started talking, he'd never stop.

But Edwards wasn't taking any chances. The envelope she had handed Smitty had contained $10,000—payment for her transportation and a guarantee she'd remain here until she was ready to go. Just a precaution that nothing would go wrong, Edwards had provided her the money as insurance.

Now all she needed was for Hawk to show himself and she could get to work.

***

Hawk lay perfectly still on the edge of the cliff. Wrapping his fingers around the binoculars' frame, he adjusted the central focusing drive until the three men with rifles were in focus. He'd been watching them steadily for several days and had almost decided they were harmless.

Until now.

A week ago he'd discovered their base camp, about seven miles away. At first they tracked deer, elk and the mountain sheep, taking nothing more with them than binoculars. By their actions today, Hawk no longer trusted them; they couldn't have followed large game into the boxed canyon. The only inhabitants of this green vale were no larger than rabbits and squirrels.

Except for his bald eagles.

The seclusion of the canyon and the prolific prey—small mammals, birds and fish—provided by the Salmon River were the reasons he chose to implant his first pair of young birds in the canyon five years ago.

As the three men craned their necks and looked toward the sky, Hawk instinctively knew they were poachers. Due to his project, this area of the National Forest was off limits to hunters. For poachers, there were no honored boundaries and eagle feathers commanded a high price on the black market. His gut tightened, anger welling up his throat just thinking of one of his eagles getting killed. Despite his suspicions, he'd need more evidence than instinct before reporting these men to the authorities.

The faint sound of whirling blades of a helicopter caught Hawk's attention. Damn! Smitty's timing for dropping off his monthly supplies was rotten.

Lowering the binoculars and crawling on his belly, Hawk left the rocky ridge confident the three men never saw him. If they were poachers, they'd be back. He'd see them again. Right now, though, he had to tend to his supplies—that or chance some forest creature getting to them first.

***

The sound of footsteps on loose gravel grabbed Jennifer's attention. She turned toward the sound, nervously stuffing her hands into the huge pockets of her belted khaki-colored safari-style jacket. Her knuckles encountered tiny plastic canisters of film and her fingers immediately wrapped around the cylinders, finding comfort in their familiarity.

He looked pretty much the same now as he did at the height of his career, only now he looked stronger, more confident, a man at home in his environment.

His had been a career many sought but few achieved. It was easy to see why he'd been a popular, much-sought-after model for the romance book covers. No one since Hawk had been as famous. The Magnificent Hawk he had been called. And he was. Magnificent.

The frown on his face, however, ruined the otherwise perfect picture.

Through her research, she'd seen hundreds of other pictures of the former male model, but only one picture—the one reproduced in the tabloid—had captured the real man. Now a respected naturalist, in his own element, it had been a picture of a man as raw as the environment in which he worked. She hadn't forgotten the way his eyes had blazed at the camera. It was the same look he gave her now and it chilled her to the bone.

Far taller than her own five-feet seven-inches, he had wide shoulders and a lean muscular frame that held not an ounce of superfluous fat. But, there was one quality the photo didn't reveal.

The aura.

It surrounded him. Goose bumps popped out on her arms. At first, the sensation reminded her of a feather tickling her skin. She decided, though, that it had to be the cool air. It wasn't until her lungs finally expelled air that she realized she'd been holding her breath.

He said nothing, his expression dark and foreboding. He moved toward her, his gaze never leaving hers. As the gap between them closed, Jennifer saw the lines around his eyes. Laugh lines on most people. She couldn't imagine this man laughing much at all. He appeared too stern. His black brows hooded his eyes and high cheekbones emphasized his Shoshone Indian heritage. Not until he stood before her, with only a foot of space separating them, did she feel fear. He towered over her like a ponderosa pine, his chest hard and formidable, his chin square and firm, his mouth an angry slash, and coal black eyes searing to her soul. She felt something else too, but couldn't put a name to the feeling that made her want to know this man.

Fear wasn't an uncommon emotion to her, not in her line of work—she encountered a variety of wild animals whenever she ventured into the wilderness and always managed to avoid confrontation. But, this was a different type of animal. This man lived with nature, finely tuned senses made him cunning and dangerous—a force one normally tried to avoid. She sensed passion would naturally accompany this man's actions. Any action. How she knew that, she didn't know. Just an instinct she had. And she'd learned, when out in the wilderness, to always trust her intuition. The one time she hadn't, she'd ended up with eighteen stitches in her calf. She thought she'd been out of reach of the cougar. Intuition told her to climb higher in the tree. She didn't and the cougar had jumped, catching her jeans. Luckily, only one nail had caught her skin. The scar was nearly invisible but she'd learned her lesson; now she listened to that inner voice she called intuition. And at the moment it was screaming, *This man has the potential to hurt you.* All her senses went on alert.

She'd much rather face a grizzly bear than deal with someone who could hurt her. It had taken her years to rise above her vulnerability, her easy trust.

Regardless of what her intuition told her, she didn't have the option of avoiding him. She would, however, listen carefully to her inner voice and proceed with caution.

She licked her lips, swallowed nervously, but stood firm. Despite the scary feeling that chilled her, she was extremely curious about him. She had done her research before leaving New York and discovered he was a complex man, an enigma, and that intrigued her even more. The more she had dug, the more she realized little was known about the man. Nowhere had she been able to find answers to her questions. It was almost as if he had been born the day he appeared in New York. Up until that time, he had no past.

Despite his hard look that probably sent most people running, she remained rooted to the spot. He was just a man after all. *Keep telling yourself that, Jennifer, and you might be convinced.* Who was she fooling? He was more than just a man. There was something powerful and magnetic about him; and yet, she felt as if she was in the middle of a maelstrom—something dark and potentially disastrous. If she had any sense, she'd turn tail and run.

When it came to her career, though, nothing swayed her except her grim determination that no one would stop her from getting what she wanted.

"Who the hell are you?" he asked, his voice low and rumbly. Captivated by the sound of his voice—smooth and almost caressing despite his anger—she didn't answer. She wanted to hear more.

He scowled. Suddenly, she was hauled up against his chest, his hands on her upper arms, firmly holding her there. "Are you deaf? Who are you? "

His hands held her tightly, and her fingers tingled with the beginnings of numbness. Despite her long sleeves, his touch burned her skin. He felt like a wall of granite.

"Let go of me! " Jennifer struggled to free herself. No matter how much she needed his cooperation to fulfill her assignment, no one treated her like this. Even if he was the idyllic image of a paperback hero.

"Not until I find out who you are, and what you're doing here. " He looked past her, and for the first time appeared to notice her luggage sitting beside his crates and boxes of supplies. The expression on his face changed to puzzlement. "Smitty left you? "

"Yes. My name's Jennifer Frost. I'm with *Wildlife and Wilderness.* Now will you let me go, Mr. Hunter? "

Hawk looked surprised at the mention of his name. He released her and stepped back. Ignoring her, he turned and disappeared into the cabin. Jennifer's mouth gaped open, then she snapped her jaw shut. He had a lot to explain, manhandling her like that, then leaving her out here alone, she thought, as she brushed down the sleeves of her jacket.

She knew from his publisher's office that Hawk's project was nearly finished. Maybe that's what made him so testy. Maybe, like herself, he hated to see his project come to an end. At any rate, he didn't have to be so rude. Nor was she about to let him walk away from her. She followed him into the cabin and found him at a table, speaking into a shortwave radio.

"Lair's Den calling Whirlybird. Come in."

A crackling sound filled the room, but there was no answer.

He tried once more, then in frustration dropped the hand mike on the table.

Jennifer winced.

He crossed the room and stopped in front of her. "Why are you here?"

"I'm a wildlife photographer. I'm here to do a feature documenting your eagle restoration."

"*Wildlife and Wilderness*?" he asked, repeating the name she had mentioned a few minutes ago.

"Yes." Finally. Now maybe they'd get somewhere.

"No one's documenting anything," he said calmly. Too calmly. "That includes you."

She wanted to react—argue right back, saying what came to mind—but she held that emotion in check. To deal with this man successfully, she'd have to use all her skills, and think before she spoke. Ever since she'd lost her one other opportunity to do a feature for *Wildlife and Wilderness* to a co-worker, she'd learned to be discreet. She wasn't about to blow what looked to be her last opportunity to take pictures she could be proud of with a byline, as well. In the process of getting this far in her career, she had also learned there was power in silence.

Besides *Wildlife and Wilderness*, Prince Publications owned and published a variety of magazines. Until now, all her wildlife features had appeared in *Scout*, a children's magazine. The editor of *Scout* had told Jennifer her talents were wasted on the children's magazine. When *Wildlife and Wilderness* had expanded their length and went to a slick page format a year ago, she had tried to obtain a contributing editor position. Her lack of experience shut her out. Edwards was glad; she had a way of getting quotes and pictures that her co-workers lacked. Edwards knew, just as she did, that her features added flair to *Personality*, a magazine that many celebrities claimed was no better than the tabloids. Lately, Jennifer had to agree, and she didn't want to be associated with *Personality* any longer.

It had taken a whole year—the longest year of her life—before this particular opportunity was offered to her.

She had to get Hawk to change his mind. She closed her eyes. She could win his trust—she had to. Patience, she told herself. Just be patient. She could get through this. There was no choice.

Opening her eyes, she wasn't surprised to see he hadn't moved. He still stared at her, and she shivered at the intensity of his gaze. She felt like a fish on a hook and forced herself not to squirm.

"I can't believe all this fuss for a few pictures of feathers," she said.

"You're creating the fuss. My world was just fine until you arrived."

"Correct me if I'm wrong," she said. "Do you have something against *Wildlife and Wilderness?*"

There. She saw it again. Every time she mentioned the magazine's name, his lips thinned. It hadn't been her imagination.

The silence became unbearable, but he'd be the first to speak—not her.

"Yes." The word sounded tortuous, as if he didn't want to admit it.

"Why? I don't understand. Everything has been arranged."

"I didn't give anyone permission to do anything," he ground out.

"But...but, everything was set up."

"Not by me it wasn't."

The muscles along his jawbone tightened even more. To say he was upset was a joke. With his eyes blazing into her own, nostrils flaring, and his mouth a line of hard flesh, Jennifer didn't doubt for a minute that this man could take care of himself under the worst circumstances—even murder, if that's what it took. Fortunately for her, her situation wasn't quite that desperate.

What would it be like to have a man like Hawk protecting her, caring for her, loving her? The idea surprised her. She had no time for a relationship. Yet, the idea both excited her and scared her to death. What drove the man? What made him give up a career that most people only dreamed about, divorce a beautiful woman—a woman whose career equaled his own—and move more than two thousand miles to live in seclusion for nearly five years?

"Who's the editor?" he asked.

Warning bells went off. "Of *Wildlife—*?"

"Yes."

"Sam Wilkerson." Something told her to be careful, not to embellish her answers.

"Not Bob Edwards?"

Because of the way he ground out Edwards' name, Jennifer kept her facial expression fixed, though the revelation that he knew Edwards astonished her. Edwards hadn't been up front with her. She didn't know what was going on, but she intended to find out.

"No." He wasn't asking her if she knew Edwards, thank goodness. "But *Wildlife and Wilderness* is tied to *Personality*."

"Yes. They're owned by the same publisher."

Hawk stared at her. Her stomach churned, and she wondered how much he knew. She kept her gaze intact, not even blinking, as he studied her. What would she say if he asked her if she was doing a piece for *Personality*?

His jaw hardened and he moved closer. Then he spoke low but in a clipped tone. "If I thought for one minute you were associated with Edwards, I wouldn't be waiting for the helicopter to remove you from my mountain. I'd throw you off it myself."

CHAPTER 2

He walked past her and out the door.

Now that he couldn't see her, she shuddered. She couldn't tell him the whole story, at least not right now. It wasn't her style to lie, and she didn't want to. She could live with keeping some facts hidden—for a while. Granted, Edwards was lower than an earthworm to remove her this far from civilization without having set up the assignment beforehand. But, the venom in Hawk's voice told her something else was at work here, something serious between Edwards and Hawk. Both men held her future in their hands, and she wanted to curse them both.

Instead, she maintained a pleasant expression on her face despite her sweaty palms, a roller-coaster stomach, and knees that threatened to buckle out from under her. Not bad considering she'd just been threatened with a visual picture of her physical departure. Hawk returned, carrying three crates stacked in his arms. She stepped aside, allowing him passage and watched him cross the room. Bulging arm muscles strained the cloth of his shirt. She half expected the material to rip at the seams. She didn't like how her body was reacting on its own to the physical feast in front of her. As much as she wanted to stop watching, she couldn't. She was impressed beyond all measure.

Setting the crates down, he turned and headed for the door again. He stopped when he reached Jennifer. "Smitty's not answering right now nor are any of the rangers," he said brusquely. "Once I can get a hold of someone, count on leaving." He stepped around her and left the cabin again. This time, she followed him. He lifted the last of the three boxes and before he straightened fully, she took the top one from him. She saw him pause, his eyebrows drawing together. She led the way into the cabin and deposited the box near the others, next to the rough-hewn cupboard.

It was time to set the man straight. She waited until he was rid of his boxes. As he bent his knees and squatted, setting down his load, she noticed the denim stretched across the tight muscles of his derriere. *He had nice buns, too.* She swallowed nervously, not at all pleased that her thoughts kept drifting back to his physical attributes. If she was going to outsmart this man, she needed to keep her concentration intact and on her goal.

Finally, he rose and she stepped in front of him, preventing him from walking away from her again.

She needed his cooperation, but she wasn't going to be bullied either. "I'm not leaving. I'm completing my assignment whether you like it or not. I've waited too long for an assignment like this. I'll succeed and finally prove I'm good at what I do."

"Prove it to whom?"

"To...to...myself."

"And who else?"

It really wasn't any of his business. But, if it would help her cause, she'd tell him anything. Anything but that she had a second assignment and who she was really working for with that assignment. She'd waited too long and wanted it too much to let this job get away from her. "To my mother."

"I'm surprised."

Now it was her turn to frown. "At what?"

"That you'd have to prove anything to anybody other than yourself. Doesn't she think you're any good at what you do?"

"What she thinks is that what I do isn't ladylike."

He gave a laugh. "And that's it?"

She clenched her teeth. It wasn't his question that bothered her. It was that slight laugh. She didn't see what was so funny. "Isn't it enough? She's never accepted my interests. I've always been an embarrassment to her because I was such a tomboy as a child. I wasn't like the other little girls who wore frilly dresses and fussed over makeup. It galls her that I work as a photographer. That I'll camp out for weeks for a wildlife shot. But, I love it, and I'm going to photograph your birds. What have you got to lose? Your project is almost finished."

His eyes became dark arrows. "How would you know that?"

"I did my research."

His face hardened. For an instant, she pictured him as a proud chief pronouncing war against his enemy. Her heartbeat quickened, and she blinked several times to erase the powerful image from her mind.

Finally he spoke. "You aren't staying. If I have to, I'll pick you up and put you on that helicopter myself."

Jennifer's mouth thinned, the muscles around her eyes tightening. She glared at him. She didn't intend to argue with the man any further, but neither would she leave. Failure on this assignment wasn't an option. If she did well here, she could probably get any assignment she wanted at *Wildlife and Wilderness* or any other wildlife magazine for that matter. She was competing with the best, and she had to be better than all of them.

She remembered her last words to Edwards—a promise that she'd get the best pictures he'd seen. His pleased smile had assured her that he counted on it. And then, his smile had disappeared and he told her if she didn't come back with what he wanted, she'd be fired. She believed he would do it. She knew he liked her work, was delighted when she got pictures of celebrities who were usually able to evade the camera lens, but he gave rough criticism and rarely gave out praise. One time, when another co-worker hadn't delivered to Edwards exactly what he'd asked, the woman had been fired on the spot. Jennifer wasn't about to place herself, or rather her job, in danger like that.

"Don't be so sure." She turned and walked out of the cabin, chastising herself with every step. It was foolish to show any sign of anger. She had to remember that it was more important to win his acceptance, and not fight him every step of the way. *Easier said than done*, she thought. The man was not only irritating, but he was insufferable as well.

No way was Hawk going to fly her back, even if she had to hide from him in the woods. Jennifer cringed at the thought. She came prepared to camp outdoors, but she'd prefer not to, not for two weeks in freezing night temperatures. Thinking of her own supplies and equipment, she went out to get her bags.

When she re-entered the cabin, Hawk spoke. "Where do you think you're going with those?" he demanded.

"I'm bringing them in."

"No need to."

Jennifer shrugged and set the two camera bags down, out of harm's way. She'd play his game and let him think he was getting his own way.

This time.

"Where's the bathroom?" she asked. It'd been a long ride up the mountain.

"Out back."

"Thanks." As she stepped out of the cabin, she smiled. From Hawk's expression, he apparently expected flak about the lack of plumbing. Well, he wouldn't get any. Only a ninny expected electricity and running water this high in the mountains. Rounding the back corner of the cabin, she saw the outhouse. As she got closer, she saw it was a bit larger than most, and that it had a window in the top half of the door that gave the user a view when seated. She laughed aloud. Now, that was different. Like herself, Hawk obviously appreciated a good view.

***

From inside the cabin, Hawk heard her laughter and frowned. It was the last sound he expected to hear from Jennifer Frost on her way to the outhouse.

When he'd rounded the corner of the cabin earlier, he'd been shocked to see her standing in front of his cabin. At first, he'd thought it was Annette—the likeness was incredible. Both had striking auburn locks, were tall and gorgeous. Then, thinking it was Annette, he had become angry. That's when he'd stomped up to Jennifer. Once he got up close, he saw she looked nothing like his former wife. Jennifer's hair was natural both in color and curl. Spray or gel couldn't duplicate those soft wind-tousled curls that covered her head. Large cornflower blue eyes, framed by naturally long, dark mascara-free eyelashes had stared at him. How his fingers had ached to touch her creamy ivory skin. It had been a long time since he had touched anything that looked that soft. Hell, it had been a long time since he'd seen a woman. Her only concession to makeup was a hint of gloss that gave her wide generous mouth a sensuous appeal. Instinctively, Hawk knew her mouth would be soft if he ever kissed her.

And then his anger had returned. First, because he still harbored some bitterness toward his ex-wife, which he didn't like to admit, especially after all this time.

Second, it didn't matter who this woman was or how pretty she was, she didn't belong here. Just the same, he was sorry he'd handled her so roughly. Damn Smitty! He had no business leaving her. Hawk didn't want a woman, or anybody for that matter, intruding upon his mountain. He had more than enough to handle right now with his eagles, the poachers, and the writing of his book. He didn't want to contend with a woman, and certainly not this one. She looked like she'd melt in the rain.

She was leaving. As fast as he could arrange it!

Grumbling to himself, he stepped to the table and picked up the microphone again. "Lair's Den calling Whirlybird. Come in. Over."

A crackling sound filled the room. "Whirlybird here. Go ahead Lair's Den. Over."

About time. "What's the deal, Smitty? Over."

"About what?"

Hawk heard the slight chuckle. "Don't play dumb, Smitty, even though it's your forte."

"Something wrong with the supplies?"

Hawk ran a hand through his hair. Smitty wasn't going to make this easy. He'd once said Hawk took life too seriously, insisted a man needed to have a little fun now and then. Hawk had replied that he had fun seeing Smitty take his leave after his drop each month. Smitty had just slapped his knee and gee-hawed. Hawk could picture Smitty now, his rounded belly a table for the microphone, his feet propped up on his desk, his well-worn oak captain's chair tilted back dangerously on two legs.

"It's the package you left—the one I didn't order."

"Nice package, wasn't it? Wouldn't mind having a package like that dropped off at my place sometime. Lucky stiff."

"If you want it, come and get it."

"No can do, buddy."

"Why not?"

"I've been paid not to."

"I'm telling you different. Come and get her. I'll compensate you for your time."

"If you can top $10,000, I'll come and get her."

One thing Hawk liked about Smitty, when asked, he told the truth. And he would do most anything—if the price was right and it was legal. Hawk knew that from the exorbitant amount he paid to have his supplies brought up the mountain each month. Smitty had a monopoly, knew it, and used his position to his advantage. Hawk couldn't help but like the guy, despite his failings. This was Edwards' doing, it had to be. It was sneaky and underhanded, just like the man himself. Despite what Jennifer said, this whole thing smacked of Edwards' conniving way.

"You know I can't top $10,000."

"Then the lady stays. Sorry, buddy. Looks like someone bought you two weeks of female companionship, like it or not. Over."

Hawk heard Jennifer's step. He spun around. She stood in the door way, her eyebrows knitted together, her skin paler by several shades. Keeping his gaze on her face, Hawk brought the mike to his mouth. "Understood. Over and out."

He placed the mike on the table. Four steps brought him directly in front of her. "Let's get your bags."

"You're angry."

"Damn right! Wouldn't you be if you were in my shoes?" He didn't wait for an answer. Instead, he headed for her bags.

***

She had to admit if she were in his shoes, she'd be angry too. But, how long was he going to be angry? Certainly not for the entire two weeks. She hoped.

Outside, she contemplated how to best approach the situation. She didn't want to get into a discussion about Edwards. He was a snake in the grass—she knew it and obviously Hawk knew it. Nor did she want to defend Wilkerson. She knew if he had contacted Hawk himself and was told no, Wilkerson would have dropped the story. So her safest bet was to stay away from talking about her assignments altogether. Easier said than done.

She decided to take a different approach. "Are you mad at me?"

Hawk thought for a moment before looking at her. Finally, in a calm voice, he said, "No. It isn't your fault any more than it's mine that you're here. You're just doing what you were told to do."

Instantly, Jennifer felt guilty. That wasn't really the truth. But, he was right. She *was* just doing her job. And, if she did it well, she'd never be put into this kind of situation again.

"Unfortunately, Smitty's the only nongovernment pilot in these parts. Until he returns, I'm stuck with you."

She was glad Hawk wasn't going to fight her the duration of her stay. She shuddered to think what Edwards was capable of and grateful that her success here would give her the opportunity to work for someone else. She wanted to question Hawk about Edwards. It was obvious that Hawk hated the man, but now wasn't the time to ask her questions. She would wait for a more opportune time.

They reached for the handle of her large suitcase at the same time. Her fingers touched his. Scorching heat traveled through her hand and up her arm. Immediately, she jerked her hand back. He scowled at her, his brows locked in a dark furrow above even darker eyes. Just once she'd like to see the man smile.

"I'll get this one. You take the smaller one," he ordered. She didn't argue. Back inside the cabin, she placed the small duffel bag on the floor next to her camera bags. "I'm sorry..." Ops, she wasn't going to say anything. "If our positions were reversed, I'd hate it too." Actually, she wasn't sure if their positions were reversed if she would hate it. Especially if she'd been without companionship for more years than she could count on one hand, and especially if someone who looked like Hawk had been deposited upon her door. *For heaven's sake*, she reprimanded herself. *Remember why you're h*ere. It puzzled her that he had such an effect upon her libido. She'd been around great looking men before. Why was he any different?

Hawk walked around the room throwing open the wooden shutters, allowing natural light to filter into the one-room cabin. When he finally spoke, he didn't acknowledge that he'd heard a word she said. "You can have the bed."

For the first time Jennifer noted her surroundings. Like all the cabin's furniture, the one and only bed was rustic and made of solid wood. It was larger than a single but not quite a double, and was covered with a large homemade quilt. A rope, rather than springs or planks, supported the mattress. Several faded quilts were folded on the low rectangular chest that stood at the foot of the bed. A window, near the headboard, gave a view of the tall pines standing near the house.

A natural stone fireplace dominated the room and appeared to be the core of the cabin, providing both heat and a place to cook. A hinged crane, supporting a black kettle, hung in the center of the hearth. Above the fireplace a rifle lay on wooden pegs, and in front of the fireplace stood a table and two chairs. Next to the fireplace was a huge buffet with a variety of pots, bowls, and eating utensils on the top shelves. Closed doors, at the base of the cabinet, hid its contents. Supplies, she guessed. A large butcher block next to the cabinet had a strip of magnet along its side that held various sized knives. Next, stood a table-like structure that was hip high, topped with metal sheeting that had a raised edge. Some kind of sink, Jennifer surmised, seeing a hand pump.

Leaning against one of the walls was a bow that stood nearly as tall as she was, and next to it was a quiver of arrows.

In the last corner of the cabin, occupying space under a window, stood a large table. Surrounded by piles of papers, books, and magazines, sat a Smith-Corona portable typewriter. The two-way radio occupied space on the left back corner.

The only luxury in the cabin—and a minor one at that—was the rocking chair near the fireplace. Jennifer imagined a grizzly bear could fit comfortably in the large wooden seat. Unlike most rustic quarters, that tended to be dark, musty, and claustrophobic, the cabin was light and airy. It was the windows, their shutters now open, that gave the outdoors sensation to the room. Turning to face Hawk, she smiled. "I like your place, but if I take the bed, where will you sleep?"

For a second, a look of surprise crossed his face. Then his brooding look that was fast becoming familiar returned, and he moved away from her side, picking up all of her bags and placing them on the bed. "On the floor. I've done it before. The bed is fairly new."

"I've never seen furniture like this before. Where can I find it?"

Hawk laughed.

She glanced at him. It was the same laugh she'd heard before, a laugh of disbelief.

"What's so funny?"

"You make it sound like you can shop for this stuff."

"You're telling me I can't?"

"Sure you can."

"Where?"

He gestured to the outside. "You've got acres to shop from. Just pick the tree of your choice."

Puzzled, she bent and took a closer look at the bed. She recognized the craftsmanship that indicated the work could have only been done by hand. The man's talents were unbelievable. "You made it?"

"This past winter. That's how I spend the bulk of my winters—

writing and making furniture."

"You made all this furniture?" She glanced around the room again. Museums would covet the pieces. The bed, like the table and chairs, appeared sturdy—like Hawk. Actually, the room *was* Hawk—hard, yet durable, tough, matching the very elements from which it came.

She grabbed the biggest suitcase by the handle and pulled until the awkward shape slid off the quilt. Bending over, she shoved it under the bed. She straightened and caught Hawk observing her actions.

"Anything wrong?" she asked. A stupid question to ask when she thought about it. Nothing had been right for Hawk since she had arrived.

"No. I just thought you'd like to unpack."

"I'm used to living out of a suitcase."

Hawk snorted in disbelief, turned away, and walked toward his desk.

"Don't you believe me?"

"Hardly."

"Why not? You don't even know me."

"I know you're a woman and it's the nature of females to nest. Before the two weeks are up, you'll have rearranged the furniture three times." He shuffled some papers around.

Laughing, Jennifer sat on the bed. "Not me." She reached for the largest of the three bags left on the bed, pulling it close to her. Quickly, she unzipped it and drew out a camera with a telephoto lens. Item by item, she checked the equipment plus two other cameras in the bag. Everything was intact.

"So, when do I get to shoot your eagles?" she asked, her hands busy loading the first camera with film, her movements precise and unwasted.

"You don't."

Jennifer stared at him. He had to be kidding. Now that they both knew she was stuck here, did he expect her to sit on her hands and do nothing? The tone of his voice told her he did. "Says who?"

He stared back at her. "Me."

The man obviously thought if he told her she wasn't going to shoot, she wouldn't. "My own mother can't tell me what to do. I don't see how you figure you can, even if you are still centerfold material." Oops, that wasn't supposed to slip out. She hurried on. "This may be your cabin, but you don't own this mountain or me. If you think I've come all this way, lugged this equipment through airports, bus stations, a general store, a ranger's station and a helicopter—a ride that made me think about having my stomach removed permanently—so I can sit here and twiddle my thumbs while you're off chasing eagles, guess again. I came here to take pictures of eagles and pictures of eagles are what I'm going to get."

"Pictures that will be plastered in the pages of *Wildlife and Wilderness*?"

"Yes, that was my assignment."

"You can take all the pictures you want."

Jennifer breathed a sigh of relief. Finally, the man was making sense.

"And you'll leave the film with me. I'll have the film delivered to you when I'm finished with my work. Then, and only then, I'll also give you an exclusive interview."

Jennifer glowered. "Leave my film with you until it's convenient for you and watch my career go down the tubes! No deal."

"Then don't plan on getting your pictures—ever." Hawk paused. The hint of a grin appeared on his face. Was it possible he was actually smiling?

Just as quickly, the smile disappeared, and he added, "Or until hell freezes over."

The look he gave her, his eyes hard and black as a pond on a moonless night, merely made her more determined. There was a time when she would have succumbed to such an intense stare. A time she would have backed down. But, not anymore. She wouldn't be used by anyone. She wanted to make a splash with her career and no one—not even this hunk-gorgeous man who not only looked as though he came from a time in the past, but lived as though he did—would defeat her.

"When hell freezes over, eh?" She gave him a small mischievous smile. "Well, I hope your long johns are warm."

Jennifer didn't think it possible, but his look hardened even more. Expecting Hawk to say something, she was surprised when he left the cabin, leaving the door wide open.

A second later, he came back into the cabin carrying the last of her belongings—a huge box. With a grunt, he set it down by the door. "Don't travel light, do you?"

Jennifer shrugged. "Usually I do. But, knowing this was going to be a longer shoot than normal, I packed a few extra necessities." She wondered if he'd ask the obvious question of what was in the box. He disappointed her. Instead, he walked over to his own supply boxes and started unpacking. As he began putting his food away, his expression darkened.

"What's the problem?" Jennifer asked.

"There are more supplies here than I ordered. Hell, some of these items I wouldn't order in a million years." He held up a pink package of Daisy shavers.

Jennifer grabbed them from his hand. "Those are mine."

"Who paid for them?"

"I did. And for the extra groceries. I figured you might not have adequate supplies, especially when I learned you get groceries only once a month."

"You figured that right," he said, his back to her as he stacked canned fruit on the cupboard shelves. "How long did Smitty say you'll be here?"

"Two weeks."

"That long," he muttered. "Isn't there a husband, a boyfriend who'll miss you?"

"None."

"Family?"

"Just my mother."

"And you don't get along with her."

"I didn't say that. Other than my career choice we're close

enough—like most other mothers and daughters I suppose. Although, we also disagree about money."

"How's that?"

Jennifer didn't consider Hawk's questions nosey. Up until now, she'd always been an open book, never one to hide anything personal, and considering how she and Hawk had started out, she was glad he was asking the questions. As long as he believed her only assignment was to photograph his eagles, she could tell him anything he wanted and tell him the truth.

Maybe if Hawk knew her better, he'd be more open to her photographing his birds and welcome her questions. *What a long shot*, she thought, but at this point, she'd try anything. "Money rules her life, as it does all her friends. She thinks I'm like them."

"And you're not?"

"No. I'd rather earn my own way doing something I love than being handed a future with stifling obligations."

***

Hawk was surprised. He couldn't name one woman in his past—other than his mother—who hadn't been influenced by the scent of greenbacks. Especially his ex-wife. He had met Annette on the job—they were posing for a romance cover. She was breath-taking beautiful, her luminous violet-blue eyes beyond description, and he had fallen in love with her instantly. During their first modeling session together, as they posed, they had both felt the heat. It hadn't been hard to pretend he was in love with her as he posed. He was. Two weeks later, they were married. By the end of three years, he'd learned what she was truly like—hard, manipulative, with her career coming first and foremost above everything else. Including him.

When he made his career change, he knew he was taking drastic steps. At the time, all he wanted to do was get away, return to his roots. Now, he knew he'd just been surrounded by the wrong people, living in a community not suited to him. Sure he had lived in style, the money he earned afforded him a great life—the best restaurants, clothes he never had growing up. But, after a while, it hadn't been enough.

Something had been missing—now, he had it. Not once did he regret the work he was doing. He loved it.

It was easy to see that Jennifer cared about what she did, that she was dedicated—like him. But, that didn't mean he was going to roll over and let her have her way. "Your mother is right. You don't belong here."

"Why? Because you agree with her or because *you* don't want me here?"

"Take your pick."

***

So much for getting better acquainted, she thought.

Silently, she helped him unpack the nonperishable goods. She'd learned long ago it was best not to defend her ability or the type of work she did. She wondered if she had been a man if Hawk would have been this stubborn about the assignment? Or would he have rejected a man just as vehemently as he did her?

She noted Hawk found a place for everything, quickly emptying the first five boxes. When he reached for the last box of supplies, Jennifer realized they had a problem. "These fresh fruits and vegetables were so appealing, I got carried away. With no refrigeration, they'll spoil."

Hawk checked the contents, then picked up the box, tucking it under his arm. "Follow me." Leaving the cabin, he led the way to a hill behind the cabin. As they got closer, Jennifer saw a small door built into the side of the hill—no building, just a door. From a distance, it was camouflaged by brush. *How odd*, she thought.

Crouching over, Hawk opened it and disappeared. Jennifer peered into the darkness and followed. She shuffled her feet cautiously, unsure of her footing, noting she was going down a slight incline. The air suddenly got cooler, and then cold. She heard a match being struck, and then a small flare of light appeared. He lit the stub of a candle and set it on a box. In the dim light, she saw other boxes, stacked one upon another so the openings were on the sides. Behind them were large blocks of ice packed in straw.

"It's a refrigerator," she said.

"Not much of one, but it works." Hawk took a few items from the box he held and put them on a shelf. Then he set the box that was under his arm on top of the shortest stack with its open top on the side.

"Where did the ice and straw come from?"

"Smitty brought them."

"How often is the ice replaced?"

"I add a couple blocks every year." He turned, his hand accidentally brushing across her chest.

Jennifer jumped, and found herself nose to nose with him. Though the touch had been accidental, she found she couldn't stop the response that hardened the tips of her breasts or the tingling sensation that went clear to her toes.

"Excuse me," he mumbled. "I didn't mean to..." His voice dropped off as he stared at her.

Her heart hammered in her chest, pounding hard beneath her ribs, and her lungs quit working. Every nerve on her body tingled with an awareness unlike anything she had ever experienced before. Good gracious, but he was a handsome devil, she thought. If her senses had gone on alert before, they were screeching at her now.

In the dark, with only the candlelight for illumination, his eyes were like black opals with fire burning behind them. Jennifer inhaled and caught the scent of him—musk and pine. It drew her even closer to him. She saw him lift a hand and a finger reached out as if to caress her cheek. She wondered what his touch would be like.

***

Hawk damned the tight space. When he had turned around, he was surprised to find Jennifer right behind him. Though his touch had been accidental, and he cursed himself for being so clumsy. He knew from the heat that was building below his belt that it would take the willpower of iron to keep from touching her again. As they stared at each other, he could feel her slight breath upon his face. In the dim light, her eyes were wide, a thin band of blue circling the dark center, giving her an innocent, yet come hither look. He felt a tightening in his chest. He thought he smelled lilacs. Even the air seemed to take on a purple hue. Her face beckoned him. He saw his own hand in the air, reaching toward her. He had to touch her, she seemed so surreal.

The light flickered, nearly going out, then resumed its steady glow.

***

In the blink of an eye, Jennifer had seen Hawk's hand reach out for her. Now his hand was gone, his eyebrows knitted together as he stared at her.

Suddenly she felt like a trapped rabbit in a hole, with a hungry wolf waiting at the opening.

CHAPTER 3

Quickly, she turned and took the few necessary steps that led her back into the sunlight. She gulped for air. This was ridiculous. What had happened in there? What was wrong with her? She'd only just met the man, and now she'd almost let him caress her. True, Hawk was attractive—heck, who was she kidding? The man was pure sex through and through. It had to be the mystery that surrounded him that had drawn her to him, making her wonder what it would be like to be held in his arms and to be kissed by him. But, to think that he really wanted to touch her? Ha! He welcomed her about as much he'd welcome poison ivy.

It had been their close proximity in the small cave-like room and the candle light that had changed everything. The charged atmosphere in there had her both forgetting where they were and what they were doing. Now that they were back in the open, things would return to normal. If she could call being stranded on a mountain with a man who didn't want her there as normal.

She heard him follow her out. Would he think she was attracted to him? She hoped not, even though now she had to admit that she was. Frankly, now that she had been around Hawk, she couldn't imagine any woman being immune to him. However, for her career's sake, she had to keep that attraction submerged. Totally. If he were Brad Pitt or Channing Tatum she wouldn't be feeling any different. Like any red-blooded, warm and breathing American woman, she had the hots for any great looking man. She had to admit, Hawk certainly fit into that category.

She groped for something, anything to say. "That's...that's an ingenious root cellar."

To her own ears it sounded like she was grasping at straws.

"It keeps the food cool," he said, shutting the door securely. He thrust a bent nail in the latch. "For predators," he explained. "The four-legged kind. Determined creatures if they choose to be." Hawk turned and pinned her to the spot with his gaze.

Normally comfortable with silence when in the company of others, Jennifer found herself searching for something else to say. The way he was looking at her, she felt like one of his birds under a microscope. Any minute, she expected her feet to turn liquid and start the metamorphosis that would turn her into a lukewarm puddle.

"Do...do you spend all your time here? Up here on the mountain?" she asked, as they walked back to the cabin. Talking about anything was better than where her thoughts were taking her.

"Most of it."

"Do you have another home?" Despite her thorough research, the material she found had been pretty skimpy. Overnight, he had become New York's most popular model, but not even the owner of the well-known modeling agency who agented Hawk knew any intimate details regarding his client's background, though they had played up his obvious physical Indian heritage. Beyond that, she'd learned nothing about his previous life, other than he'd been married for a brief time, then divorced. No one knew why the marriage had broken up. She did know, however, from her research that he'd presented his program of rehabilitating the bald eagle to the Salmon River Mountain area to the government and received approval.

Hawk stopped and turned towards her, his eyes mere slits, the lines in his face unyielding, his jaw square and firm. "Are you going to grill me every minute you're here?"

"I...I just wondered if you had another home? That's all." This was not the same man who moments ago had almost stroked her cheek. She loathed the way he had her feeling—skittish as a newborn colt trying out its legs. She couldn't remember ever feeling this way. Ever.

"As part of your interview or to satisfy your female curiosity?" he growled.

When she conducted her interview for *Personality* it would be done with his knowledge and permission. It wasn't her intention to be devious and obtain quotes on the sly. "Neither," she said honestly.

By the expression on his face, she could tell he didn't believe her and questioned her motive. She needed Hawk to be cooperative. If he gave her no choice, she would have to find another way to get her interview. She wondered how he'd feel if she used a nameless third person as a source. For once, she wanted to do this piece up front and with the interviewee's knowledge. She hated that her notes would be handed over to someone else who would write the actual article. It had been hard for her at first, but she had prevailed and became good at getting information even the best writers often weren't able to obtain.

"Human interest," she said.

His eyebrows shot up.

"Human interest is a far cry from female curiosity," she added and walked away.

She entered the cabin and sat on the bed. She hated the fact that he disturbed her so much. Neither her nerves nor her heartbeat had been steady since she first met him. She tried to concentrate on her cameras. Inspecting the equipment, cleaning the lenses, and loading the cameras with film. She wanted to be ready for shooting. The difference between an amateur and a professional was in being prepared.

With her head bent, she opened a new canister of film. Suddenly, she was in shadows. Startled, she jerked her head upright, losing her concentration and dropping the film.

Hawk bent, retrieved it from the floor, and held it out to her. Without looking directly at him, she accepted it, mumbling her thanks. Darn the man! She never heard him approach. Her gaze followed him as he crossed the room and settled himself at his desk. She noticed he hardly made a sound as he moved. Quickly, he was engrossed in his own work, seemingly not affected by her presence at all. It irritated her all the more that he affected her quite the opposite. She never had a problem concentrating on her work before. Once she had changed film while being surrounded by elephants, and she hadn't acted nearly so clumsily as she did just a few minutes ago.

She turned back to her cameras. Carefully, she replaced the ready cameras into their appropriate slots in her bag and set it by the wall. Once more, she found her gaze directed in Hawk's direction. The click-clack of the keys were steady and rhythmic. As far as he was concerned, she didn't even exist, and for some unknown reason that bothered her even more.

Determined to finish her task, she checked her small camera bag, the one she carried in the field. It contained different filters, rolls of new film of various speeds and extra lenses. That bag quickly joined the first one. Finally, she checked her supply bag. In it were a few emergency items she carried when traipsing in the wilderness— flashlight, fire starters, matches, plastic raincoat, a few first aid supplies, crackers, a tin of meat, and a Swiss Army knife. She carried the small duffel bag not so much for fear of being stranded or lost as she did for those times when she found she couldn't leave a site. Sometimes, she waited hours before an animal appeared on a trail that it followed regularly. She enjoyed tracking and stalking her subjects, but waiting was always the hardest.

Her inspection complete, she stretched. Hawk was still at it, typing rapidly. From all appearances he made few mistakes, if any at all. She watched as he pulled one sheet of paper out and inserted a clean sheet into the typewriter. In an instant, with no wasted movements, the task was completed, and he resumed, moving his fingers across the keys. It was only then she noticed that he was a two-finger typist. Without any hesitation, his fingers were tapping out words that she had a sudden desire to read. What was he writing? And for whom? She wondered if she'd get the chance. Didn't the man ever take a break?

She watched the muscles in his back splay against his shirt as he moved. The sun, low in the sky, shone through the window by his side, and the strands of his black hair glistened in the filtered beams of light. She squelched the urge to go and stroke his hair. Jennifer curled her fingers into her palm. Feeling grubby from her day's travel, she decided to take a shower—a cold one.

As she rummaged through the large heavy box Hawk had brought into the cabin earlier, she found him watching her.

He wore a puzzled expression. "I'm going to take a shower," she offered.

"Refrigeration, to a degree, I can provide. A shower?" Hawk snorted. "You're out of luck, Lady."

Jennifer smiled and continued her search. When she looked up again, he was still watching her. Raising her eyebrows, she asked, "Male curiosity?"

"Just human interest," he mimicked. "A far cry from curiosity."

***

Jennifer laughed and stood. Hawk got up, crossed the room, grabbed a handful of kindling from the box next to the fireplace, and placed it on the hearth. If they were going to eat tonight, he'd have to get the fire started now, so they'd have some coals to cook by. With practiced ease, he took a match and struck it against the mantle. In seconds, a flame engulfed the wood chips layered on the hearth floor and ignited the kindling. Purposefully, he tried to ignore Jennifer but found he couldn't. His hands, reaching for a small log, halted in mid-air. Jennifer stepped to the dry sink and started filling a two-gallon container, the kind used to spray herbicide on a lawn, with water.

Slowly, he added the wood to the fire, all the time watching her. As her hands grabbed the water pump, he noted her fingers were long and tapered, the nails free of polish and neatly trimmed. Though her hands looked fragile, they maneuvered the pump expertly with long, easy strokes.

A strand of hair fell from behind her ear, caressing her cheek as she moved. He envied the strand as it lay against her cheek. He watched her hand move up, tucking the tendril back behind her ear, never missing a beat with the pump handle. Her hair had to be soft to the touch, he imagined. Threads of silk. He admired the trim figure clad in form-fitting jeans and noticed how her derriere wiggled slightly whenever she brought the pump handle down. Her hips moved rhythmically. It had been a while since he'd been with a woman. He wondered if her hips moved as easily in bed. Moving slightly, he shifted his squatted form from one foot to the other and nearly groaned aloud, as his growing arousal rubbed uncomfortably against his jeans.

"Hellfire!"

Jennifer turned and looked at him. Hawk pressed his hand against his mouth. "What happened?" she asked.

"Got burnt," he told her. In more ways than one.

"Oh? Sorry to hear that. You ought to watch what you're doing when playing with fire." The container full, she set it by the door.

He liked seeing the way her blue eyes twinkled when she teased him. Her wit was sharp. Frankly, he was enjoying their exchanges. "Movies are a rarity around here," he told her. "I'd rather watch you. You're providing enough entertainment to last me...oh, at least a year. What is this that you're presenting. A comedy?"

"You don't recognize an adventure when you see it?"

Fascinated—and curious—Hawk followed her movements with his gaze. She pulled the suitcase from under the bed, fished out a large towel and returned, once again, to the door. With the towel draped over her arm and some folded, cream-colored plastic in her hand, she reached into the box again with her free hand.

Hawk laughed aloud when she pulled out an umbrella. "That's adventurous all right. But, more in the way of fantasy I'd say. There's hardly a cloud in the sky."

Jennifer glanced over her shoulder and gave him another quick smile, then stepped outside.

Through the window, Hawk saw mare's-tail clouds had created a colorful canopy for the sun that was starting its descent. Mare's tails didn't bring rain, so what did she need the umbrella for?

Following her outside, he watched her open it under a small tree, and hang it upside down on a limb above her head. Next, she shook out a sheet of plastic and fastened it on the tips of the umbrella.

Not realizing he'd continued moving, Hawk found himself

standing within a few yards of her. She had hung a shower curtain on the umbrella! "I'll be damned," he muttered.

Jennifer heard him. Finished, she stood back a step to admire her work. "Nifty, huh?"

"Where'd you learn that?" It was so simple and yet such an effective contraption.

"I confess," she whispered, looking both to her right and left, pretending to look for eavesdroppers. "I was a Girl Scout."

Hawk eyed her coolly. She was a cheeky one. Didn't anything bother her? She certainly bothered him. First, he was to believe she liked his cabin. No way. The cabin was built for a man. Only one other woman had ever stepped inside it. He could still see the expression on Annette's face when she realized he expected her to live there, could still hear her acid laughter as she left it and him behind forever.

Second, there was the incident in the root cellar. He had wanted to kiss Jennifer. As much as he wanted to then, and still wanted to now, it was for the best that he hadn't. When Jennifer had backed out of the root cellar, it appeared she couldn't get out fast enough. He was grateful that she wasn't fawning all over him like he remembered so many other women doing when he was a model. The last thing he needed was for her to be attracted to him. And yet...why wasn't she? What would it take to ruffle her feathers. Didn't she find him the least bit appealing? *Now you're being ridiculous*, he thought. Fewer entanglements meant fewer complications later.

In less than a year's time, his book would be finished and delivered to his editor. Until the book was published, and his eagles solidly implanted in the valley, he couldn't risk early publicity bringing tourists to the area and disturbing the success he'd achieved so far. Yes, Jennifer Frost definitely bothered him.

He turned and retraced his steps back to the cabin.

"Hey, don't you want to see how it works?" Jennifer called after him.

"Not interested," he declared over his shoulder. Actually, he was...but, only a little bit. All right, so he was interested a lot, but he didn't want her knowing that. Without looking back, he disappeared into the cabin.

From the window at his desk, Hawk watched as she stood hidden from view inside the curtain, except for her bottom part of her legs, and tossed her clothes to the ground, item by item. He noted only a couple scraps of beige accounted for underwear. Instantly, a picture of her wearing nothing but those two scraps of material crossed his mind.

Eagles, think eagles, he told himself, forcing his eyes to turn back to his typewriter.

A screech filled the air.

Hawk bolted out the door, fear knotting his stomach. Several steps out of the cabin and striding into a run, he heard Jennifer laugh aloud. "Woo-wee, that's cold."

He stopped short—she wasn't hurt. His limbs trembled against the useless adrenalin that still flowed through his body. He took a deep breath forcing his racing heart to slow down a bit. He swore. The last thing he needed was Jennifer getting hurt. He cursed the responsibility he suddenly felt for her welfare.

As he studied the contraption Jennifer had made hanging from the tree, he saw an arm reach out, grab the towel that lay across a nearby branch and shake it out. Then the towel disappeared behind the shower curtain. When the towel reappeared, it was wrapped around Jennifer Frost.

Hawk couldn't have moved if he'd wanted to.

She was all leg. He inhaled sharply. The towel barely covered her assets. Her breasts jutted out with cleavage nearly as deep as the mountain gorges. He could easily imagine her nipples, right now well covered, but beginning at the edge of the towel. In just a few hours, she had him responding to her like an adolescent discovering a stash of his father's *Playboys*. At the end of two weeks' time, at this rate, he'd be as resilient as a soft stick of butter. All but a part of him that was now as stiff as a flagpole.

He cursed again. That mosquito of a towel was the sexiest thing he'd ever seen on any woman. Damn, if he wasn't continually aroused every time he looked at her. Why hadn't he kissed her when he had the chance? Anything to satisfy this teenage-like curiosity.

Just then, Jennifer noticed him. Though she gave a slight start, she didn't try to cover herself further. She couldn't have if she tried. "Is something wrong?" she asked.

Was there ever. She was on his mountain, and he had the most uncomfortable bulge pressing against his jeans than he'd had in a long, long time.

Jennifer repeated her question. This time he could have sworn there was a catch to her voice. Was she nervous? She certainly made him nervous.

Hawk snapped. "Nothing." Nothing a quick tumble between the sheets wouldn't fix. He turned and stalked to the back of the cabin. At the pile of wood, he stopped. He picked up an ax and hammered it into the log that was standing upright on an old stump. It splintered into two. He swore when one of the pieces fell close to his foot. This woman was getting the best of him. No one had ever been able to do that. Not like this. Not in a long time.

Soon, he was peeling off his flannel shirt and undershirt, his bare torso gleaming with perspiration, with the wood on the receiving end of his frustration.

***

Back inside, dressed, and standing by the window as she towel-dried her hair, Jennifer watched him. His muscles rippled with every movement. His dark nipples were taut, telling her despite the sheen of perspiration that covered his body, he was feeling the cooling dusk air. His jeans were worn low, almost indecently, on his hips. Jennifer licked her lips. She could almost taste the salt and smell the musky scent that would be on his skin.

His activity was almost frenzied, as if he was trying to exorcise some demon. Too bad. Years ago, she'd learned that life was too short to go through it as a grump or angry at something she couldn't change. When he'd startled her earlier as she emerged from her shower, she could tell by the way the muscle in his cheek twitched that he was aggravated had asked. about something. Fearing she'd done something wrong, she had asked. Instead of telling her what was wrong, he remained silent. She couldn't help it if she didn't know what the problem was. Unless the problem was her. She was here for two weeks and nothing he could do would change that. She knew from experience the two weeks would disappear all too quickly, and she'd soon be returning to the noisy city of New York.

Jennifer hated living in New York. She much preferred the majestic mountains to the streams of automobiles and people. But, until she was established as a wildlife photographer, she needed to be based in New York. Someday she'd have the ability to work wherever she wanted, but until then she had to pay her dues.

After today's revelations, she had to wonder if Edwards had been holding her back. Would she have gone further with a different editor? Would she have felt any different about the work she did for *Personality* if she'd had a different editor? She doubted it. She had learned through her association with Edwards that he wasn't always a fair man, and she hadn't allowed him to get the best of her. Until now.

If Hawk had been one of Edwards' victims in the past, she could well understand Hawk's hatred for the man. The work, as little as it was, that she'd done for *Scout* had been her salvation. If she failed here...

No, she couldn't think that way. She couldn't fail.

In the meantime, she'd cherish every moment while on the mountain. Maybe one day she'd have a cabin like this.

Hawk was a challenge. She'd seen traces of humor in some of his responses. Would he surprise her, revealing a facet of his personality few had seen? Or, would she find that the frown he wore was as natural as his bronzed skin? She hoped for the former. Jennifer looked out the window again and saw Hawk stacking the wood he'd chopped.

He paused in his movement, his gaze fixed on something out of her sight. He bent and picked up something brown and small, stood and held it out, his hand just inches above the tree stump he had been using to split the wood.

What was he doing?

For several minutes, she watched as he stood rock-still in that position. And then, she saw a chipmunk skitter across the ground toward him, pausing at the stump. Jennifer held her breath. She could see Hawk's mouth moving. He was talking to the chipmunk!

The chipmunk twitched his tail several times, then jumped to the top of the stump. On his hind legs, he reached for Hawk's hands. With his front paws he rolled the object in Hawk's hand toward him. The chipmunk appeared to be chattering, twitched its tail again, and grabbed what Jennifer could now see was a nut with his teeth, then scampered away. She'd never seen anything like it before. It was as if the chipmunk and Hawk had been talking to one another and understood each other.

When the chipmunk disappeared from sight, her gaze went back to Hawk. He, too, was watching the chipmunk disappear. His expression had softened, but she couldn't tell if having a chipmunk eating out of his hand had delighted him or not. It certainly had tugged at her heartstrings.

Come to think of it, she hadn't been able to get a genuine smile out of him, yet—not unless she called that smirk he used just before he'd said "When hell freezes over" or those guffaws of disbelief earlier. Nah, those didn't count. She'd continue to try to discover the real man, the one hidden beneath the gruffness and tough exterior. It wasn't like her to give up on anything or anyone once she decided to do something.

Anyway, one thing was guaranteed. She was going to have a good time here no matter what happened.

Her stomach growled. Figuring they had to eat and not sure how they'd divide the chores, she decided to go ahead and start dinner. Her stomach couldn't wait until Hawk came in, and the way he was aggressively handling the ax, she didn't want to bother him. With experienced movements, she stoked Hawk's fire until it roared. She filled the kettle with water and left the cabin to retrieve some vegetables from the *refrigerator* while the water boiled. By the time she had returned and had the carrots and potatoes cut, the water was ready. Bent over the pot, she held the wooden cutting board over the kettle and with the knife, and slid the vegetables into the pot.

Hearing the door open, she continued, and at the same time, peeked under her arm. Hawk stood there, his arms full of chopped wood. She saw him staring at her behind, then his eyes rolled. She grinned and returned to her task. Good. She affected him. It only seemed fair the way he was affecting her.

The door slammed shut. The noise startled her, and she rose quickly, bumping her head on the hearth. A few pieces of carrot plopped on the stone flooring in front of the fireplace.

Neither said a word as they stared at each other. A tiny coal popped out of the fire and hit her leg. She jumped. "Oh."

"Did it hurt you?" Hastily, he took steps to the wood box, dropping the wood into it haphazardly, then bent while brushing her leg. "Are you burned?"

"No," she said, wishing he would stop that. His hand burned more than the coal ever could have. "I don't think so." She took a step back away from him and brushed the leg herself—more to wipe away the heat he left with his touch than anything. She found where the coal had touched the denim, burning it, but it hadn't made a hole. She dismissed it with another brush of her hand. "It surprised me more than anything."

Hawk rose. Looking up at him, Jennifer trembled. *Darn it all.* Every time she got next to him she trembled. She felt like melted mountain snow rushing toward the ocean. All thoughts turned to mush when he was this close, and she felt she was tumbling headlong down a long river with far too many rapids.

Purposely, but with wooden movements, she turned back to the pot and forced her shaky hand to stir its contents. Finished, she banged the wooden spoon on the rim of the kettle. "With all the vegetables I brought, I decided to fix stew for dinner," she said. "I hope that's okay."

"Stew's fine."

"Speaking of dinner, I hope you're not expecting me to fix all our meals."

"Why would I do that?"

"Because I'm a woman."

"I'm not most men."

Just looking at him, she knew that.

"Do I look like I've been starving?" he asked.

Without thinking, her gaze slid down to his chest, and his stomach. She wanted to look further, but forced herself to stop there. When her gaze returned to his face, his eyes were dancing, daring her comment.

"Nope. You look healthy enough to me." *Good Lord, did he ever.*

"We'll rotate as cooks."

"And whoever cooks, the other cleans up."

"Deal," he said.

With that settled, Jennifer turned to the stew and gave it another stir. A draft of cold air swept over her. She heard the door close.

Jennifer turned around and discovered she was alone again. She muttered to herself. "Boy, a real conversationalist, that one."

A minute later the door opened again. Hawk brought a wrapped package to Jennifer.

"Oh, for me? How sweet." She saw his eyebrow lift at her syrupy words.

"It's venison. For the stew."

To her way of thinking, he was being too serious. She wanted to tell him to lighten up. "Darn. And here I thought you were warming up to me."

"Not in this lifetime, Sweetheart."

"Oh, golly. My first endearment. There is hope."

"You're touched."

"Not by you I haven't been." She could have bitten off her tongue the moment the words escaped, easily remembering when he had touched her. By the look in his eye, she knew he was thinking the same thing.

"That can be easily remedied," he said, huskily.

Her body reacted instantly. A shiver sped down her back, her nipples puckered, and her toes curled in her shoes. With just a few syllables, he had taken the words that she had tossed out casually, twisted them around, turning them into something warm and appealing. It was all she could do to hold onto the wooden spoon. She squelched the desire she felt, and bit her lip. She dared a glance at him, and found she couldn't look away.

Stealthily, with complete silence, he'd moved closer to her.

He was going to kiss her.

Her mind screamed at her to stop him, but the words were paralyzed in her throat. All she could do was open her mouth in hot anticipation.

Instead, his eyes darkened and he moved around her. Her gaze moved to the package in her hand. She didn't want to feel vulnerable, nor let him think she'd actually been waiting for him to kiss her. If he thought he'd gotten the best of her, she'd be under his thumb for the entire two weeks. She had to stay tough. *Look him in the eye*, she told herself. *Don't you dare let him know how he affects you. If he discovers that, your mission will be over. At least right now, you've got half a chance to complete your assignment.*

She squared her shoulders, then looked at him again. This time her gaze didn't waver from his.

Rooted to the spot, Jennifer was relieved when finally, Hawk turned away and went to his desk and plopped into his chair. Picking up the pile of papers he had typed, earlier, he flipped them over and started reading.

Jennifer inhaled deeply. The man had to have nerves of steel, and here she was shaking like leaves on a poplar tree. He bothered her a lot more than she wanted to acknowledge, and it was her embarrassing blurt that had started the whole thing. She could kick herself for that.

Jennifer's lips broke into an upward curve. But, at the same time, his actions just now, told her she affected him more than he liked. His back and shoulders were stiff and even though she only had a profile of his face, his jaw seemed tighter than usual. She grinned even more.

At first, she had thought that the signs she'd seen earlier—the way he watched her, and his earlier attack on the wood was because he was aggravated at her being here. However, the way he had watched in the refrigerator, and then before and after her shower, she sensed he found her attractive.

Okay, so they were both unwillingly interested in each other. That wasn't earth shattering considering he had fascinated her since she first saw him in that underwear ad years ago.

Nor was it unusual that she and Hawk were attracted to each other, considering the circumstances they found themselves. All they had was each other. For two weeks. After that, he'd be alone again, and she'd continue with her life in New York. Nothing unusual about that. People were stranded together all the time. It didn't mean they would get married or anything. Suddenly, Jennifer wondered what kind of husband Hawk would make.

Enough, she told herself, shaking off the thought. This isn't a movie. She'd get her pictures, he'd finish his project, and they'd go on to live their lives—separately.

Despite being shaken at the strong attraction she felt toward Hawk and their brief encounter, their exchange of words had been quite stimulating. It wasn't often she found a perfect sparring partner. Actually, she had enjoyed jabbing at him, wondering how he'd react. She always found it a challenge to get a grumpy clerk to talk to her or to put a smile on a waitress who was obviously having a bad day. Hawk was no different except he spent most of days—and nights—alone. How he responded to her when it came to his birds would really tell a lot about his personality. Did his birds bring a smile to his face? Or, had he become jaded to his surroundings, silent like the giant trees outside his door?

***

"What was that?" Jack stood and looked around nervously. The scar that extended from the corner of his right eye to his jaw appeared pale in comparison to his leathered skin. He'd only been out of prison for a few months, and this was his first illegal hunt. If Angus, formerly his cellmate and now his companion, hadn't convinced him of the money to be made out here, he doubted he would have ever left southern California. He was a city boy, used to hearing guns, sirens, and screams. He hated the sounds out here. In the dark, everything sounded spooky.

Both Angus and Stick, who was Angus' cousin and was tall and thin, laughed. A fourth man, who lay on his side with his hands tied behind his back, his feet tied, and a rag stuffed in his mouth, glared at them. His uniform was that of a ranger. His face was heavily lined. Thin, and much older than these men, he hadn't been able to resist when they'd grabbed him when he walked into their camp moments ago, surprising them.

Angus wiped grease from his mouth and scruffy gray beard with the back of his hand and guzzled down the rest of his beer. "A mountain lion, Stupid." Built like a bull but standing only five foot five, he'd been given the nickname in prison after another prisoner half again as big as him tried to make him his lover. By the time Angus was through with him, the man would never be able to make love again. To the tied up ranger, Angus smiled. "One animal that won't be screaming much longer." He laughed as the old man struggled against the ropes in vain.

"Angus, if I didn't know any better I'd say Jack here is jumpy," Stick said.

Jack poked at the coals, stirring them with agitation. "Damn right, I'm jumpy." He glanced at the stranger. "What are we going to do with him?"

Stick answered hotly. "For chrissake, he's an old man. You almost sound like you care."

"Do not!"

"Ah, shut up! Both of you," Angus said. "He's history. You want to join him?"

Both Stick and Jack looked surprised, and the ranger stopped struggling against his bondage. Angus took another greasy bite. "Either of you got a problem with that?"

Jack looked at the victim uneasily. "No." He knew Angus well enough to know that if he said anything else, he would be next in line after the ranger. "How can you be sure there won't be more rangers following him?"

"Trust me," Angus said. "I don't take chances. This one's a loner. He's got a cabin close by." He leered at the ranger. "Didn't know I'd been watching you, did ya'. This isn't my first trip into the forest. No, sirree, not by a long shot." To Jack and Stick, he bragged. "Nobody's going to stop me this time. This boy knows his way around the forest."

Stick grinned. He wasn't about to doubt anything Angus said or wanted. Angus had kept him out of prison by taking the rap the last time they'd been caught with illegal hides. It had been more important for Stick to be on the outside, enabling them to be here now, as soon as Angus had been released. "Besides, by the time he's discovered missing, we'll have what we came for and we'll be gone."

Angus wiped his hands on his pants, leaving wide dirty streaks. "Well, I guess there's no more waiting. I've had my dinner." He bent over and picked up a knife, then walked to the ranger.

The man's eyes widened. As Angus grabbed what little hair the man had and yanked his head back hard. The ranger screamed but the sound was muffled. Angus slashed the ranger's throat from ear to ear. Blood bubbled, as he took a last dying breath, hearing for the last time the mountain lion's scream.

CHAPTER 4

An hour later, Jennifer announced that dinner was ready. Hawk's quick ability to immerse himself in his work surprised her. He didn't even jump earlier when she'd noisily dropped the apples into the sink.

Jennifer stirred the apples, celery, and raisins one more time before setting it on the table, snitching one of the raisins. Mmmmm. Not having any mayonnaise, she'd used a packet of ranch dressing, dry milk and water. She mixed the ingredients and watched him scribble notes on a pad of paper. She filled two glasses with water and saw he was finished with his reading. As she set down the glasses, she glanced his way and saw him reach across his desk for another ream of paper, his muscles taut and supple beneath his shirt. Water spilled on her hands. She was startled to see her hands shaking. Quickly, she set the glasses down and mopped up the spillage.

Finally, she went to get the pot of stew. Taking no chances on burning herself, she wrapped a thick towel around the handle, protecting her hands from the heat. It took all of her will power not to glance up to see what Hawk was doing now, but she could tell by the sound that he was typing again. Slowly, she lugged the heavy kettle to the table. With a thud, she set it down.

Hawk continued typing. Once more, she told him dinner was ready.

He still didn't respond. She called to him, louder this time. Nothing. He continued pounding away at the keys. Maybe he was at a point where he wanted to finish his thought before he stopped, she mused. Or, was he ignoring her on purpose?

Whatever the reason, Jennifer shrugged, but felt a twinge of disappointment that he could dismiss her so easily. She retrieved the foil-wrapped biscuits from the coals where they'd been cooking. Opening the foil, she dropped several biscuits into her bowl and covered them with the rich smelling, thick stew. Maybe he wasn't hungry, but she was. The last meal she'd eaten had been breakfast. She dug her spoon into the bowl heartily.

"Why didn't you tell me the stew was done?" Hawk dragged a chair out from the table and sat down opposite Jennifer.

Astonished, she stared at him. "I did call you, but you didn't hear me. In fact, I called you several times."

He scooped a huge portion of stew and biscuits into his bowl. From the way he gulped down his first spoonful, he appeared as hungry as she was. A surprised look appeared on his face, then he quickly shoveled up another mouthful. "This is good. I guess I didn't hear you."

Jennifer dropped her spoon into her empty bowl and lifted it up to the pot for a second helping. It had been a while since she'd had a dinner cooked over an open flame. She'd forgotten how much she enjoyed these campfire meals. "Obviously. And thank you." Judging by the huge pile of typed papers stacked beside the typewriter, it had to be the book manuscript. She watched as the third spoonful of stew went to Hawk's mouth. "You were buried in your book. When's the deadline?"

She was guessing. She couldn't remember at what point in her research she had discovered he was writing. Everywhere she went, she'd been told it was to be a series of magazine articles, but now she didn't believe it for a minute.

"November," he mumbled. Then Hawk's head snapped up and he stared at her.

Jennifer calculated quickly. His book would be on the stands by next summer. "Just in time for tourists and bird watchers." Watching bald eagles was a growing industry. Many small communities advertised eagle populations to bring interested tourists, along with their money, to their area. It'd be just a matter of time before people—

hikers and climbers—would be traipsing over these hills, eager to see eagles that had been brought into the area.

She had been prepared for Hawk's penetrating stare, but he kept staring at her, focusing his gaze at the bridge of her nose. She hated to admit it, but he was beginning to rattle her. In an attempt to cover up her nervousness, she grabbed the apple salad and spooned a generous portion into her empty bowl. She speared a chunk of apple with her fork and brought it halfway to her mouth, and then said, "Are you aware that you frown quite often? Really unflattering considering you're such a good looking man. Do you know who your illustrator's going to be?" She brought the fork to her lips.

***

Hawk watched as the apple disappeared from her fork. Her tongue licked at the corners of her mouth.

It was all he could do not to imitate her movement with his own mouth. Right now, he sorely regretted not having kissed her earlier, sensing she would have tasted of pure heaven. He felt himself growing hard again; she was turning him into a quivering flesh of nerves that were turning raw. His mouth was hungry to taste hers. *If you don't stop thinking like this you're going to end up reaching for her across this table and having a different kind of meal entirely!* he thought. Not that he wouldn't mind—not in the least. But, he figured Jennifer would have something to say about that. So far, she'd had something to say about everything. In fact, her comment about his frowning was meant to distract him, he was sure of it. Realizing he *was* frowning, he lifted his brows. He couldn't help but be amused. She was good. He'd just told her something no one besides his publisher knew. He couldn't believe he'd given her information as easily as one of his eagles gives food to its young. She was fishing, and he'd told her. Preoccupied with her delicious stew—and her delectable mouth—he'd been thinking how to best present his final chapter. It'd be a challenge to stay ahead of this one.

Maybe, Smitty was right. Maybe, he did need some fun. Had he been up on the mountain so long and shut himself off in his own little world that he'd become a modern-day Scrooge? When was the last time he'd simply enjoyed himself? Hawk couldn't pinpoint a definite time; he only knew that the time could probably be counted in years.

Jennifer Frost was going to be here for two weeks. Why not make the best of it? The fact that her face had turned several shades of pink during their earlier conversation told him she wasn't immune to him. She had spunk. But, how would she react if he pushed her into a corner? Would she turn tail and become submissive? Or would she challenge him face on? He hoped it'd be the latter.

"You tell me," he said, then consumed another huge spoonful of stew, all the while keeping his gaze on her. Then, he let his gaze drop down. He knew how it flustered her, and after being without the companionship of a woman for such a long time, it was hard not to appreciate her slender but curvy form.

***

Jennifer froze. Then she glanced down at her chest, inspecting her clothing.

She looked back at him. "Why do you keep looking at me like that? Did I spill something on me?"

The cabin rumbled with his laughter.

The sound delighted her. His mouth curved sensuously, revealing perfect white teeth. His eyes sparkled, the corners crinkling. Her heart fluttered against her ribs. "You should laugh like that more often. It becomes you."

Instantly, the laughter stopped and he became solemn again, attacking his stew with a vengeance.

It was like a switch had been flipped. "Did I say something wrong?"

"No."

"Why don't I believe that?"

He shrugged.

"Brother, you flip your moods faster than a fish that's just been landed."

Hawk dropped his spoon. It clattered loudly against the dish. The noise made her blink.

"Why are you sucking up? It won't get you any closer to my eagles."

Jennifer gasped. "Sucking up? I was doing no such thing."

"Then why the compliment?"

Suddenly, Jennifer understood, and she smiled in disbelief. "You're telling me I'm sucking up because I said you look good when you laugh?" She chuckled. "Boy, are you paranoid."

"I am not."

"Then what do you call it?"

"Cautious." A look of frustration crossed his face. He ran a hand through his hair, then sighed. "Look, I'm sorry. It's an old habit."

"You don't trust people do you?"

"Not much."

"Is that the reason why you're here?"

***

The sincerity in her face was real enough, but was she asking as a journalist or as a person interested in another person? "Is this off the record or on?"

He had to be realistic. She was going to be here long enough to get a good grasp on what he was doing. If he thought he could really keep her away from his work, then he was fooling himself. He might be able to keep her from shooting pictures and having them published, but he doubted he could stop her curiosity. She'd be relentless in her pursuit of answers, and she did seem genuinely interested in his work.

He'd spent too many years protecting his Indian background to have his privacy invaded now. Granted, he'd soon be moving into the next phase of his work—enlightening and educating the public—but he wanted that step taken when *he* was ready. Even then, he'd still protect his private life. Was it possible that Jennifer could help him when the time was right? Could he trust her to help him keep private what he didn't want the world to know?

"I'd prefer on the record," she started, but upon seeing the determined look he gave her, she added, "But off the record is fine, if that's what you want."

"It is."

"You have my word, then."

For now, it was all he had—her word. Only time would tell if he had judged Jennifer correctly. It'd be far better to explain his work to her off the record than to tell her nothing and let her draw her own conclusions and publish something damaging and untruthful later. He wanted nothing distorted. Right now, all he knew was Edwards and how destructive he was, and the fact that she worked for the same company. He didn't trust Edwards. Just the thought of her being in the same room as that bastard annoyed him. He would hate to see Edwards soil someone as fresh and spirited as Jennifer. It was enough that she knew him.

But then suddenly, none of it mattered. For the first time in a long, long time he wanted to talk. What was it about Jennifer that made him want to tell her things he'd never confided before?

"It was my great-grandfather, Two Eagles, who brought me to the Salmon River Mountains," he finally answered.

"How'd he do that?"

"He died."

"I'm sorry."

***

"He was old, extremely old. A hundred and four. His time had come. He always wanted to come back here, but he never did." Hawk stared out the window. Jennifer saw a faraway look come into his eye. "He made me promise I'd restore the bald eagle in his homeland. Idaho was his birthplace, and he'd lived here as a young brave."

Jennifer pictured a proud, young Indian brave riding through the trees, traveling through these mountains, and goose bumps rose on her arms.

Hawk continued. "He was a great storyteller. When I was young, every night on the reservation, we kids would gather to hear his tales."

"Reservation! I had no idea." In her research, she hadn't been able to discover Hawk's origination. It was as if all of a sudden—poof—he had appeared in New York. He hadn't talked, given interviews, or appeared on any of the talk shows. "What was it like...living on the reservation?"

"Okay, if you didn't know anything different. But, once I stepped off the reservation and saw how the rest of the world lived, I realized how poor we actually were."

There wasn't any bitterness in his voice. Frankly, Jennifer wouldn't blame him if he were bitter. She'd seen the conditions some Indians had to live under. Houses that were no better than shacks. Unemployment was high. Infant mortality higher than the national average. Few of the young people went to college. Many ended up drinking too much.

Hawk's eyes softened as he spoke of his great-grandfather again. "Two Eagles spoke of the hunts. I envied his youth—still do—the sight of hundreds of thousands of bison roaming the prairie. Can you imagine? Being able to see nothing but prairie and the blanket of dark fur as the animals grazed? What a sight that must have been.

"In his later years, with the buffalo nearly gone, grandfather participated in only a few hunting parties. It was the last for any of them. He'd talk of the summers he spent in this area. How the waters ran cold and clear. How the skies were filled with the great birds."

The picture Hawk described fascinated Jennifer. He had learned well from his grandfather the art of storytelling. Two Eagles would have been proud of his great-grandson.

Hawk continued. "During his lifetime, grandfather watched pollution, forest fires, drought, pesticides, and poachers after the valuable feathers destroy the birds until none remained. He was the last generation to live on the open plains, living in tepees, living as his ancestors had lived for hundreds of years. He cherished the land and all the creatures that shared it with him.

"As the old man lay dying, he made me promise I'd come back and re-establish the bald eagle in his homeland. I couldn't say no."

"Was this promise made before or after you became a model?"

"Before. I knew to keep that promise I'd need money, so I left the reservation to get a job. It was never my intention to live in New York or become a model—it all happened by accident. In Deadwood, I found my first job. That area in South Dakota was always popular with the tourists. Back then, I was a tour guide by day and pumped gas at night. The secretary of a modeling agency vacationed out there, saw me, and told her boss about me."

"And after a few years you just turned your back on all that, built this cabin, and set out to fulfill the promise you made to your grandfather?"

Hawk nodded. "What I saw made me sick."

"I don't understand."

"As I grew up, Two Eagles warned me that man—all men, regardless of their color, even the Indian—would destroy his own world. He was right."

"It's true," Jennifer said, thoughtfully. "I've seen waters too polluted to drink, and everyone knows the air is no longer clean. Your great-grandfather was a wise man."

"Even wiser than he knew. When I lived in New York, our friends—including my wife—had no concept of the number of animals that were destroyed for our lifestyle. If they did know, they didn't care. They scoffed at the idea that they were destroying species of animals. After a while, I couldn't stand it. Nor could I stomach the person I'd become. I was like one of them—superficial and uncaring. I became so self-absorbed in my own fame that I failed to realize I was doing the very things Two Eagles had warned me about."

Jennifer liked to believe her work made a difference, bringing awareness to the public, her photos showing the wilderness as something beautiful and worth saving.

"I'm curious about something. Is your name really Hawk Hunter?"

"No. It's Hawk Who Flies Alone."

It suited him. He was very much a man with a mind of his own, who sought his own way through the wilderness of life. It was obvious by the years that he'd spent on the mountain solo that his life suited him. "Then, how did you come by the name Hunter?"

"It was my agent's idea. She said I'd do better with a more

conventional name. At the time, I was reluctant to give up my real identity. Now, I'm glad I did. I was Hawk Hunter in New York. Now, I'm Hawk Who Flies Alone again. I don't ever want to be connected to that man I once was in New York."

"Was it that bad?"

"No, not in the beginning."

"How did you meet your wife?"

"Like me, she was a model. We posed together for a number of romance covers."

"You met after you'd become a success."

"Yes. After that, my life changed completely."

"How?"

"When I first met Annette, she was engaged to Bob Edwards. She dumped him. For me."

Jennifer eyes widened in disbelief. She'd had no idea.

Hawk continued. "Then Edwards used his position at *Personality* to take a pot shot at me, claiming my heritage was anything but Indian. What was worse, people believed him. But, I wasn't about to set them straight. I figured people like that weren't worth my time. After Annette and I were married, he did another article on us. This one was no more flattering than the first. In fact, he tried to infer that I wasn't a man at all, that I was using Annette as a cover-up. Annette demanded that I fight back, take Edwards to court. I wouldn't do it. When I decided to stop modeling, my fans were disappointed. But, modeling just wasn't fun anymore. I'd been thinking about coming back here for some time, started to make some long range plans—all Edwards did was speed up my time table. I'd never planned to make modeling my career. It was just a means to an end, and for a while, I'd forgotten my promise to Two Eagles.

"Annette was furious at both of us. At Edwards for what he was doing to her through me, and at me, claiming I was walking out on her. I invited her along, but she wanted no part of this life. "Living like an Indian," she called it. She wasn't suited to living in the mountains of Idaho any more than I was suited to living in New York City. If I'm honest, Annette did me a favor leaving me. So, how could I stay bitter at her?"

"Aren't you being hard on yourself?"

"Maybe. I realize I can't solve the country's problem regarding the extinction of the eagle, but in my own small way, I'd like to think I'm making a difference. Needless to say, that was the beginning of the end of my career and my marriage. By that time, I was so disgusted with our friends—really it was a crowd Annette ran around with—I wanted to leave anyway. Annette wanted nothing to do with me if I was dropping out of sight. She loved the fast lane, no matter how shallow it is. She came out here one right after I moved—for what reason I still don't know—but she no sooner got here than she left telling me it was over. After she left me, she quickly attached herself to a Chippendale dancer. I know now she saw me only as a stepping stone. I was nothing more than her current toy. A boy toy."

"I'm sorry. I had no idea." Though she had seen the two articles he was talking about, she hadn't known what to make of them. Working for *Personality*, she knew exaggeration took place. But, not knowing the players in those two articles, it had been hard to separate fact from fiction. Thank goodness she hadn't drawn any hard conclusions from them. She liked to think that she kept an open mind about everyone and everything until she had unveiled the facts for herself. Would she have reacted any differently if she'd been in his shoes?

Finished with her meal, Jennifer pushed her bowl aside and rested her arms on the table. "Now that you're doing something wonderful, don't you want the public to know?"

"I'm not doing it for the public. I'm doing it for Two Eagles and myself. And for the birds."

"But, doesn't the public have a right to know about your work and the difference you're making? We need more people like you."

"Eventually, the public will know what I've been doing. But, when the time is right. That time hasn't arrived yet."

Though she could understand Edwards wanting revenge for

Hawk taking away his fiancée, it didn't explain Hawk's venom for Edwards. There had to be more. Hawk had said he was glad to be out of New York. If Edwards had a hand in that, it didn't reason that Hawk would hold *that* against Edwards. "Did something else happen between you and Edwards?"

"He wanted an interview. Twice before when I had turned him down, he printed something anyway. By then, I'd finished building the cabin. As secretive as we—meaning the government, myself, later my publisher—kept my project, somehow Edwards found out from the Department of Interior that I was bringing a pair of bald eagles into this area. To this day, everyone denies telling him."

"But the Department doesn't hand over a pair of valuable birds to just anyone."

"Exactly. Once I detailed my plans and received clearance, I got all the help I needed. But, Edwards had sniffed out a story and was determined to get an interview. I told him no, but he persisted. Unable to find transportation up the mountain, he tried to climb it—and nearly made it too. Had he been an experienced climber—which he wasn't—things could have been different. "Unfortunately, he put his hand into a rattlesnake den, got bitten, fell, and broke his leg. If I hadn't found him, he'd have died from exposure or from the bite. Or both."

Jennifer shuddered. She always wondered how Edwards had acquired his limp.

"Edwards blamed me for the accident."

"Blamed you! But you had nothing to do with his fall."

"To his way of thinking, I did. I wouldn't allow anyone to provide him transportation to my cabin, forcing him to make the climb, so he claimed."

"But, you didn't force him to do anything. That's ridiculous."

"As the medics carried him to the helicopter that day, he swore he'd get his story one way or another."

Hawk watched as she digested the information. "That's why I think he's behind your being here."

She couldn't say anything. She didn't dare. But, at the same time, she hoped her silence didn't tell him more than she wanted him to know. Now she understood the sneer Edwards had every time he spoke Hawk's name, and why Hawk wanted nothing to do with anything that had Edwards' hand in it.

"Other than my agent, publisher, the department, and the local rangers, no one else knows how far along I am in my project or what I'm doing. You were guessing with your earlier questions, weren't you?"

"Some."

"Anyone who was determined to get to me—like Edwards—wouldn't have had any more problems getting the same information you did. Who verified your information?"

Jennifer debated whether to reveal her source or not. She didn't want to snitch, but it wasn't wise to hide too much either. He had told her so much already. She didn't want him to lose confidence in her. "Your publisher's assistant," she finally said. "He didn't give me a whole lot of information—."

"I'll be talking with him."

"No, it wasn't it fault. Not really."

Hawk studied her, then admitted, "I haven't talked this much in my entire life. All you did was ask a few questions. I gushed like a maple tree that had been tapped for its sap for syrup."

"Your assistant was the same way. He didn't say much."

"All I can figure out is that Edwards pumped Smitty. Smitty's a good ol' boy and wouldn't intentionally hurt my project, but someone, like Edwards, could have pieced it all together if he got the right information. Remember, Smitty picks up and delivers all my supplies, and mail—including any communications with the Department of Interior.

"Could Smitty be bribed that easily?"

"Smitty fixes a price tag to everything he does. He'd let himself be used just to earn a few extra bucks. Big bucks in this case. Smitty wants to move to Florida, buy a fishing boat, and charter it. Even though I don't like what Edwards did, I can't believe Smitty told him anything.

I'd bet that Edwards had someone at the ranger station snooping around. You may have noticed on your ride up here that Smitty has a fondness for the language—he never shuts up."

Jennifer laughed. It was true.

"Smitty could have said things without realizing he was setting me up. Besides, I know Smitty doesn't play dirty. He just likes to even his odds, sort of speak. He knows I'm close to finishing my project, which means my monthly payments will soon be coming to an end. I can't blame him for taking Edwards' offer, if he did. To Smitty, it was just a job. But, Smitty was used. Just like you."

She couldn't deny it. Even though she didn't call it by the same name, Edwards had paid Smitty a handsome fee to keep her here and not let Hawk talk Smitty into coming for her any sooner. Though, at the same time, she willing acknowledged she was using Hawk to further her career. She didn't like thinking she was no better than Edwards. If she was using Hawk, and Edwards used Smitty, how were they any different?

"I assume you're relatively new to the industry. What are you, twenty-two?"

"Twenty-six."

"You look younger." Hawk paused, then went on. "One thing's for sure, Edwards didn't underestimate your eagerness. He played on it."

His chair scraped against the wooden floor as he rose taking dishes to the dry sink. He pulled a large bowl from the shelf underneath, put it in the sink, then went to the hearth. With a towel wrapped around the handle, he carried over to the sink the bucket of water he had earlier placed by the coals. Water splashed as he poured the steaming liquid into the bowl.

"He always has," she admitted.

Hawk appeared surprise at her confession.

"Edwards likes to have his staff competing against each other. Clawing over each other. I know I've never felt like I could confide in anyone there, always wondering if everything I said would be twisted and retold. After a while, I just stopped talking with my co-workers. At least regarding anything personal." And wasn't that exactly what Hawk was protecting himself from? An interview in Edwards' publication that was twisted and incorrect? The more she thought about it, the more she realized just how disgusted she'd become with the magazine. All the more reason to leave it. Which brought her back to the reason why she was here. Though she had known Edwards was wily and not to be trusted, his revenge to get back at Hawk could have really put her in danger.

Right now though, it didn't matter how she came to be here. Granted it wasn't fair to Hawk or herself, but if she didn't come back with a story, she'd have no job. That had to be her main concern.

And what a story it was. A man and his mission. If Edwards was using her, she could just as easily use Edwards.

But could she live with herself by doing that? She wouldn't be using just Edwards, she'd be betraying Hawk. Why did it have to be so confusing? In the wilderness, the animals were either predator or prey. She certainly didn't want to be prey, but could she stomach being the predator? She didn't know what was right anymore. So much was at stake. For both of them. Why did everything have to be so complicated?

Jennifer gathered her dishes together.

"What are you doing? I'm washing the dishes."

"Does that mean I can't even clear my place?"

"No. At least not tonight."

He took her dishes and plunged them into the hot water. Jennifer stood staring at him. Despite his tough exterior, there was a gentleness in him that surprised her. When he spoke of his great-grandfather, she could tell he not only loved the old man but held him in the highest regard. Maybe there was a chance she could appeal to this gentler side to convince him she had a job to do and that she was on the same side as he was. She didn't want to destroy his work, only enhance it.

Hawk noticed she still stood at his side. "It'll only take me a few minutes to wash up. Get another cup of coffee and go sit down."

Their eyes locked, and the air became ladened with tension. His gaze slid to her lips, lingered, and suddenly she longed for him to kiss her.

She became conscious of wet hands on her shoulders and watched as Hawk lowered his face to hers. When he was so close that her eyes could no longer focus, she closed her lids, aching for the moment their lips would touch.

It was all she could do to hang onto his forearms. He felt so good.

Lips, warm and possessive, softly rubbed hers. She felt as if she were being kissed by the sun, but when she finally breathed in, she amended that feeling to being kissed by a sun drenched in pine and dusted with the song of the meadowlarks.

She felt his tongue rub along her lower lip. She nipped at his lower lip in return.

And then he was gone.

CHAPTER 5

Blinking her eyes open, she saw that he had hardly moved a hair's width away from her. She wondered how she had ever thought this man was hard and unreadable. His eyes spoke volumes, and they told her he had enjoyed the kiss just as much as she had. She was captivated by this tender, sensitive side of Hawk, a side she felt he had hidden from the world for too long. As a model, Hawk had radiated sex in his ads—hard, manly sex. This was different. He still radiated that sexual appeal, but now there was something added. A vulnerability. And, she wanted to experience more of what she had tasted only briefly. His mouth touched hers softly one more time, and her eyelids drifted closed.

Like a hungry baby bird eager for nourishment, she opened her mouth welcoming the tip of his tongue. Her heart raced and she rested her hands on his chest, feeling the thud of his own racing heartbeat. Her legs went limp. Fearing she'd topple any moment, she leaned into him. Feminine muscles contracted involuntarily and she shuddered. His arms encircled her, crushing her to him. His lips captured hers completely, claiming full possession over her erogenous flesh. She gave in to him willingly.

Too willingly.

She straightened, and pushed away from him. Hearing his ragged breath, and feeling her own ragged impulses that made her want to forget what she needed to say and escape back in his arms again, she looked down, summoning up all the strength she could muster.

Hoping she was in control of her emotions again, she risked a look at him. His dark eyes were nearly her undoing. Like warm chocolate, his eyes studied her face intensely. His need was as great as her own, and yet she was going to deny both of them of what they wanted. She took a step back. "I don't think this is such a good idea."

"Why not? You want it and so do I."

Jennifer inhaled sharply. He was honest, if not blunt. All the more reason for her to put a halt to the kiss. Had she not, it could have easily led to other things. Her gaze slid to the bed, and she instantly regretted doing so. Tingles of desire spread through her body, making her even more conscious of the man standing in front of her. She squashed her desire as best she could. "Since we're sharing such close quarters, this was bound to happen."

"This happens to you often?"

"No!" Darn it, he was rattling her and she didn't like it. Nor did she like the wicked gleam in his eye. "What I mean is—"

He leaned toward her. "I'm a man and you're a woman—

"And we've both got our jobs to do."

He stiffened and she wondered if she had said the right thing. "You're right." He turned his back on her and returned to the dishes. Even while doing this mundane chore, his movements were fluid and gentle, belying his brute strength. He was as comfortable doing this simple chore as he was slicing through hard wood with one powerful clean stroke of the ax.

Relieved that he was no longer pursuing her, she felt equally bad that this situation wasn't turning out more amicable. She'd get nowhere with her assignment unless they came to an understanding. "Hawk," she said, softly. "I think we need to establish some ground rules."

"I'm listening."

She felt like she was trying to tiptoe through broken glass. Hawk had been up here for five years—alone. No company, no women. And then here she was, a temptation to a man who clearly had basic needs. But, she wasn't going to be a willing sacrifice to any man. He didn't care about her, not the way she would have liked. If she thought for one moment—

No. To even think such a thought was ridiculous. She'd only been here one day. How in the world could either of them know each other well enough to feel anything beyond a physical attraction. That's all this was. Physical. She had to admit, his body next to hers felt wonderful, but there was more to life than her physical needs—or his—being met. There was his work and she was here to photograph it. Beyond that, nothing more mattered.

But, she couldn't say that to him. He'd have his defenses well in place before she even finished her first sentence. She had to win his confidence, and at the same time achieve her goal. Not an easy task, not with this man.

She started again. "Hawk, we can make this difficult or we can make this easy. I'd prefer to think you'd want the latter. I'd hate to think I'm going to be spending two weeks fending off...I don't think it would be in either of our best interests to get involved."

When he didn't respond either by word or movement, she bit her lip. It was like talking to a wall, high and impenetrable. Right now, she needed to distance herself from him.

Taking a flashlight, she decided to visit the outhouse before she turned in. She was tired, and it had been a long day.

***

Hawk heard the door close softly. He expected the cabin to be empty, and when he turned around it was. He had run her off. There was so much he had wanted to say. He wanted to respond, but he couldn't. He knew it was his pride. She had rebuffed him and it had hurt.

But, she was right. Nothing good could come of a physical relationship. There were already so many problems with her being here. Getting involved with each other would only complicate matters more.

If only she wasn't so spunky, so beautiful, so full of life it would be easy to agree to everything she was saying. He tossed the dishtowel on the table. He could wring Edwards' neck for doing this to him.

He grabbed a mug, its bottom scrapping the wood as he dragged it across the cupboard. Angry, frustrated, and feeling he'd been backed into a corner, he poured the last of the coffee into the mug. He sat in the rocker and stared at the flames.

It was going to be a hellish two weeks. He took a deep swallow, finding the heat as it traveled down his throat something tangible that he could focus his thoughts on. He leaned back, closed his eyes, and meditated on the warmth, feeling it spread into his stomach. He felt his muscles start to relax, his thoughts becoming calmer.

The moment he heard her footsteps outside, however, the tranquility he had established shattered. Instinctively, he rose. As she entered the cabin, her gaze searched the cabin until she found him, then locked in on him. Instantly, he saw she was having as much a problem dealing with the situation as he was for she appeared nervous, cautious, and hesitant.

"I...I guess it's time to turn in," she said finally. "It's been a long day."

He saw her hands tremble as she went to her suitcase and pulled out her nightshirt and toothbrush. The toothpaste fell to the floor. Quickly, she retrieved it.

"I'll just go...and..." She stopped.

"Change?" Hawk finished for her. He smiled. Seeing her skittish appealed to him, though he much preferred the gutsy, outspoken Jennifer he'd first met. He moved toward her and stopped when he stood before her. Gently, he rubbed his knuckles against her chin. "Did you forget there's only one room?"

She nodded. He felt her warm breath on his knuckled fist. Quickly, the warmth spread to other parts of his body. He felt about as solid as whipped cream. Before his body could betray him and reveal to her how much he wanted her, he reached for the door. "I'll leave you alone for a few minutes. Don't be too long," he said softly. He closed the door behind him.

For a moment, Jennifer stood motionless and stared at the door. Despite the short length of time she had been kissed, never had she been kissed as solidly and thoroughly. Any kiss she'd received in the past melted into nothingness compared to his kiss. It excited her. It scared her. She'd always known exactly what she wanted. Now she felt muddled and confused. The step she was taking in her career was still uppermost in her mind, but Hawk was throwing her a curve. For the first time in a long time, she had forgotten her career. Even though it had only been for a few minutes, the feeling had overwhelmed her.

The hoot of an owl brought her out of her trance. Quickly, she stripped off her clothes and pulled her nightshirt over her head, tugging it down over her hips so its hem rested mid-thigh. A collage of a giraffe, tiger, and an African elephant decorated the front of her Banana Republic shirt.

Then she went to the sink. Finished brushing her teeth, she swished her toothbrush in a bit of water. At the sound of the door opening, she spun around.

***

The first thing Hawk noticed was the way the nightshirt hugged Jennifer's curves, just barely covering her upper thigh. The second thing he noticed was how huge her eyes appeared as she stared at him. She was gorgeous. Few women stood up to him as she had done earlier, yet now, she appeared frail and timid, like a mouse caught in an open field with an owl circling around, closing in.

Her hands were braced against the seat behind her, hanging onto the counter's edge. The action forced her breasts to jut out against her shirt. Her nipples, now pointed nubs, contrasted against the soft globes. He envied the shirt, the caressing touch it gave her as it lay against her skin. His hands ached to feel her breasts. Both of them. And he wanted her naked, him naked too. Skin against skin.

He clenched his fists and shut the door securely, pulling the leather thong inside. It was the only protection he needed against the night. He had no fear of people entering his cabin. Only the animals.

"I...Would you...Ah...Goodnight, Hawk."

She moved away, then looked at her hand and the toothbrush she still held. She thrust it into a glass and it rattled noisily. With a heavy clunk, Jennifer placed the glass on the shelf above the dry sink.

As she crossed the room, he couldn't help but notice how her breasts swayed beneath her shirt. If he thought he'd been aroused earlier, he was doubly so, now. As she climbed into bed and scooted down, her nightshirt climbed up and he caught a glimpse of her bottom. The air in his lungs was trapped. For a moment, he couldn't breathe. Then, the sheets and blankets settled on her slender form completely.

With her back to him, she remained frozen in her position.

Mesmerized, Hawk stared at Jennifer's back. Did she have any idea what she was doing to him? He clenched his fists and willed himself to the spot. Every pore in his body, every thought in his soul demanded he take the few steps to her bed and finish what they had started earlier. Instead, he closed his eyes willing himself back in control. It was the hardest thing he had ever had to do in his life. All he could see in his mind was the image of him going across the room, flinging back her covers, lying next to her, pulling up her nightshirt and sucking on the rosy nipples that had been exposed to his view earlier.

When he'd first come back into the cabin, he was going to mention the curtainless windows. Seeing the expression on her face, he decided against it. Apparently, she hadn't given it a thought or been aware that outside, Hawk had seen her change. He hadn't meant to watch. He, too, had forgotten there were no shades or curtains until he had turned around and seen her pull off her T-shirt. After that, he hadn't been able to stop himself from watching. Though he knew he shouldn't be watching, his feet had remained rooted.

Now he was in pain—severe pain. His jeans had become uncomfortably tight. He wanted release. He needed a woman.

He opened his eyes, arched his neck back and stared at the ceiling and breathed deeply until his jeans finally didn't feel quite so tight.

Lord. How was he going to get through two weeks of this? With great difficulty. It wasn't her fault. Not really. She'd just found herself caught between Edwards' manipulative actions and his own goals.

Despite the fact that she had continued to deny any knowledge of Edwards being behind all this, his gut reaction told him Edwards was. She was too good for Edwards, she didn't deserve to even work in the same building as he did. She was too trusting, and when it came to wildlife that was a vulnerable trait to have. And now with the poachers, the area lurked with unseen dangers.

Somehow, he had to make sure she would remain at the cabin. If she stood up to him like she did today and refused to honor what he wanted, he was going to have his hands full. Undoubtedly, she'd want to accompany him with her cameras. She wouldn't be content to stay at the cabin. He ran a hand through his hair in frustration. A battle was guaranteed to take place tomorrow.

It didn't matter, as long as he won the war.

He walked to the fireplace and banked the coals. Then, he placed two large logs, to keep the cabin toasty, on top of the coals. Though it was late summer, the temperature outside would drop below freezing during the night. Jennifer remained huddled under her blankets and still hadn't moved.

Once again, he saw mental images of him in her bed and their doing anything and everything but sleeping. Frustrated that he couldn't stop thinking about her, he rolled out a sleeping bag with a snap, lay it on the floor, shed his clothes, cupped his hand over the top of the oil burning lamp, blew it out, and slipped into the sleeping bag. Only now did he consider that he was sleeping in the nude—just like he did every night. He considered getting back up and at least putting on some underwear. But, for what purpose? So she wouldn't be uncomfortable?

No, he decided. He wasn't about to change his ways. She had invaded his territory, his lifestyle. If she was going to be uncomfortable about his nudity, so be it. She had certainly left him uncomfortable—downright in pain at times.

He heard Jennifer's sigh. The bedcovers rustled as she settled down. He could still see the silhouette she made as she lay on her side—away from him—her hair feathered on the pillowcase, her hips rounded, legs slim and long, the line tapering to the points of her toes.

Hawk bent an arm back under his head and stared at the ceiling. It was going to be a long, long night.

***

When Jennifer finally heard Hawk's even breath that told her he was asleep—which had seemed to take forever—she turned around so she lay on her other side. With an arm resting beneath her pillowed head, she fastened her gaze on him. His entire length was outlined wonderfully against the backdrop of the glowing coals, and even though he was asleep, he still had the ability to stir her senses.

His wide chest rose gently with each breath he took. Despite the slight chill she felt in the cabin, his only blanket came up to his waist. His golden bronzed skin looked supple, yet she knew the muscles beneath the skin were hard and strong. The washboard contours of his waist were smoothed out; she ached to feel the texture of his body. His hair curled slightly around his face, and his brows were lines low on his forehead. From here, his lids were in the shadows, but it was easy to remember the velvet brown as he had gazed at her after their kiss.

Her gaze traveled down the length of his body, then back up again to his midsection. There was no disputing the bulge that lay between his thighs. She swallowed heavily, closed her eyes, and forced herself to move on her back. When she opened her eyes again, she saw shadows dancing on the ceiling. Almost like the aurora borealis, she thought. The shadows mesmerized her, lulling her into a trance.

Suddenly, she saw Hawk dancing among the shadows, dressed in full uniform of a Shoshoni warrior, including a headdress of feathers that reached his heels. And then with the shadows at his back, he turned to her, stalked her, and when he was so close so thought they would be one, his image disappeared.

She blinked. A strange heat passed through her, a pulsating beat hummed through her veins. And then, she thought she heard the beat of a drum.

She darted a glance at Hawk. He hadn't moved; he was still asleep, in the same position he had been just moments ago.

Biting her lip at the strange sensation, she thought about the day. Had it only been hours ago that she had met Hawk? It felt much longer than that.

Punching her pillow, Jennifer purposely emptied her mind of all thoughts and let her weariness slide her into sleep.

***

She woke with a start, the dream still vivid in her mind. She'd been running down a long, dark tunnel. Someone was chasing her, but she didn't know who it was. She only remembered the eyes. Hawk's eyes. When she emerged from the tunnel, she fell into the embrace of the person who'd been chasing her, and welcomed the arms that encircled her.

The arms started moving, hand caressing and touching in her places that she hadn't been touched in a long while. Her hips rose to meet fingers that probed and she ached with unfulfilled desire.

That's when she had woken up. It had all been a dream, yet she felt flushed and excited. Her heart raced.

She sat up and combed her fingers through her hair not understanding the dream at all, but feeling unnerved at the intensity of emptiness it had left her with. She glanced out the window. Judging from the sun's angle in the sky, she determined it hadn't been up long. She certainly didn't feel like she'd gotten a full night's sleep.

At the sound of a pop, she turned her head toward the fireplace. The kettle hung over the fire. She sniffed the air, unable to detect any clear distinct odor. Rather, she heard a bubbling plop every few seconds. Oatmeal? A quick glance told her she was alone in the cabin. She scooted out of bed, dressed, washed her face, and tied her hair back into a ponytail with the aid of a small mirror fastened to the wall above the dry sink.

Going to the door, she pulled the handle. It swung open too easily. Hawk filled the doorway. "Oh." She jumped out of the way.

Hawk stepped into the cabin, his arms piled high with wood. His dominating maleness jolted her. Before he had entered, the cabin was just a functional building filled with sunshine, and warmth from the fire. Now, all she noticed was how he seemed to permeate every corner. The room had a vibrancy that was missing before. And, she felt the heat, as if someone had turned it up by at least five degrees.

"Sorry," Hawk replied. "I didn't know you were there."

"Just on my way out to...to the powder room."

"That's a new name for it."

After he passed her, she smelled earth, pines, cold air, and a hint of musk in his wake.

No man should look that good before breakfast, she thought walking out back to her spoken destination. There ought to be a law against such a thing. She wondered if he missed the women. When he was in New York, he could have had his pick. Easily. She also wondered if any woman had ever been able to say no to him. A few minutes ago, when he had walked into the cabin, she would have said yes to most anything. Well, almost anything. As much as she wished things were different, she couldn't forget her assignments.

By the time Jennifer returned, breakfast was nearly ready. The bacon, fried to perfect crispness, already sat on a plate on the table. The remaining fat in the pan spit, occasionally jumped into the fire, making the flames leap high. Slices of bread, speared on a long thin piece of iron, hung in a corner just above the flames where it was hot enough to toast, but not too hot to burn. Hawk deftly broke open half a dozen eggs in the bacon fat, each egg sizzling as it hit the grease. It was nice seeing a man who was comfortable in the kitchen—such as it was.

All that remained for Jennifer to do was to set the table. Both finished their chores at the same time.

She sat back in her chair while he dished up the eggs. The sleeve of his blue flannel shirt caressed her cheek, and it felt soft. She wondered if he washed his clothes by hand up here or if he went to a laundromat now and then. No, it didn't make sense that he had them cleaned elsewhere. When Smitty had dropped her off along with his monthly supplies she didn't remember seeing Smitty pick up anything remotely resembling a bundle of clothes when he left. In fact, Smitty hadn't taken anything off the mountain or from the cabin when he'd dropped her off.

So how did Hawk get his clothes so soft? she wondered. She couldn't help herself, she had to know. She sniffed at the fabric hoping to catch the familiar scent of some fabric softener. Instead, her nostrils were rewarded with the scent of Hawk. Smoke, pine, and musk. Each scent was a strong, distinctive scent, but when combined, it was a heady fragrance that made her dizzy with weakness.

Instantly, she jerked her head back, reeling from the way her senses spun out of control, feeling guilty as if she'd been caught in the act of doing something wrong. A glance to his face told her Hawk hadn't detected her action. She bit her lip, conscious of her accelerated pulse. She noticed the taut cording of his muscles forearms as he handled the wooden spoon. His movements were fluid, and he didn't drop even the tiniest bit of egg.

Once he moved away, she took a breath, and hoped her face wasn't as flushed as it felt to her. She felt exhausted all of a sudden, like the time a wolf had walked past her—so close, she could see the pale blue of its eyes. For some reason, she had gone undetected that time, too. From the time she had first spotted the carnivorous animal until he was safely gone, she had held her breath. It amazed her that she felt like that now.

Her eyes continued to follow his movements. All over again, she felt his prowess, the magnificent aura that exuded around him, and now all he was doing was sitting opposite her and biting off a piece of toast. The sensation shook her. She picked up a slice of toast and mimicked him. "What's on the agenda today?" she asked.

"The usual. I try to check on at least two nesting sites each day. I need to warn you, though. I think there are some poachers in the area."

"Poachers? Have you reported them?

"Can't. I don't have any proof yet. But, I will. Sooner or later, they'll reveal themselves. It's just a matter of time. For now, I'll keep watching them."

"Are we safe?"

"For now—they've stayed north. The closest they've gotten is about three miles from here. Yesterday, I saw them about seven miles from here. They've been moving around a lot, and I try to find them each day while I'm out."

"What are they poaching?"

"I'm not sure yet."

"Then how can you know they're poachers?"

He spoke in a tone that told her he didn't want to discuss the matter anymore. "I just know."

Though Jennifer knew poachers were dangerous, their presence added an exciting element to her story. She was anxious to get going—she wanted to see these men for herself. She didn't mind his not wanting to talk about them right now. She was patient, she could wait.

Breakfast over, Jennifer stood and stacked the dishes. Her gaze strayed to Hawk. He picked up the last piece of toast and it quickly disappeared. She was grateful he'd made no mention about last night. Apparently, he accepted and agreed with everything she had said. Even though she knew the kiss last night was still affecting her—more than she would have liked—it was best this way. But, she wondered as tender as his kiss had been, if he'd be as tender a lover.

Wondering, however, was the only luxury she'd allow herself. Despite her inquisitive nature, there was no way she would let her curiosity or her attraction to Hawk get in the way of her priorities. It was a new day, and she needed a new course of action—mainly, to get going on her project.

Hawk was accepting her presence, and she couldn't do anything to upset that. Since he hadn't said anything about her not going with him today, she assumed he'd changed his mind.

Hawk's chair scraped the floor. He reached for the bucket of hot water in the hearth while Jennifer took the dishes to the sink.

She stepped back allowing him room to pour the warm water into the dish pan. His elbow brushed against her breast. The effect was the same as if he'd caressed her. She found it difficult to swallow, let alone breathe.

"Sorry," Hawk said. "I didn't mean...to bump you."

His gaze dropped to her breasts. Instantly, she remembered her earlier dream, and the way his hand felt when he touched her yesterday. And later, the bone melting kiss they'd shared. She saw by the smoldering look in his eyes that he was remembering it too. But then, the look was gone, like a door had been slammed in her place, and he quickly re-focused his attention back to his chore. She closed her eyes in agony. This was not going to work. How could she possibly live with this man for two weeks and ignore the way her senses reeled every time they got close to each other? She opened her eyes.

She jumped seeing he wasn't standing next to her. She swiveled around and found him banking the fire. She hadn't heard him move. As much as she admired his ability to move around silently, at the same time she cursed it; she never knew where he was. If she didn't know any better, she would have sworn he was a ghost, a figment of her imagination. But, she did know better than that. She knew from his powerful kiss—one that had literally knocked the breath out of her—that he was a living, breathing man. The word *magnificent* came to mind, once again. It was easy to see how he'd earned the nickname.

Her hands, deep in the dishwater, paused. She wondered who had given him the nickname. His wife? His agent? A fan?

All of a sudden, she wished she knew. Not that it meant anything, she told herself. Just curious.

She thrust her hands deeper into the water, grabbing the first dish. She had to re-evaluate the situation rationally. She'd already spent too much time thinking about Hawk and his magnificent form. Instead, she should be focusing on her job. That was her first priority. She took a deep, calming breath.

Second, this was a vacation for her too. She wanted to enjoy her time here. She had to stop worrying about what might or might not happen. As long as she kept talking to herself like this, keeping herself focused, everything would be fine.

Contemplating seeing her first eagle today, she thought about the different types of pictures she'd like to capture.

Ten minutes later, she rinsed the last dish, setting it to air dry with the others. She picked up the dish towel, turned and said, "I'm all set to go..." Her voice faded in the empty cabin. "Darn it all! Where did he go?"

She went to the door, opened it, and looked around. Not seeing

Hawk, she raced around to the back of the cabin. He wasn't in sight, nor was he in the outhouse. He'd left her!

"You just wait," she said aloud. "You just wait."

Slapping her thigh with the dish towel, she walked back to the cabin with determination. If he thought he had her stymied, he was wrong. He didn't know Jennifer Frost!

Inside the cabin, she put on the khaki jacket, hoisted the small camera bag onto her shoulder, slung two cameras over her neck and slipped her supply bag onto her other shoulder.

After circling the cabin's outer perimeter, Jennifer determined that Hawk's freshest tracks—if she could call them that—led west. The track he left wasn't like anything a man his size would normally leave. There was no full footprint. Only a slight indentation on the ground. If the earth weren't quite so damp, she doubted she'd have been able to pick up a track at all. Quickly, she followed his trail. Once she was away from the clearing, she knew without a doubt that this was the way he had come. It was as if he had left his scent behind for her to follow, which was truly idiotic when she thought about it. A person's scents didn't linger in the air—not unless it was someone who hadn't bathed in several weeks.

So, how could she account for the fact that she *knew* he had been on this very path earlier? She couldn't. Not unless Hawk had something to do with this uncanny sense she was feeling. Even then, she didn't think his powers extended to guiding her to him in the wilderness. First of all, why would he be doing that after he had deserted her at the cabin?

"Listen to you. You're acting like he's some mystical god with—ooooooo—supernatural powers." She kept walking. "He must have powers. He's got you talking out loud to yourself, doesn't he? You've never done that before, have you?"

She stopped in her tracks, then shook her head. "Don't answer that."

About a mile later, she encountered an owl sitting on a low branch and took his picture as he swung his head around, staring at her with round eyes. She continued on, looking for signs that kept her aware of Hawk's movements. A few times, she lost the trail and had to retreat a bit until she found another sign. Hawk definitely followed the ways of his ancestors, leaving behind little evidence that he'd been in the area. It was hard to see the slight image of a footprint—just the softest impression of the back of his heel or the ball of his foot. At other times, a leaf was fastened to the ground tightly as if someone had stepped on it gluing it to the dirt, making it stand out from the surrounding leaves that ruffled in the breeze. She grinned, wondering if he'd be surprised that she'd been able to follow him.

A few hours later, she paused, leaning against a large lodgepole pine that had grown twisted from the mountain winds and uncapped her canteen. She drank thirstily, wondering how much farther she'd have to go before catching up to him. It was stupid at this point to think she'd catch up to him; he'd be traveling so much faster. It was time-consuming following such as she was.

Twigs snapped in the underbrush. Slowly, she recapped her canteen, allowing it to slide down her side until its weight was on the strap on her shoulder. She sniffed the air. She couldn't smell anything. She was downwind of whatever it was. Not knowing what was out there, she didn't want to make any sudden movements. She hoped it was Hawk. And then, she remembered Hawk's talk of poachers.

Her heart climbed into her throat. She couldn't swallow.

Suddenly, it was hard to breathe.

She could hear every shallow breath she took.

If she moved, they'd be able to hear her too.

She heard the rustle of leaves and then the bushes in front of her parted.

CHAPTER 6

A huge black bear stood only twenty yards away from her. *This isn't good*, Jennifer thought. She'd encountered bears before, but never this close. The bear sniffed at the wind.

It hadn't seen her yet. Thank goodness the animal had poor eyesight and couldn't see her, not unless she moved. And, with the wind blowing from the north, neither of them was downwind of the other; so, the bear hadn't smelled her, yet.

Another lucky break.

Suddenly, behind the bear, two cubs burst into the opening their mother had made. Jennifer's eyes widened and she held her groan. A bad situation had suddenly gotten worse.

The wind swirled around them.

The bear sniffed the air again and rose on her hind legs. Jennifer had just been discovered.

Fear numbed her, and her body turned cold.

She clamped her teeth to keep from making the slightest sound.

As much as she wanted to yell for help, she couldn't risk it. She needed to get rid of the baggage on her shoulders, knowing the bear could smell the crackers through the thin wrapper, but she couldn't do it.

To move unnecessarily meant danger. The tinned meat, thank goodness, would remain undetected.

Silently she cursed, knowing in the future—if there was a future—all foods she carried would be contained far better. Slowly, not looking the bear in the eye, but still keeping track of mom and the two cubs, she lowered herself, noiselessly, to the ground. In a prone position, face-down, Jennifer covered her head with her arms, putting as much face into the ground as she possibly could, keeping her hands hidden in her sleeves.

Then she froze, breathing as deeply as she dared without making any movement.

She heard the bear moving towards her, sniffing the ground as she approached. A chill ran down Jennifer's spine and through her legs.

Would she survive this encounter?

Her mind raced, thinking of everything she'd learned of bears.

She knew she'd done the right thing. If she had run, the bear would have immediately given chase believing prey was getting away. Fortunately, this was a black bear, not the dreaded grizzly. Grizzlies attacked anything nearby; black bears attacked but only when provoked.

The unlucky side was this bear had cubs—mothers were always unpredictable.

Jennifer felt the hot breath of the bear on her fisted hands through the material, and then, on the back of her neck.

She wanted to gasp for fresh air as she smelled the foul carrion-like scent of the bear. Jennifer closed her eyes tightly, praying fervently that the next few moments would pass quickly.

***

At a fast pace, Hawk walked through the jack pines that stood tall in the forest. The thick carpet of needles muffled the noise of his footsteps as he took care not to step on branches or twigs. Even though it was his nature not to leave a trail, it was even more important now that poachers were in the area. He wanted to keep his presence and whereabouts a secret as long as he possibly could. He wanted the element of surprise on his side, not theirs.

He'd been gone longer than expected. Wanting to check on a pair of nests where eagles were near fledgling, a nest the poachers were close to discovering, he didn't want Jennifer following him, but he didn't like leaving her alone at the cabin either. He knew she wouldn't be content to stay there alone long, so he had taken the necessary precautions, earlier, of securing his manuscript safely from Jennifer's curious eyes.

After he reached the first nest, he start rethinking about having left Jennifer alone and berated himself for doing so. It was a stupid thing to do, especially with poachers around. How did he figure she'd be safe if he wasn't around? It was because he'd been so intent on checking up on his eagles without Jennifer, everything else escaped his consideration. He'd feel better once the poachers were apprehended and Jennifer was safely back in New York.

But, would his life ever be the same again? Somehow he doubted it.

Thinking how he could appease Jennifer's appetite to fulfill her quest and yet keep his birds safe from publicity, Hawk almost missed the signs. There was a bear up ahead. Under his feet were bear tracks. A female with two cubs. A bear to avoid. Then he heard it, a low menacing growl. It was closer than he thought. Finally, he smelled her. He froze. Before he moved any further, he needed to know its exact location. The cubs were growling now, and then he heard...cloth tearing?

Slowing and silently, Hawk crept up to a hedge of bushes. The bears were on the other side. Carefully, he squatted down and moved into the bushes, not touching any of the branches allowing them to crack and reveal his position.

He saw them. The cubs were only a few months old. And there was something else. Jennifer!

Terror gripped his heart. Instinctively, he held back the desire to burst through the bushes, yelling and drawing the bear's attention to himself. In doing so, she could be injured.

Was she hurt already? She lay so still. From this distance, he couldn't tell if she was breathing. Not knowing if she was dead or alive, he could do nothing. If she wasn't hurt so far, the safest thing for him to do was wait. Maybe the bear would depart on its own, leaving her unharmed.

The cubs were playing tug of war with a strap of some kind. He saw a canteen, ripped of its cloth cover, with scratches on its metal exterior. The mother had her nose in one of Jennifer's bags and withdrew a package of crackers. With a jab of a paw, the package was opened and swiftly consumed. Then, the bear started sniffing at Jennifer, trying to get her nose beneath Jennifer. Hawk held his breath. Did the bear think Jennifer was a log and that there might be insects under it?

Unable to move Jennifer with its nose, the bear took a paw and moved it from Jennifer's shoulder down to her elbow. Hawk heard the fabric tear. Jennifer still didn't move. Was she conscious?

Then, he saw the torn fabric on the back of her jacket. How long had Jennifer been there? Wasn't there anything he could do?

No, he told himself. There were no other apparent wounds, no bleeding of any kind. Be patient, the bear will lose interest and move on in a minute.

They were the longest moments Hawk had ever endured.

With a snort, the large bear swatted at the last bag in obvious disgust that she hadn't found any more food. A camera fell out of the bag onto the ground. With one final sniff at the camera, the bear waddled away. As soon as she was out of sight, the cubs dropped the ravaged piece of cloth and scampered after their mother, calling at her.

Hawk waited a few seconds, making sure the bears—all of them—were gone for good. He ran to Jennifer's side, bent down, and rolled her over, not knowing what he'd find. If anything had happened to her, he'd kill Bob Edwards!

"Jennifer! Are you all right? Talk to me!"

Jennifer's eyes popped opened. She looked at Hawk, then smiled weakly. Her tense body sagged with relief seeing him. "Talk about Goldilocks and the Three Bears."

Hawk gaped at her. "It's no joke."

She struggled to a sitting position. "Would you rather have me hysterical? Sorry to disappoint you."

"You had no business being out here alone."

"You were out here alone."

"That's different."

"Because you're a man?"

"Because I told you to stay at the cabin."

"Not this morning."

"I told you yesterday."

"Yesterday doesn't count."

He was getting nowhere fast. "You could have been seriously injured."

Her feet flat on the ground, she rose. Hawk helped her up. She winced as he touched her arm. She took a deep shaky breath, then confessed. "Actually, I was scared out of my skin."

Hawk could tell. Though her blue eyes shone brightly, her teeth started to chatter and her body shook uncontrollably. Instinctively, he opened his jacket and gathered her close to him, offering her as much body heat as he possibly could.

He held her within the circle of his arms, content for the moment to keep her there. "I shouldn't have left you alone thinking you'd stay at the cabin." Unable to stop her chattering, he shrugged out of his jacket and wrapped it around her. "I took a chance that you would. I should have known better."

"How...how...how could...you...you have known? You...you don't...know me and how stub...stubborn...I...can be."

The woman was incredible! And incorrigible, he thought. He'd never met anyone like her. She'd just been thoroughly inspected by the worst kind of bear—a mother with cubs—and she was bantering with him as if they'd just finished a Sunday stroll.

"Oh, I think I've seen some of your stubbornness. He held her a few more minutes until her teeth stopped chattering and he felt her start to relax in his arms. "You need to take your jacket off."

Jennifer looked up at him, sighed, and pressed her lips together. She wanted to cry, but she wouldn't, not in front of him. She could tell he expected her to cry. Well, she wouldn't. "What for?"

"I want to check your arm and back," he said grimly.

She handed him his jacket, then accepted his help in pulling hers off. She prided herself that she was good in an emergency situation but acknowledged that she fell apart afterwards. For once, she was glad she wasn't alone. Hawk kept her from dissolving into tears.

He grimaced, seeing the long red bleeding lines on her arm. "Take off your shirt."

"No way."

"I want to look at your back."

"Then lift the shirt up."

Jennifer turned her back to him and Hawk lifted it. He sucked in air as his eyes took in the angry crisscross of lines—some bleeding, some just welts. He wished it had been him instead of her. She took a step away and pulled her shirt down.

"Does it hurt?" he asked. She had to be in pain. He saw through the disguise of the fierce don't-touch-me look she gave him. There was pain in her eyes, and her mouth trembled slightly. All he wanted to do was comfort her, hold her close to him again, and let her release her suffering.

"Like fire," she said, raising her head, sticking her chin out.

He felt the edges of his mouth lift up. She was tough and unafraid. He liked that. No matter what she might be feeling, she wasn't going to go soft and whiny on him.

He helped her put her jacket on again, then draped his over her shoulders. Her teeth were chattering again, but not nearly as severely as they had before. He probably should have waited until they got to the cabin to inspect her back, but he had wanted to make sure she wasn't bleeding badly. He picked up her equipment. "Let's go back to the cabin. I want to clean those wounds."

She didn't argue with him and led the way.

Once, Jennifer's foot slipped on some wet leaves. Hawk reached out for her and saw her cringe when he grabbed her arm to keep her from falling. He had grabbed her injured arm. After that, he walked at her other side, a hand at her uninjured elbow—just in case. He didn't want anything more happening to her before they reached the cabin.

Back at the cabin, he motioned for Jennifer to sit at the table. First, he placed some water over the fire to warm, then retrieved the first-aid kit from the cupboard.

When Hawk turned back around, he saw she had removed her jacket and shirt. All she had on above her waist was a lacy bra. He couldn't help but notice how her breasts threatened to spill over the edge of her bra. A fierce protectiveness filled him. He wanted to punish the bear for marking her. It was all he could do to wrap his arms around her protectively and hold her close to him. And yet, at the same time, his hands ached to cup her breasts, to feel the smooth satin of her skin against his fingertips, to unveil the dusty rose-colored nipples and rub them until they were tight nubs.

He hated the fact that he was aroused. Here she was injured and all he could think of was what it would be like to make love to her.

She turned her head, trying to see the scratches, then turned back.

"It's not a pretty sight," he said, referring to the scratches and moving behind her. He took a wet cloth and started wiping away the blood.

"I didn't expect it to be pretty."

He held his breath when the cloth snagged against her scratched skin. She didn't move, but he felt her muscles tense. She was a beautiful woman, but appeared oblivious to her own beauty, her natural sensuality. Glancing up, he saw her lip quiver slightly. She was trying to hold onto the last threads of her courage and not collapse in front of him. If nothing else, he admired her strength.

"I think you'll want to remove your bra and not wear it for a few days. Your friend didn't miss much. These scratches won't heal if your bra's rubbing against them." He unhooked it for her and slid the straps carefully off her shoulders. The bra dropped into her lap, exposing her breasts—full and ripe. She held her T-shirt to her chest. His fingers shook. "You need to lower your jeans too," he said, softly. He heard a catch to his voice. Did she hear it as well? He cleared his throat. "The edges of a couple scratches disappear into them. We should treat all of your injuries."

The T-shirt fell, once again revealing her breasts, as Jennifer, still sitting, unsnapped her jeans and tugged them down a couple inches.

Hawk clenched his hands, then flexed his fingers, then clenched them again. Oh, how he wished the circumstances were different and that she was pulling down her jeans for other reasons. He nearly groaned aloud. He knew her motion wasn't meant to be sensual, but to him it was.

Her voice, when she spoke, was at a whisper. "How's that?"

He gulped. Other than the scratches, her skin was like ivory—smooth and luxurious. He would have preferred running his hands over her skin, stroking her tenderly compared to what he was about to do. "Fine. Just fine."

It was anything but fine. She didn't appear embarrassed that she had just exposed her breasts. It was hard to blot out the picture of his hands cupping them, his mouth sucking on the rosy tips. Instead, he concentrated on putting a cotton ball on top of the open antiseptic bottle, tipped it upside down, and let it absorb some of the healing liquid, while Jennifer, once again, held her T-shirt to her chest.

"This is going to hurt," he said before he applied the wet ball to one of wounds. The last thing he wanted to do was hurt her.

***

Jennifer stiffened and swore softly at the first application. Wasn't it enough that she was sitting here practically nude? She was both glad that Hawk was acting like a gentleman and equally upset that he didn't seem to respond to her nudity. It was as if he were made of rock. *No. Even rock gets hot or cold depending how much heat it gets or lacks.*

He tended to her wounds with a soothing voice and gentle hands, much as he would a child.

"Sorry," Hawk apologized. "I'm trying to be as gentle as I can."

"Forget gentle," she answered through gritted teeth. "Just do it fast." She wanted the whole business over with. To be dressed again. To not feel helpless like this. The air was so thick with tension, it practically crackled.

He cleaned her wounds as she requested. Fast. She watched his expression in one of the window's reflection. He winced every time he heard her inhale sharply. Not once did she cry out. Finished, he put the antiseptic down. "What do you want to wear?" he asked, wiping his hands. "It should be something loose."

She didn't answer. She couldn't. The pain had overwhelmed her, but not once did she utter a sound. He stood up and took a step around her, When she lifted her gaze to his, she noticed the breath that he held.

***

His heart swelled for her. Her eyes had been closed, with, her face wet from silent tears. "So brave," he thought, when she looked up at him, with a look that said she was okay. But, she wasn't.

"You're trembling." He rubbed her uninjured shoulder, then reached around her to gather her into his arms. "I wish I could take your pain away.

She took a deep shuddering breath, turned in the chair so she was facing him, and leaned into him. "I'm okay." He didn't believe her. She wasn't as strong as she let on. She wanted a shoulder to cry on, more than she wanted to admit.

Although she said she was okay, Hawk noticed she didn't push him away. Her skin felt warm, smooth and silky, just as he had imagined.

He put a hand to her head. Her hair felt like spun silk, and despite the leaves still entangled in her curls, her hair smelled like a strawberry patch. He looked down at her face. White streaks, where the tears had tumbled down her dirty face, were visible. Another tear spilled over her lashes. With his thumb he erased it from her cheek. His lips followed the trail his thumb had made.

When she raised her face to his, he kissed her softly. A huge sigh escaped, and her arms encircled his waist. She clung to him, her shirt held in their embrace as her breasts flattened against his chest. He inhaled sharply.

The kiss deepened. More than anything, Hawk wanted to gather her next to him as tightly as she held him, but her injuries stopped him. Instead, he ended the kiss and pressed her head onto his shoulder again. Another shudder ran through Jennifer, and then she quieted.

He waited a few minutes, then gently unwrapped her arms from his waist and placed her hands on her shirt. Instead of covering her nakedness, she let the shirt fall to the floor, then turned toward the table again. Hawk forced his gaze to remain on her face. It took the strength of steel to keep his hands at his side as he went to fetch one of his own undershirts for her to wear. She wasn't even conscious that she was naked from the waist up; she had to be in shock. He hadn't wanted to look at her nakedness—not like this, but he was a man after all, and he had looked, the whole time hating himself for his weakness.

She was beautiful, and he would wait until she was healed before making her his.

The thought stopped him in his tracks. She would never be his! How could he forget his eagles? Had he been without the company of a woman so long that he was willing to throw five years of his life away? As much as he wanted her, he had to think rationally, to think with his head, not with other parts of his anatomy.

Grabbing a clean T-shirt, he went back to Jennifer. He pulled it over her head and helped her ease it down her back, this time refusing to notice the lush curves of her breasts, and the tips that had tightened to russet peaks.

None too steady, he sat down in the chair next to her. Her face looked as white as the shirt she wore. It dwarfed her, the shoulders seams sagging halfway to her elbows. She looked so young, so adorable, and still vulnerable. Silently, he called himself every name he could think of for having such lewd and lascivious thoughts while she had sat here suffering. "Tell me exactly what happened."

She looked up, her blue eyes huge against the pallor of her skin. "We simply surprised each other."

"What were you doing out there? Taking pictures of the scenery?"

"No, I was looking for you. You really didn't think you could leave me here all day did you?"

"I wasn't going to be gone long."

"You shouldn't have left without me."

Hawk frowned. "How did you know where I'd gone?

"Easy. I followed your trail."

Hawk gaped at her. "Then you're better than most, if you can pick up any trail I might leave."

She shrugged her shoulders.

Now she had him curious. "How did you become so knowledgeable in tracking?"

She pursed her lips, cocked her head to one side, then gave him a coy look. "I'm not sure I should give out all my secrets."

"I told you about my great-grandfather, didn't I?"

"Off the record."

"Then you can tell me your secrets—off the record."

Jennifer laughed. He enjoyed seeing her smile again. He didn't realize how much her pain had affected him until he heard her laugh. "All right, off the record. I was sent to camp for a month every summer ever since I can remember." As she talked, he put the first aid kit back together. "I loved it from the beginning. I thought it was great substituting swimming for baths. Eating, cooking, and sleeping outdoors. My mother wanted me to stay home. She wanted nothing to do with the camp. She thought it was vulgar sending me to live outdoors for a month, living in tents the whole time. To her way of thinking, accommodations are nothing short of having insulation in the walls. I was living in bug-infested tents and using slimy showers, I think were her words. The only arguments I ever remember my folks having were over my summer camping trips.

"Dad thought it was a great experience. I heard him telling Mom I needed to get out from her frilly apron strings, learn to live in the real world—not the sheltered life of teas and clubs that she took me to and enrolled me in. As long as he was alive, I was able to go to camp. I learned about animals, trees, plants, how to recognize animal footprints. I was curious, wanting to know what made the tracks I found.

"When I was thirteen Dad bought me my first camera. I took it to camp and had a ball. Dad always encouraged me, taking me on hikes during the year. No matter what I did, he told me I was the best and that I should always do my best. I guess that's why I want to be the best in my field."

"I bet he's proud of you."

"He never knew. He died when I was fifteen."

"I'm sorry."

Jennifer continued. "Mom thought that was the end of the outdoorsy episode of my life. Instead, it became the beginning of the battle between us. She stopped my summer camping for a few years—until I turned eighteen—then I left home. But, she hasn't given up trying to convert me. I keep telling her it's a lost cause."

She shook her head. "Anyway, with money from my dad's trust fund, I went to college and got a degree in zoology, and combining that with my love of photography, here I am."

"That still doesn't explain your excellent tracking skills."

Jennifer shrugged. "From books, experience on the trails, I don't know. I had a counselor tell me once that I was a natural. All I know is that I follow my instincts. It's when I don't that I get into trouble."

"Is that what happened with the bear?"

Her smile disappeared. "No. I never heard her until she came into the small clearing. I don't think she knew I was there either. Maybe I wasn't paying close attention to my surroundings, concentrating on your trail too much."

"In another mile or so you would have found me," Hawk admitted. "You're the first non-Indian to do that. No one has been able to track me down since I was a kid."

"So, does that mean I get to go with you from now on? That you won't leave me behind?"

Hawk studied her. She had a point. She'd proven she could stalk him. And, she would be safer with him than alone. After seeing that bear with her, he didn't want anything more happening to her. "Yes, for more than one reason. How did you know to lie down when you saw the bear?"

"*Reader's Digest* I think. One of those Dramas in Real Life articles.

But, that was years ago. My classes reinforced everything I'd learn or read on my own up until that time. What are your reasons for letting me accompany you from now on?"

Hawk paused, then decided to be honest in his response. "Because of the poachers," he finally said.

She didn't like the idea that the only reason she was going to get to see his birds was because he felt he needed to protect her. She had seen poachers before; she knew they were more dangerous than an injured bear. She wasn't stupid. But, at the same time his need to take care of her was going to allow her to achieve her mission—to get close to the birds. If that was the case, she was determined to take her cameras. She didn't see how he could stop her from taking pictures. Let him think the film was going to remain behind. She didn't care— she knew differently. "You think they're after your birds don't you?"

"And anything else that's considered a trophy, an aphrodisiac, or brings a high price on the black market."

"I hope you're wrong."

"I hope I am, too," Hawk said.

Later, as Hawk watched Jennifer wrap a few apples—cored and stuffed with brown sugar and raisins—in foil for their dessert, he found himself thinking about the bear and her confrontation with it. He was amazed all over again at her ability to deal with a wild creature that even he gave wide berth to, and her determination to get back out in the environment. She had wanted to trek right back out after the attack, but he had convinced her he had work to do around the cabin. Actually, he'd have preferred making his usual rounds, checking on his eagles. He tried to visit each site twice a week, but since he went out every day, he could afford the loss of one afternoon.

He wanted to make sure she was as good as she said she was. That she had fully recovered. He wasn't surprised when she resisted his suggestion that she rest. Instead, she mended her jacket and camera case as best she could. When he had seen her use regular sewing thread for the camera case, he gave her some fishing line telling her it would hold better. When he wouldn't let her help fix dinner, she went out and gathered a few pine cones, then put them in a bowl for a centerpiece. And now, she was putting together a dessert. When he had protested, she told him in no uncertain terms that she wasn't going to sit around and twiddle her thumbs. She needed something to do.

It had been a quiet afternoon with her sewing and him doing small chores around the cabin he'd been putting off. And the whole time, he felt like a clock that had its coil wound too tightly. He hadn't been able to stop watching her, the way his shirt hugged her ripe curves, the way he could see her nipples brushing against the cotton material. The way she kept tugging her hair back behind her ear, and the way it kept escaping and dropping back down into her face every time she looked down at what she was doing.

It wasn't until he had started fixing dinner and they started talking that he felt more at ease. It had been an uncomfortable afternoon for him—in more ways than one. At least, while they talked and he concentrated on what he was doing, he wasn't able to watch her thoroughly. Consequently, his pants fit a bit more loosely. He hated how he no longer seemed to have any control over his body.

Their conversation continued through dinner and while he cleaned up after their meal. Politically, he learned she was an independent like himself, that she preferred boisterous adventure movies to his mysteries, that she liked Dan Brown's books, adored Liam Hemsworth, and that they both enjoyed the operas and Broadway shows that New York City had to offer. He confessed the shows were one thing he missed about New York. That and the fresh-baked bagels with large piles of cream cheese. Jennifer offered to ship him some when she returned to New York.

Now, they sat in front of the fire—Jennifer in the huge rocker and he in a chair, straddling it backwards. He leaned his chin on his hand as his other hand reached around the back of the Shaker-like chair, twirling the marshmallow speared on a long stick over the coals. Fire flared around the marshmallow's perimeter. Quickly, he brought the end of the stick with the burning marshmallow to his mouth and blew out the fire. He offered the burned marshmallow to Jennifer, having discovered she preferred marshmallows well-done, while he chose those toasted to a golden brown, but just barely.

He watched as she cautiously extracted the hot, puffed confection from the green spike. Opening her mouth wide, she stuffed the whole thing in at once. Caught in the act, she grinned at him, white goo appearing between her upper and lower teeth. She covered her mouth, giggling, trying to swallow it at the same time.

She gulped the confection down while still laughing. "Don't watch me like that," she finally said. "It's hard to swallow when you do."

Hawk smiled. Such a delight to watch—so innocent at times, and so sexy. And yet, so tough when she needed to be. He found himself enjoying her company, reluctant to turn in. She yawned.

Sticking a raw marshmallow on the end of the stick, he held it over the coals and waited for the fire to perform its magic. Minutes later, he drew his marshmallow, golden and slowly cooked to perfection from the fire and ate it. Grabbing another marshmallow, he pushed it down on the stick. "How do you want this one—burned black as sin, or burnt just on the edges?"

He glanced her way. Jennifer's head rested on her left shoulder, her long lashes more noticeable.

She was asleep.

Hawk rose and propped the newly-loaded stick against his chair. Gingerly he picked her up, careful to keep his arm's pressure against her back to a minimum. She snuggled her head into his neck.

"Whatcha' doin'?" she mumbled.

"Putting you to bed." He smelled strawberries again. The scent used to turn him off. One summer, he had eaten too many strawberries, and ever since then, he had hated the smell. Now, he couldn't get enough of the scent.

She sighed. He sighed too. Jennifer affected him, turning his insides to puffs of cotton.

One minute he wanted to ravish her, the next he wanted to protect her from himself. Never in his entire life had his emotions been on the roller coaster as they had been today.

He walked to the bed, finding her lighter in weight than he expected and fitting comfortably in his arms. Reluctantly, but gently, he lay her down. Moonlight filtered softly through the window, allowing him adequate light to remove her shoes and socks. He debated whether to remove her jeans and then decided he should. He didn't want her scratches—the one or two located in her lower back— getting infected because they'd rub against the denim during the night.

"Jennifer," he said softly. "You've got to take off your jeans."

"'kay."

He waited, but she remained motionless. He'd have to help. He unsnapped them and pulled down the zipper, all the time watching her face. All she did was sigh again. His heart expanded at the tenderness he felt.

"Lift your hips."

She did, but not nearly enough to be helpful. Easing the pants down her hips and then her thighs, he knew it'd be impossible to remain impassive. But, he wasn't prepared for the gut-wrenching desire that gripped him when he saw her slightly rounded belly and the briefest of pink silk that she wore.

Quickly he pulled the jeans off her legs and covered her with the blanket.

She moved in her sleep, settling on her side with her hands tucked under the cheek that lay against the pillow. She looked so sweet and angelic, he couldn't resist kissing her other cheek. She sighed, digging deep into the covers, then was still again. Yes, she certainly appeared angelic now, but what would happen tomorrow when she discovered he'd emptied her cameras of film that morning before she had awakened? He had watched her working over her camera bag, mending it, waiting for her to start readying her equipment for the next day. The wait had been for naught; she hadn't checked anything.

Tomorrow would he still consider the look on her face angelic when she learned what he'd done?

Gently, he slipped a finger beneath the strand of hair that had slid down her face, letting his fingers feel the texture of the spun gold in the moonlight before moving the strands away from her face. He wondered if he'd ever get to touch a hair on her head again, already wishing he hadn't removed the film. He feared her retaliation would be swift and final—that she would never want him near her again. He could try to put the film back, but somehow he knew she'd be able to detect the slightest tampering. What was done was done.

CHAPTER 7

The morning mist shrouded the forests in pearly gray. The trees nearby looked like sentinels surrounding the three men as they sat hunched over the fire drinking the last of their coffee.

"It feels like winter," Stick groused.

Angus growled. "Ya' know what? I'm gettin' tired of your complaining. I told you it was gonna be cold. Come on," he said, pouring the dregs of his coffee into the fire. It hissed and white steam rose into the air. "The day's not gettin' any longer. The sooner we get our merchandise, the sooner I can be rid of you. And, make sure those furs and horns are stashed properly. We don't need anyone else snooping around. I didn't come here to dig graves."

"Haven't we got enough already?" Jack asked.

"No." Seeing Stick ready to add something to Jack's question, Angus beat him to the punch. "And, we won't have it all until I say we do. Now, are you coming or not?"

Stick knew better than to say anything more. He'd seen Angus lose his temper and kill men for less than this. He wasn't about to incur any more of Angus' wrath. He shot Jack a warning glance, then they both did as they were told.

Minutes later, they were stalking through the woods. They hadn't gone even five hundred yards when Jack raised his rifle and fired at a deer that had just run out in front of them—a buck with an eight-point rack. If nothing else, they'd have meat for dinner.

Stick laughed. "Ya' missed."

"I hit him!"

"He's halfway up the mountain by now," Angus said.

"Damn."

"Forget the deer. We've got better game to catch. I want that bear we heard last night. We'll find us a deer later."

***

Jennifer worked with her equipment, her thoughts drifting to the day before when Hawk had been solicitous and gentle. What a change from their first disastrous meeting. Yesterday, trying so hard not to cry out at the stinging antiseptic, she'd been surprised when he held her and equally surprised at how safe she felt in Hawk's arms. She wondered if this was how addicts felt, wanting something they knew wasn't really good for them, but unable to resist—

Jennifer gaped at her opened camera. The film was gone. Frowning, she tried to remember if she had taken it out yesterday after they'd gotten back. After the bear attack.

She distinctly remembered readying the cameras the day before yesterday in preparation for yesterday's outing, but she certainly didn't remember removing any film between that time and now. What happened to it?

Curious, she reached for her second camera and opened it. It, too, was empty. And, there wasn't any film in any of the camera bags either. Anger filled her.

Quickly, she checked the suitcases where she had hidden the rest of her film. In the beginning of her career, she used to store all her film in one place. Ever since the airline lost that one piece of luggage—the suitcase that had all her spare film in it—she learned to divide her film. If her luggage was ever damaged or lost again, at least she wouldn't lose everything. When Hawk first told her she wasn't going to photograph his birds, she suspected he might pull something like this. Finding the first two dozen rolls of film, she breathed a sigh of relief. If he hadn't found this cache, it wasn't likely he had gone through the rest of her luggage. It didn't look like he had. Just as quickly, she rehid the film and slid the big suitcase back under the bed.

A shadow crossed the window and she looked up just in time to see Hawk disappear and that he was rounding the corner of the cabin.

Seconds later, the door was kicked open. Hawk entered, his arms loaded with wood. He went to the hearth and stacked the wood next to it.

She jumped up, walked over to him and stood with her hands on her hips. She was on the warpath, and by golly he was going to know it. He had no right to do what he had done.

He looked up at her. His express changed immediately and it was obvious he knew why when he said, "Oh, oh."

She wanted to laugh at his little boy I-got-caught-with-my-hand-in-the-cookie-jar expression, but she didn't want him to think he was getting off lightly.

He stood, dusting his hands off, then turned to face her. "You want to beat me now or save it for dessert after dinner tonight?"

She couldn't help herself. She laughed. Calling him names would settle nothing. Yelling wouldn't resolve anything, either. How did he expect her to react? She was furious, but if she reacted that way she'd go nowhere. Literally. She needed to surprise him, keep him off guard. That way he'd prefer her with him, and that was exactly where she wanted to be. It was the only way she was going to get the pictures she wanted.

She smiled sweetly. "For dessert sounds great to me. The anticipation will make it all the sweeter. Think you can wait that long?"

She watched as his eyes expressed surprise, amusement, then wonder.

She wanted to scream at the way his gaze traveled down to her toes, then back up again, hesitating slightly at strategic points. She was still wearing his T-shirt, and she could tell by the way his eyes lit up that he enjoyed seeing her wear it. She had tried to wear one of her own, but it was tighter than his and rubbed against her back uncomfortably. He'd been right about suggesting she not wear a bra—it would have been too irritating. Now, though, she wished for the pain the bra and the too-tight-of-a shirt would have given her rather the disturbing way she now felt under his gaze. Her breasts swelled. She knew without looking that her nipples were standing at attention and straining at the fabric.

Hawk's voice drawled and dripped with eroticism as he repeated, "Can you?"

She responded with a shudder. She inhaled sharply at the erotic sensation of her nerves tingling, knowing full well the shudder had done nothing to relax her nipples.

Softly, he said, "I don't think I can." Then, he dug into his jeans pocket. Her gaze followed his movement and she watched as he shifted his jeans to accommodate the handsome bulge beside his zipper. Muscles in her lower abdomen contracted wildly, and a throbbing pulsed through her body. She swallowed a lump in her throat and looked up.

Hawk examined her face. "Is it warm in here, or...is it just you?"

"I...ah...don't know what you mean."

"Your face. It's all red."

Her hands went to her cheeks. "Must...must be warm, then."

He laughed. "Little girls shouldn't tell lies. You were thinking about dessert, too. Here," he said holding out his hand, his fingers closed in a fist.

"Huh?"

His eyes twinkled as the corners of his mouth turned up even further. He reached with his free hand for hers. He dropped two canisters of film into her palm. "Your film."

"Does this mean you've changed your mind about dessert?" Horrified, she couldn't believe she'd said that.

"Not for a minute. Desserts are my favorite course of the meal. That is, unless you've got something else in mind," he said huskily, his gaze dropping to her chest again.

Oh, how he rattled her. But, then, she had no one to blame this time but herself. "Ah...let me think on it." She knew how inane her statement sounded, but when he had her befuddled like this, she couldn't think clearly.

Hawk's gaze flew to hers. Seeing the expression on her face, he laughed, and this time she laughed, too. Better to laugh with him and let him think she was amused than to have him draw any other conclusion.

She stuck her hand out, open and palm up. Hawk raised his eyebrows. "Didn't I give you what you wanted?"

"Not by a long shot." He moved toward her. She put both hands on his chest, halting his progression toward her. She didn't want to be hauled into his arms again. Not right now. If he kissed her now, she'd forget her train of thought and he would have gotten away with tampering with her equipment. Beneath her fingers, she could feel his heartbeat racing just as hers was and that his eyes had darkened considerably. "I want the rest of it—the film you removed from my bag as well."

"Oh. That." Hawk turned and went to his desk. With his back to her she breathed a sigh of relief, rubbing her hands against the sides of her hips. The sparks they created were getting to be too much; if they weren't careful the cabin would burn down around them.

With a dozen rolls in his hands, he returned to her and gave them to her. Her cache of film back, she retreated to the bed.

"That's not much film, not for two weeks, anyway."

Jennifer sat down and stashed the spare film into her bag. "No, it's not. This will probably be good for two days—at the most." She looked up and met his gaze. "But, don't you worry, I've got lots more." It did her heart good to see him with the flabbergasted expression. "You figured you'd gotten it all, didn't you?" she asked.

"Yes," he answered without hesitation. "If you had more, why did you ask for the film I'd taken?"

"Because it's mine, and I wanted you to know that I'd found you out." She looked up at him. Her eyebrows came together as she thought. "Wait a minute. Considering everything you said yesterday, you gave it back to me too easily. Why?"

"You're not returning to New York with it anyway, so what difference does it make if it's developed or undeveloped."

"That's what you think."

"That's what I know," he informed her.

That's what he thought, she said to herself, silently.

Half an hour later, Jennifer was ready to go and hoisted a camera bag onto her shoulder. The strap rubbed the back of her shoulder. She grimaced. She darted a look at Hawk. Too late, he'd seen her.

"Let me see your back."

For just a second, she considered arguing with him. At this rate, they'd never get outside. Reluctantly, she put her equipment on the bed and went to where he stood. She turned her back to him and felt him tug the shirt out of her jeans and up. Cool air caressed her skin; her body reacted to the sensation. Thankful that she had her back to him, she faced the bed. But, seeing the bed brought another vision to her mind...with Hawk pulling out her shirt, their limbs entangled, their breathing heavy. Jennifer closed her eyes tightly. Suddenly, she remembered the previous evening. Her eyes flew open. The last thing she remembered was that she had been sitting in the chair eating marshmallows. Vaguely, she remembered being carried to bed. Had Hawk undressed her? She couldn't remember undressing herself. She thought about asking him, then snapped her jaw shut. She wasn't about to invite another intimate conversation. Not after the one that had occurred earlier. It had been bad enough getting ready to leave, knowing Hawk was watching her every movement.

"You need some more ointment. The welts are nearly gone, and most of the scratches are minor, but there's two here that need more doctoring. Remind me to take a look at them again tonight."

"Okay." She wanted to say more but didn't for she was afraid her voice would squeak or catch or reveal how he was affecting her as he rubbed the first-aid cream onto her skin with his fingertips. He wasn't hurting her; in fact, he had the opposite effect on her. She didn't want him to stop. Hearing him twist the cap back on the tube, she stuffed the shirt back into her jeans, not once turning around.

"Are we ready now?" she asked, picking up her equipment again. Fresh air. Once she took a deep breath of the clean country air, her head would clear.

She could only hope.

Feeling the weight of her shoulder bag being lifted from her, she looked over her shoulder seeing him place the bag on his shoulder.

"I know I am. Are you?"

The way he looked at her, she didn't know if he meant that as a double entendre or not. Her eyes wanted to gaze lower and check him out, but she forced her gaze to remain on his face.

"Yes," she croaked.

On their way out the cabin, Hawk grabbed his bow and arrow. "You're going to use that?" Actually, she thought the weapon was just for decoration, but if she had given it any real thought, she would have realized that nothing in the cabin was ornamental.

"Yes. I plan to find a rabbit or some other small animal. For dinner."

"You're allowed to hunt?"

"Only for my food. I was granted a special permit. And even then, I don't hunt much. I can't keep meat for any length of time in the refrigerator during the summer. The venison we had the other night was the last meat that I had. And until the temperature stays below freezing, I won't be hunting big game." He didn't tell her he often hunted with a gun, but since spotting the poachers, he hadn't fired one shot. He didn't want to do anything that might attract their attention to him.

After leaving the clearing, they headed north. Soon they were submerged in the undergrowth of bushes. Hawk led her through the dense cover, holding limbs and branches until she'd passed through safely. Taking a look around, she saw a slight path leading to the right. It was an old path, one made by an animal. She looked up. Hidden behind the greenery was a smidgen of darkness on an otherwise green incline.

"What's up there?" she said, pointing to the area. "A cave?"

Hawk looked back and followed her finger with his eyes. "You've got good eyes. How did you spot it?"

She pointed to a place just right of her feet. "The leaves are pressed down here and a few small twigs are broken. Obviously, it's a path of some kind. The dark patch there tells me it's a cave."

"I'll camouflage that path when we get back."

"Am I right?"

Hawk nodded. "Three years ago a bear hibernated there. It's been empty ever since."

"Is the cave large?"

"Not too. It's big enough to stand up in and it jogs around so that anyone or anything in it isn't exposed to the opening. I found a few Indian artifacts—actually just pieces of broken pottery and a couple arrowheads—the first year I was here."

"Do you think your great-grandfather might have used this cave?"

"It's possible."

What a connection. She envied his rich history and the fact he was literally following his ancestor's footsteps.

About three miles later, he stopped. During the last two miles, the terrain had changed. First the dense undergrowth disappeared, leaving western white pine forests and the earth covered with multi-layers of pine needles. In addition, she'd noticed the air thinned the higher they climbed. At one point, she stopped long enough to remove her khaki jacket and tie it around her waist.

Catching her breath, Jennifer looked around. Finally, the ground was leveling off. It was rocky, with occasional huge boulders jutting out of the ground, some sitting precariously at an angle. It wouldn't take much for those to go tumbling down the mountain, she thought.

Hawk spoke with his voice at a near whisper. "Just around the corner is a drop-off and the nest. There's only one eaglet in it. The other died two weeks ago."

"From what?"

"An older sibling, twice his size, pecking him to death."

"That's a shame," Jennifer remarked. She knew the laws of nature were tough, extracting heavy prices from the weak, guaranteeing the survival of the strongest. "Isn't it late for the birds to be nesting?"

"This one's just about ready to fledge. You won't see any other birds quite as young. But, to answer your question, yeah, it is later than usual. Up in the mountains like this, summer is short. And, it was made shorter this year because of the freezing temperatures through May and our last blizzard the first week in June. So the birds got a late start nesting. The parents of this bird were first-time parents."

Jennifer's eyes lit up. "I guess I'm fortunate, then, to see a bird still in its nest. Great. Think I'll be able to get close enough to get some good shots."

"I know you will if it's still there. But, from here on, we don't talk."

Jennifer nodded.

He signaled with his hand for her to follow him.

She did. Just as they rounded a boulder the size of a small house, Jennifer found they were on a rocky ledge. She watched as Hawk crouched down and silently moved along the ledge, so she mimicked his movements. He stopped and then lay on his belly. She crawled up beside him and duplicated his movement.

They were at the edge of the precipice. Below them, about twenty feet, was the largest nest Jennifer had ever seen.

Her eyes widened. In the middle of the nest, sat the eaglet, a juvenile flapping its wings—that easily spanned to seven feet. Other than lacking the distinctive white *bald* head, it looked like its parents. Jennifer smiled as it flapped its wings and hopped around in a gangling-like manner. A typical teenager, she thought.

She looked at Hawk. He had watched her the whole time, his expression reflecting her joy and surprise. He was proud and had every right to be.

She grinned at him. Slowly, she slipped her hand to the camera looped around her neck, sliding it forward. With easy movements, she focused the camera and started shooting. Within minutes, her first roll of film was gone. From the way the bird approached the edge of the nest, she knew it wanted to test its wings. She reached for her second camera. Hawk's hand stopped her. He shook his head.

She raised her eyebrows and questioned him. He pointed to the automatic rewind and mouthed a word. At first, she didn't understand him. Then, she realized he was telling her that the automatic rewind would be too noisy. She nodded her head, telling him she understood. She switched to her last camera and started shooting. In ten minutes, she had shot an entire roll, again.

She reached into her bag and extracted a new roll of film. Quickly, she manually rewound the first one, then replaced it with the second roll. Poised for her first shot on the new film, she heard a screech from above.

She lowered the camera an inch and looked up. Another eagle—most definitely an adult—sat perched on the rock above the nest, a rock that was in their direct line of vision. She held her breath. The animal was gorgeous. White feathers coated its head, the beak bright yellow in contrast. The eyes were penetrating and stared at the younger eagle as it flapped its wings, rising above the nest a few inches. The older bird cocked its head right and left, looking down at its offspring.

Moving her camera to her eyes, she aimed it at the adult bird and squeezed off three or four shots before it took to the air. Following the bird through the viewfinder, she gasped as the larger bird swooped at the adolescent and watched as the young bird tottered at the edge of the nest. Then, it was gone.

She lowered the camera and saw the young bird's first flight end as it landed, rather clumsily, on the branch of a jack pine on the mountainside below. Struggling to sit up, she accepted Hawk's assistance. The scene had been impressive beyond any measure.

"Wow! That was fantastic," Jennifer said. She knew she sounded like a teenager who'd just seen her favorite rock star, but she didn't care. She'd never seen anything so majestic, so powerful, and yet so maternal.

Hawk pointed to a tree near the youngster's perch. "See, there's Mom still watching out for him."

"How long will she stay by him?"

"Until he catches his first dinner. It could take several days or just a few hours."

"That has got to be one of the most breathtaking scenes I've ever seen. Thanks for sharing it with me."

Hawk's expression softened. "You're welcome." Now that they were out of the cabin, the bright light softened the color of his eyes, reminding her of milk chocolate. With a deliberate slowness, his gaze dropped to her mouth, then back up to her own gaze. There was a hopeful glint in his eyes, and she felt her heart and then her throat well with an emotion she couldn't name. Though he hadn't even looked at her breasts, she felt her nipples tingle, then pucker. She opened her mouth slightly and expelled the air that was caught in her throat.

It was just the two of them, high on the mountain, occupying a space so small, they sat side by side, arm touching arm, thigh touching thigh. Hawk shifted his leg slightly, and the movement sent electric shocks along her own leg. He bent toward her, his hand under her chin as he tilted her head toward his, then gave her a kiss that was light as the air that circulated around them. As his lips lightly touched hers, she found herself hungering for more. She had tasted and felt his passion before; she wanted to feel it again.

As he drew away. she saw each individual hair that made up his eyebrows, and she wanted to take her fingertips and smooth the few stray hairs that rebelliously refused to lay down.

A gust of wind whipped the ends of her ponytail into her face. She blinked at the sting to her eyes, then hurriedly brushed the offending strands of hair away from her face. The moment had passed, but the feeling of ecstasy lingered behind.

"Ready to see more?"

She doubted for a minute that anything, or anyplace, could be better than this. The brilliance of the blue sky, the first flight of a powerful hunter, the air crisp and clear, and a man beside her as primeval as the view were riches beyond words. "Is it possible to top this?"

"We'll see," he teased. "Ready?"

"Let me tag this film first."

Hawk watched as she took a small roll of labels from her pocket, peeled a label off, and stuck it on the film.

"How do you label your film?

"By using any word or two that'll remind me of the pictures I took. This one will be..."First Flight."

Finished with the task, she put the unused labels back in her pocket and the used film in a zippered pocket of the small camera bag. "Now, I'm ready."

About two hours later, they arrived at the second nest. Jennifer was excited to see the mother sitting on the nest, and her mate arrive with a fresh catch of fish. Enthusiastically, she snapped the shutter a few times. "I thought you said we wouldn't be seeing any more eaglets. It would be fantastic to get some pictures of newborns."

"They aren't going to hatch."

"How do you know?"

"She's been sitting on them too long. Even if they did hatch, the birds wouldn't survive. They'd be too young to survive the winter. By the end of September we'll be in snow."

"Can't you do anything?"

"No. Sometimes interference won't change anything. This was the second mating for these two birds. Both times her eggs failed to hatch. Any number of things could have gone wrong, but my guess is the female is sterile."

Sometime later, after they'd left the last site and when they had stopped for a brief rest, Jennifer twisted her head around, a puzzled expression on her face. She could have sworn she heard voices. Glancing at Hawk, she saw by the look on his face that he had heard the slight sound also. He signaled for her to stay put. She did. Not knowing where he got all his energy, she was glad for the brief rest while she waited.

While in the city, she worked out every other day for an hour or two at a neighborhood health spa, plus she ran about twenty miles a week, but she hadn't been quite prepared for these steep hills. New York had nothing like them, not unless she stopped taking elevators and started using the stairs. Next time, her legs would be ready for an expedition this vigorous.

She watched as he crept up the slight incline, not making a sound, then crouched down next to several trees and shrubs at the crest. With a flick of his wrist, he motioned for her to come up, and he put a finger to his lips indicating she was to be quiet.

Trying to avoid any twigs or leaves that could snap or rustle beneath her feet, she moved slowly, crouching down like he had as she approached him.

He pulled her next to him, then pointed.

It hadn't been necessary for him to point them out, as their laughter gave away their position. She tapped on Hawk's shoulder and waited until he looked at her. "Poachers?" she mouthed without making a sound.

He nodded once.

For a few moments, she studied them, then Hawk tapped her shoulder indicating they were leaving and that she was to stay low. When she thought they were a safe enough distance away where their voices wouldn't travel back to the three men, she finally spoke. "Are you sure? I didn't see anything suspicious."

"No, I'm not sure. I told you, it's just a feeling I have. They've moved from their original camp. I don't like it."

"If they were poachers, wouldn't they be more quiet, more secretive? Couldn't they just be regular hunters?"

"No. This area's been closed to the public."

"They must feel they're pretty safe to be that loud," she said.

"Or that dangerous that they don't care. I don't want you wandering around these woods without me."

She couldn't promise that she'd be by his side every minute for the remainder of her stay, but she wasn't about to do anything foolish either. "It's not right that we have to wait until they kill before reporting them."

His voice was filled with frustration. "Like it or not, we have no choice. It's the law. And, I don't trust them."

She wasn't sure what to think at this point. She knew Hawk's instincts were sharply honed. She had to believe that he was right, that he knew what he was saying; she'd only been here for a few days. As far as she was concerned, the men looked innocent enough. Granted, if these men were poachers, they were here to exploit the area. They were dangerous. But, what if Hawk was wrong?

Did he still think she was here to exploit his birds? His project? Though they hadn't discussed it since she first arrived, she assumed he still planned on taking her film before she left. He studied her cameras and her movements fervently whenever she loaded or unloaded them. Was he keeping track of how many rolls she had exposed?

Jennifer felt she and Hawk had grown closer. Other than her father, she couldn't remember when she had as much fun being with a man. They had much in common—love of nature, a desire to educate the public through their work. Hawk was a purist, she realized. His goal, right now, was to preserve the eagle, to help it strengthen in number so it could prosper again. For the first time, she wondered at her motive. Though there was nothing wrong in wanting to be the best in her field, was it wrong to go against Hawk's wishes and continue to believe she'd remove the film off the mountain even though he'd been explicit about what he wanted? Didn't he care anything about her? Oh, she knew she was turning him on, and that they were becoming friends. But, did he care about her emotionally? Did he care that if the film remained when she left, that her career would be lost? Or, that she'd be set back several years?

She grew weary of trying to figure it out. The way she felt every time she was around Hawk, she almost believed she was in love. But, then, when she started thinking about her job and what she wanted for her future, she couldn't fathom how she could love someone who had the potential of ruining her plans. Besides, how long had she known? A couple days?

Hawk swore.

"What?"

"There's blood."

Jennifer looked around, but couldn't see anything. "Where?"

"There." Hawk pointed to a spot well ahead of them. She was beginning to believe that he had the eyesight equivalent to the bird he was named after. She still couldn't see anything. Following him, she soon saw the spot he had indicated.

Hawk knelt down, examining the ground. "It's a deer. This might be the proof we need." He rose and appeared to be following a trail. As she tailed behind him, she saw the hoof prints. At one point, there was blood on the leaves, as if the animal had rested for a while.

Hawk moved on, and she continued to follow.

Then suddenly, Jennifer noticed the tracks changed. They lengthened as if the animal had been running.

Hawk stopped and searched the area beyond the tree line, about a hundred yards away. A growl sounded.

She spotted the cougar the same time he did. A monstrous cat, it sat on a rock that gave it a vantage point from all directions. It had probably watched them approach, but it wasn't interested in them. He was more interested in his meal.

"Is that your deer?" she asked.

"Yes."

"So it wasn't poachers?"

"Doesn't look like it. Not this time."

CHAPTER 8

The next day, they had been hiking for an hour in silence, but Jennifer wasn't seeing the landscape. Instead, her thoughts kept drifting back to the night before. She had chosen to use her shower just as the sun sank beneath the horizon. By the time she returned to the cabin, darkness had descended and the cabin's light was spilling out. Seeing Hawk through the windows, she'd stopped in her tracks. He was at the sink indulging in a quick sponge bath.

Bare chested, he splashed water on his chest, then over his arms. The water glistened, and she swallowed heavily, watching as he ran a cloth up and down his muscular arms then across his chest.

It was such an intimate act, and yet, this morning he had done the same thing outside the cabin in plain view. Obviously, he wasn't bothered by it, but she was. In fact, every time he so much as changed his shirt, her gaze was drawn to him.

Even now, she found herself watching him as he hiked in front of her. Observing the way his thighs bulged when walking up hill, and the way his bottom tightened when he walked downhill.

Never had she been so aware of a man, as she was of Hawk.

Always before, when she'd been the least bit attracted to a man, she'd found silence awkward and uncomfortable. And yet, here they'd been hiking for over an hour, nary a word between them. She didn't feel the slightest need to fill the silence. She wondered if Hawk found the silence unusual.

No, she thought. He probably didn't even notice. In fact, she'd bet he was glad of it, preferring silence to chatter.

Earlier, they'd talked while sharing the cooking and cleaning duties as if they'd been doing it for years rather than just four days. What was it about Hawk that created this feeling? Despite the brief time they had spent together, it was obvious to see they worked well together. Or, so it seemed. Time would tell soon enough if her observation was true or not.

Now they walked along the top of the ridge, putting more distance between them and the cabin.

"Is this a normal route you take every day?" she asked, careful not to step on any loose pebbles and turn or twist her ankle.

"No, I have about fourteen different lookouts and try to visit two each day."

"Do these include nesting sites?" Hawk extended his hand, and she grabbed it, letting him pull her up a huge boulder. When he let go of her hand, she wished for an excuse to touch him again. When she had awakened with cramps in her calves this morning, she knew it was from all the climbing she was doing and decided to be easy on her body today and accept Hawk's help any time he offered it.

"Most of them. Though the nests are all pretty much empty, the young birds tend to remain nearby."

They started down the ridge again, quickly reaching the forests. Soon the vegetation changed once more, back to the undergrowth of vines and bushes.

Looking at her feet, rather than watching Hawk, Jennifer bumped into his back, head first. "Sorry," she mumbled. She hadn't seen him stop.

"Shh," Hawk said softly, holding up his hand to indicate silence.

Jennifer listened. All she heard was the whisper of wind, a few leaves rustling as they were shook free from the tree limb above them and fluttered to the ground. Then she heard it, a soft mewing sound.

She watched as Hawk slowly and silently parted the limbs of a large bush. A fawn, still covered with its camouflaging dots appeared tangled in prickly vines. It caught sight of them and she could see its little heart pounding away in its chest.

Taking a step toward it, she found Hawk's hand on her arm

stopping her. She glanced at him, puzzled.

"I want to make sure it's alone." Cautiously, he looked around the area. "If its mother is nearby, I don't want to scare her off."

After a few minutes, Hawk tugged on her hand, indicating it was okay to go forward. Slowly, they moved toward it. Hawk spoke to it, but she didn't recognize the words. Was he speaking his native language?

Miraculously, the fawn didn't struggle. Jennifer watched as Hawk gently unwrapped the vines from around its legs. It barely moved under his gentle touch; it was as if it sensed what Hawk was doing. It wasn't until the fawn was finally free that Jennifer realized she had been holding her breath.

The animal nudged its head against Hawk's hand. She envied the strokes he gave it. She knew his touch to be gentle and she felt a kinship to the fawn. She, too, wanted more of Hawk's touch.

A bleat sounded from the other side of the bushes, and Hawk's hand stilled. He leaned back on his knees and looked at the baby. The animal looked back, with adoring huge brown eyes. Jennifer wished she'd had her camera out. The moment was precious, worth capturing on film. This was the second time she'd witnessed Hawk communicating with an animal. An understanding had passed between the small mammal, even though it was a wild creature, and man.

With an answering bleat, the fawn trotted off, responding to her mother's call. From around a bush, the head of the mother suddenly appeared, and Jennifer froze. The fawn went up to its mother and accepted a lick on the top of the head. Jennifer grinned. The large female raised her head, looked at them, then turned, and disappeared. The fawn followed. And then, the forest was silent again.

Jennifer stared at the bushes. She'd seen many things in the wildlife—a moose with triplets, an opossum traveling with nine babies all trying to ride on her back, spilling and scrambling for position, and a hummingbird feeding its young in a nest no bigger than a thimble, but never had she seen anything as majestic as the eagles or as poignant and tender as Hawk with the fawn. It was a side to him that she'd guaranteed no one had ever seen before.

Hawk was a man's man, able to live solitarily for years at a time, and in just a few days he was sharing his world with her, letting her delight in the wonders he lived every day. At times, she felt Hawk shared what he was doing only because he'd been forced to. She wanted to believe their comfortable camaraderie was because they liked each other, had become friends. She didn't want to believe once she'd returned to New York that he'd forget about her. She knew she wouldn't forget about him that easily. If ever.

"Everything okay?" Hawk asked.

Jennifer blinked. "Sure," she said. "Why do you ask?"

"You looked like you were a million miles away."

Only a couple thousand, she thought, standing. Images of Edwards' headlines regarding Hawk's story had flashed before her. "Hawk Dumped Fans for the Birds," or "Hawk the Magnificent Goes From Wild Life to Wildlife." She shuddered at the harm such headlines could do. Hawk could lose his credibility as a naturalist. Edwards wouldn't be content to do a piece on Hawk as a man doing something good and right, but rather as a man who turned his back on his fans, left his wife, and chose to live like a hermit—a man soured on life.

Feeling pangs of a longing in wanting to do the right thing, Jennifer watched Hawk slap at his jeans, shaking off the leaves and dirt at his knees. Then, he straightened and grinned at her. Distress tore at her heart. She hated that Hawk was starting to trust her. Right now she didn't feel worthy of his trust, not with the secret she kept from him.

A few hours later, Jennifer looked up at the sun. By its position in the sky, she knew they were south of the cabin. They had made a complete circle around the cabin, traveling more miles than she cared to count.

They stopped at a small brook. Delighted with the opportunity to rest her tired feet, Jennifer took off her boots and was ready to stick both feet into the water when she hesitated and stuck one toe in first. Shocked at the icy temperature, she jerked it back out. Then, determined to ignore the cold, preferring a few seconds initial numbness to stuffing her worn out feet back into boots, she plunged them into the stream. Gritting her teeth, she sucked air into her lungs with a hiss. A few seconds later, she was swinging her feet, enjoying the freedom from her boots.

She reached for her bag and pulled out two apples. Holding one in each hand, she turned, one hand outstretched to offer Hawk one. She laughed, seeing him holding two apples, too.

"Great minds think alike," he said, putting his away and accepting hers.

"That's a cliché."

"All right, then, we're attuned to one another."

It was true, they were. At times, they seemed to be reading each other's minds. It was eerie. She considered herself an okay cook, but once she tasted Hawk's meals, she realized he was far superior in the kitchen. She enjoyed the lessons he gave her on herbs, and once she returned to civilization, food from the microwave would taste flat compared to the dishes Hawk cooked over the open fire. Nor could she ignore their closeness when they worked side-by-side in the kitchen, bumping into each other, feeling his heat as he stood next to her. Even the smell of him kicked her senses into high gear.

Since her bear attack, he had continued to apply suave, each application feeling more sensual than the last. She didn't know if it was her imagination or not, but just the thought of his fingers and hands spreading the healing medicine across her back sent ripples of desire up her spine and left the rest of her body tingling with anticipation.

Earlier this morning, when he told her the scratches were nearly healed, she'd looked at him in amazement. In only two days?

He had responded, "I didn't tell you I'm a descendant of a medicine man, did I?"

Even now, she hated and looked forward to each time he helped her over the rocks. Hated it because every time they touched, she could feel the tension building, wondering if he would ever kiss her again. And looking forward to his help, because she couldn't get enough of his touch. Though there had been several opportunities in the last two days where they could have shared a few more kisses, she had been puzzled to see Hawk back off.

Every time she looked at him, she caught him watching her. He was friendly enough toward her, in fact, he volunteered a lot of details about his birds, showing her his charts and the progress that had been made. Slowly, she had come to the realization that he didn't want to get involved with another woman. Hadn't he said as much the first day? Maybe it had something to do with all the women who'd chased him when he was a model.

"Tell me about that underwear ad," she said. Hawk, wearing bikini briefs, had been plastered on billboards, buses, and back covers all across the country at the beginning of his career, some years back. Later, the ad was reprinted as a poster—a fast selling and highly profitable poster.

An astonished look crossed his face. "I had forgotten all about that ad."

"You gave American females something to dream about."

"Did you?"

"Dream? Yes, I did. Though...I can't remember if it was you...or what was his name? There's been so many."

Seeing Hawk's pained expression, she laughed. "Tell me. Didn't it bother you, posing like that, practically naked?"

"Not the first ad. But, as they became more popular, I remember feeling like...meat on a rack."

"I didn't think men felt that way."

"I did."

"But, you were a hot property."

"That's right—a property. I was peered and pawed at, women talked about my pecs, my hair, my eyes, my rear end as if I wasn't there. I never did a totally nude shot, but the speculation about my physical endowment was...embarrassing. The romance conventions were the worst."

"How?"

"I was their ideal man. Their white knight. The fantasy come alive.

I was paid to be a hunk, so a hunk I was. Don't get me wrong. The readers were great. I loved those women—but it wasn't always fun being mobbed and some people ended up hating me."

"Who?"

"Unfortunately, some of the writers. One publisher wanted me to pen a romance novel. I wouldn't do it, I had never been interested in writing a romance. Just because I was a cover model that didn't make me a writer of the fiction. A few writers got word of the offer and were quite upset. Frankly, I didn't blame them. I was offered an advance of over $100,000. Annette thought I was stupid to turn it down."

Jennifer remembered the book covers and of course the famous underwear ad. "You were something," she said. "Are," she added, unable to look him in the eye.

He reached out and touched her hand. "I'll admit I'd like to know you better," he said.

"You're talking about sex." Might as well get it out in the open.

"You bet I am. How can I not think of sex? From the way you sashayed that little bottom of yours in that thing you call a nightshirt the first night, to the way your skimpy underwear turned me on the other night when I undressed you. And now with you going without a bra, it isn't doing a thing to calm my libido. Not a bit. Right now, I'm as hard as these hills. Hell, I'm harder. I'll admit it. I'm no saint. I think Edwards wanted this to happen, and I'll also admit I've been without a woman long enough to wonder what it'd be like to go to bed with you."

As he talked, her heart beat faster. The intensity of his desire scared her. If they weren't careful, it would only be a matter of time before they their mutual lust ruled their heads. "I appreciate your honesty." What else could she say? That she'd had thoughts of going to bed with him, too? She wasn't about to let him know that her feelings were just as intense as his. At least, they both had the good sense to know a physical relationship was out of the question, no matter how much they each wanted it.

"Sorry that I was?"

"No," she answered, truthfully. On one hand, his response pleased her. He couldn't deny he was attracted to her. But, on the other hand, she knew a physical relationship would only make things more difficult.

"How old are you?"

The last thing he expected her to ask was this. "Thirty-three. Does it make a difference?"

"Not a bit. It's a nice age," she commented.

"Nice?"

"What do you want me to say, you look well-preserved for over thirty?"

He hooted. "You never cease to amaze me."

"What are you going to do after this project is over?" She wondered if he was going to remain on the mountain, or move somewhere else.

"I'll continue what I'm doing—working with wildlife. I've enjoyed writing this book and I'd like to write more books."

"I've always known what I wanted to do—photograph wildlife, traveling throughout the world. Although, I have to admit I never thought I'd be living like this. Camping out in the back yard is a far cry from living on a mountain peak with a helicopter being the only transportation out."

"It's possible to hike down."

"Coming up in the helicopter, it looked to be a tough hike. How many miles and days?"

"As the crow flies a day and forty miles."

"And as the crow doesn't fly?"

"At least two days and nearly sixty miles. There's no easy or straight path down the mountain. And unless you're an experienced mountain climber, I don't recommend it. Only under the most extreme emergency would I do it." He paused, then asked he, "Don't you miss the amenities of life—hot water, telephones, cable TV?"

"Not a bit," Jennifer replied. "Not having any brothers or sisters, I learned how to entertain myself. I've always been able to find something to do, no matter where I am. In fact, I don't own a television. I'd rather read, take walks. What about you? Any brothers or sisters?"

"No. My mother couldn't have any more children, and she died when I was seventeen. I think it was the poverty that killed her—she had to scrape for every small luxury we had. Luxuries most folks take for granted—like fresh milk, new jeans. My dad died when I was a baby—he was an alcoholic."

"Is that why you didn't take you father's name as your last name?"

"No. That was my mother's decision. They weren't married, and once she was pregnant with me and discovered what my father was really like...she just decided I'd have a better start in life with no father, than to have a father like him."

She couldn't begin to imagine what it would be like not having a father. True, she had lost hers when she was fourteen, but she'd have memories of him for the rest of her life. Hawk had nothing. "Didn't that bother you? Did you miss not having a father?"

"I don't know. How can you miss something you never had? I can't fault Mom for anything she did—everything was done with my best interest in mind."

"Did you ever learn who your father was?"

"No. And I don't want to know. If Mom felt it was important enough not to give me his name, then I trust her judgment."

"Were there any male figures in your life? Besides your great-grandfather?"

"I had a couple uncles and cousins, but I don't think it was the same."

"No, probably not. It must have been difficult for your mother." She envisioned Hawk as a boy living in a trailer or some shack as some Indians did, while living on the reservation, and it saddened her.

"It was, but I wasn't the best son either. I could have made it easier for her. I remember the first time I drank beer, I was at a friend's house trailer. He was usually left alone, a wild child. I looked like a saint next to him. I was twelve at the time, and there were four of us. We were on our second six-pack when my mother came looking for me. She walked in and found us and sent the other kids home, telling them they were not only stupid but perpetuating the system that was killing our tribe. My friend, the one who lived there, just laughed at her and told her there was nothing else out there for us.

"I remember mom taking me home, dragging me by my ear—it hurt for days—and then, she took a belt and thrashed me soundly. I couldn't sit down for twenty-four hours I was so sore. She told me if she ever found me drinking again, I'd be as good as orphaned—she'd want nothing to do with me. She told me then how my dad was so drunk the night he died that he drowned in his own...well, you get the picture."

"How awful," Jennifer said.

"She told me I was better than that and if I didn't think so, at least she did, and I'd better not disappoint her again."

"What'd you do?"

"I never drank again. Not even to this day."

She was proud of Hawk, for his determination as a young man. "She never saw your success." At that moment, Jennifer felt that his mother knew of Hawk's achievement and was proud, too.

"She always believed I'd do well. For her, that was enough."

"How'd she die?"

"Cancer."

"I'm sorry, Hawk. She sounds like she was a wise woman."

Jennifer pondered over Hawk's history. What had he been like as a boy? In her mind, she saw a lanky kid about nine or ten with untidy hair and scruffy sneakers.

"How did you spend your time growing up?" she asked.

"There was always someone to play with. Our mothers all kicked us outside, telling us to find something to do. We usually did."

"Like what?"

"My favorite was cowboys and Indians."

Jennifer laughed. "You're kidding? I bet I know who won—"

"The Indians," they said, in unison.

"Or we'd go fishing or swimming in the creek. We'd catch tadpoles in the spring and an occasional crab now and then. I had my fair share of fun."

"I think you'd be a good father. Have you ever thought about having kids?"

"At times. Annette never wanted them. Said it would spoil her figure and her career. I certainly couldn't raise a family here, this is too remote."

"That's true. Plus there's schooling. But, the cabin would make a great vacation home."

"It would, wouldn't it? What about you? How many kids would you like to have, or don't you want any?"

"I've always wanted a dozen. Growing up as an only child had a few redeeming factors, but I think a family with lots of kids would be fun. Certainly never dull."

"What about your career? How would you handle it with your family?"

"I'd like to think I could do both. But, I know I couldn't. My photography takes all my time. I've got friends who are trying to juggle a career and a child—some are single, some have husbands—and I can't say any of them feel they're doing an excellent job. Just a so-so job. In fact, one friend says she feels like a forest ranger, just going from one fire to the next, trying to keep everything smooth, everyone happy. I don't want that. If I have to choose, I guess it'd be my work; I love it too much to quit.

"Whenever I think that I could do both, I just remember my friends, especially the ones who have had to give up their jobs because they couldn't handle the stress."

"I think you're stronger than that. I think you could do both if you really wanted to."

Jennifer glanced at Hawk. Their gazes met, and he smiled. He really meant it. It warmed her that he had that much confidence in her, and she felt her heart swell with emotion. She loved him.

But, she couldn't tell him that. Unable to finish her apple, she pulled her socks and shoes back on. "Where do we go from here?" Seeing Hawk's puzzled expression, she asked, "What is it?"

"I scare you, don't I?"

"I don't know what you mean." *Liar, liar, pants on fire.*

"Yes, you do. I saw it a moment ago in your eyes."

She couldn't deny her attraction or her love, nor would she completely hide from it. "You're right. You do scare me. I'm attracted to you, and I'm also scared if our relationship goes any further, it'll be used against me when it comes time for me to return to New York."

"You haven't changed your mind? You still intend to follow through with your assignment?"

"I don't have a choice."

"Yes, you do. We all have choices. You've made yours."

But, she hadn't made the choice. Edwards had made it for her. To keep her job meant she had to return with pictures and a story. She now knew how important the success of this assignment was to Edwards, the real reasons, and she knew if she returned empty-handed, her career at that magazine would be over. She also knew the clout Edwards had with other publishers. If he chose to blackball her, there was nothing she could do. He'd said as much in his subtle threat before she had left.

"Jennifer?"

"What is it?"

"I hope you realize everything I just told you was still off the record."

Jennifer bristled that he felt the need to state it. She had assumed anything he told her was off the record until he said otherwise. But, then again, she thought, maybe he didn't trust her. Yet. Totally. She'd prove to him one way or another that she could be trusted.

"We'll check out some golden eagles I saw recently," he said, without expression.

Jennifer knew he was disappointed that she was continuing with her assignment. She couldn't blame him. If she were in his position, she'd be disappointed too. Only, he didn't know the half of it. Why did one of them have to lose in order for the other to win? It wasn't fair. It just wasn't fair.

CHAPTER 9

"Oh, look," Jennifer said some time later, pointing to the rocks above them. Instinctively, Jennifer raised the camera and aimed at the Rocky Mountain Bighorn sheep standing on the sheer side of the mountain. The sheep stood still for a few moments, then something, probably by his and Jennifer's movements, set them in motion. Fifty yards away from the original point where Jennifer had spotted them, they stopped.

"This is Billy Goat Pass," Hawk whispered. "Any time I'm here, the area's alive with goats and wild sheep."

"They're beautiful."

Hawk looked around "I don't see Gruffy."

"Who's Gruffy?"

"He's a big ram, the patriarch of this herd with huge horns. One of the tips is broken off, about a third of the way down, giving him a lopsided look. Strange he isn't with them."

Jennifer kept snapping pictures of the sheep as they, in turn, watched her and Hawk. "I thought it was a goat that was named Gruffy, as in "Billy Goat Gruff."

Hawk settled himself on the rocks, his elbows on his knees, as he raised the binoculars to his eyes. "In this case, it was a sheep that had the nasty attitude."

"I'm going to see if I can get a little closer."

"Good luck. They'll probably take off seeing you approach."

Cautiously, Jennifer climbed up the rocks about twenty yards, then rested against a boulder. She looked up and sure enough, they had taken off again.

"Hawk?"

"What is it?"

Even before she could say anything, he was already scrambling up toward her. Quickly, he reached her. "What is it?" he repeated, his voice filled with concern, seeing her resting against the stone. His gaze scanned her body, his hands ran up and down her legs. "Are you all right?"

She swatted his hands away. "For crying out loud, I'm fine." Health-wise she *was* fine. Emotionally, she was a wreck every time he touched her, even casually like this. She could still feel the imprint of his hand upon her skin. She pointed to the patch of white. "Take a look."

As he rose, he told himself that she was right. He was over doing the caring concern thing. He couldn't help it. When he had looked up at her, she was reclining on the rocks. He had thought she had tripped or sprained her ankle. He hadn't seen her get in that position of her own free will. From now on, he vowed he wouldn't react quite so fast or so dramatically. He never used to do that. Why now?

He knew why. He wanted to protect her, despite the fact she only stood as high as his shoulder and could give him the what-for every time he did the wrong thing. He'd as much told her she made his tomahawk stand upright at a salute every time he got close to her. Hell, he didn't even have to touch her to be aroused these days. All he had to do was smell her familiar shampoo—from the bottle or her hair, it didn't matter—see the cuff of her jeans and he was hard instantly.

He turned in the direction she pointed, then cursed aloud. He clenched his teeth, seething at what he saw. "Damn poachers!"

***

Seeing Hawk's grim expression, she stood, too, gathering her equipment, then followed him as he strode quickly to the object. Up close, she saw it was the remains of a sheep with huge horns, and one of the tips missing. "Oh, Hawk. It's Gruffy, isn't it?"

"Yes."

It saddened her to see the once energetic creature that had defied gravity as it ranged the mountain cliffs, now lay battered and emancipated. It saddened her even more that Hawk was taking the animal's death so hard. What else did she expect? To him, these were his animals, they were under his care. At the same time, though, he was too personally involved. But, would she care for him so much if he weren't?

"If it was the poachers, why didn't they take the horns? Is he alive?"

Hawk bent down and ran his hand over its fur. "Yes, he's alive. Just barely. He probably ran off after getting shot, most likely into an area where the poachers couldn't follow." His hand rested on Gruffy's chest.

Jennifer raised her camera to her face, focused and squeezed the shutter. In rapid succession she had three or four pictures.

"What are you doing?" he asked.

"Getting the proof you need to turn them in. Unless you plan on bringing him back with us."

Hawk shook his head. "He's too heavy. If you're going to take pictures, we've got to show the bullet wound. Let me flip him over." By grabbing Gruffy's legs, Hawk was able to turn him to the other side rather easily. Gruffy gave a shuddering last breath, then ceased to breathe again. Hawk paused. She could see the muscle in his jaw working.

Now, she couldn't bring the camera to her eye. She wouldn't be able to see clearly enough through the lens. She grimaced at the amount of blood that had stained Gruffy's white coat. Hawk searched for the wound. Finding it, he cursed again, then sat back on his heels.

"What is it?" she asked. "Did you find the bullet?"

"There's no bullet. It looks like another ram injured him. I was wrong. It's not unusual for a younger, stronger ram to oust the leader. Unfortunately for Gruffy, his injuries were fatal."

She lay a hand on his shoulder and squeezed. He patted her hand, then rose. "Take pictures, Jennifer. Take lots of them. Get a few close-ups too, will you?" Then he walked away, his head down.

Jennifer complied but didn't quite understand why he wanted the pictures if Gruffy's death wasn't the result of a poacher's hand. She didn't question his motive, however; she took the pictures.

***

Several hours later, Jennifer noted they were still traveling south. They had just crested a hill and were starting down the other side when Hawk grabbed her and yanked her to her knees, then pushed her head until she was flat on the ground. Down below, amongst the trees, were the same three men she'd seen before. They sat in front of a small campfire, carefully circled with rocks. At least, they knew what they were doing with fire in the forest, Jennifer acknowledged. The last few summers had been dry and it wouldn't take much to tinder the area.

Hawk tugged on her sleeve, indicating for her to crawl back. Once they had retreated behind the hill again, and the men were no longer in sight, Hawk spoke softly. "Did you see any guns?"

"No," she whispered. "Hawk, I think you're making a mistake. I think these are just three guys out camping, having a good time and somehow they've stumbled into an area they don't belong. We've seen them every day for the past four days and we've seen nothing suspicious at all. You've seen them long before that and you admitted you hadn't seen any guns."

"I know. It's just a gut reaction I have. I don't like the way they keep moving their camp."

She didn't question him further. She couldn't. To do so meant she doubted him, and she didn't want him to think she didn't trust him. She did trust him. This was his home; he was on familiar ground, not she. She knew how she relied on her instinct when she was in the wilderness, so she couldn't doubt that Hawk sensed something was wrong. But, it was getting frustrating that they couldn't gather any incriminating information. "Are you sure they couldn't have gotten special permits to be in this area?"

"No, but we can find out quick enough. When we get back to the cabin, I'll call the ranger station. But, I know they're poachers. Before you arrived, I had been following them, and they were tracking moose, pronghorn elk, and my eagles."

She had to give him the benefit of the doubt, though she wondered if maybe he'd been alone too long. No man could live alone as long as he had without becoming paranoid about something.

Together, they turned in the direction that would take them back to the cabin. "If they're poachers, you'll have all the proof you need."

"How's that?" he asked, taking long strides up the hill. Jennifer had to take two steps to his one to keep up with him. She patted her camera bag. "With this."

He stopped, put an hand on her arm to stop her forward movement and turned her around to face him. His eyes bore into hers. He looked angry. "You stay away from them. They're dangerous men."

"But if you need proof—"

"I mean it, I don't want you anywhere near them. I don't want you hurt."

What was he afraid of? She wasn't about to jeopardize her own life. "Trust me," she said seeing the concern in his eyes and mistaking it for anger. "I'm smarter than that."

"I wonder," he mumbled and took off.

She gaped at him. She caught up with him, sputtering, "Now what is that supposed to mean?"

He stopped and so did she. They faced each other like two bears defending their territorial rights. "I don't know if I can trust anyone who was so easily hoodwinked by Edwards, and on her first day here manages to tangle with a bear."

"You conceited, overgrown—." She stumbled for the right word. "Boob!" she finally blurted out in exasperation.

Hawk laughed aloud. "Is that the best you could do?"

Infuriated, she fisted her hands and started beating him on the chest. It was like throwing a small rock at one of the peaks that surrounded them and expecting to inflict heavy damage. Her hands just bounced off his expansive chest. Too make it worse, he was still laughing. Angry, she pushed at him.

Instantly, her arms were locked against her side by his hands. His fingers felt like talons around her flesh. "Enough!"

"It's not! You've got no right!"

His eyes darkened. Suddenly, she feared him. She'd just unleashed the animal in him, the predatory animal she'd witnessed the first hour after her arrival. What had possessed her? Even though she knew she had been wrong to attack him like that, she couldn't back down either. What had happened to her sense of humor? She was appalled at her behavior, but pride refused to let her admit it. She jutted out her chin and stood her ground.

He growled, then roughly pulled her forward until she crashed into his chest. His arms snaked around her quickly and held her tightly. At the same time, his mouth raked over her mouth, then took final possession, his lips hard against hers.

At first she fought him, holding her mouth tightly, keeping her teeth firmly together. But then, an overwhelming yearning deep within her soul flooded her emotions; her anger disappeared, and she found herself kissing him back with every ounce of energy she had. His tongue parted her teeth, and she welcomed the intrusion.

Hawk's hands moved to her behind and pulled her up, then against him so she could feel his hard length. She heard a moan, and realized it was she who had made the sound. A throbbing between her thighs made her tilt her hips so that she cradled him against her perfectly, if not for their clothes. She cursed their clothing.

Suddenly, Hawk tore his lips from hers, and stepped back, his hands once again wrapped around her upper arms. His breathing was ragged, his chest straining against his shirt every time he took a breath. Her heart raced and each breath she took was as ragged as his.

"Is that what you wanted?"

"No." What a liar she was! She couldn't let him know the power he held over her. If he did, he'd use it against her. A minute ago, she would have denied him nothing. Even now her soul, every ounce of strength she possessed, her very foundation, wobbled. It wasn't the thin air that made her dizzy. She couldn't let him do this to her; she had to regain control, and the only way she could do that would be to act casually, use humor, and hope she could throw him off guard. Only thing was, she had no appropriate retort.

She turned and walked in what she hoped was the right direction. At this point, everything was topsy-turvy including her usual unfailing sense of direction.

Soon they were back at the cabin. It hadn't helped any once Hawk passed her, that she had been forced to follow him, watch his thighs harden as he climbed the subtle upgrade, and how his soft jeans pulled along his backside, the material hugging his hips, emphasizing his beautiful, perfect shape.

Now, as she sat in the rocker in front of the fireplace, she gladly admitted he had cute buns. Nice, lean, firm. A picture of him wearing a loincloth crossed her mind. She knew he would be magnificent, all muscles and sinew, his skin bronzed as copper. She had felt his hardness when she had been crushed against his body. And yet, when she had leaned against him, his actions had softened, his kiss becoming tender and sensitive.

She'd witness his sensitivity other times as well. He cared about a lot of things; in fact, through his actions, he had shown he did care about her. He tried to protect her, to keep her safe. Actually, this was the first time she could remember when she wasn't bothered by a man's desire to take care of her.

And she had to admit even though he frustrated her at times, she enjoyed their verbal sparring.

All she could think about were his kisses and how she responded. What must he think of her? What did she think of herself? She groaned aloud. She didn't want to think about it at all, but over and over, various scenes replayed themselves in her mind. Remembering that she had called him a boob, she grinned. It sounded so silly now.

***

Outside, Hawk dropped the ax next to the woodpile. His purpose in coming out here had been to exorcise all thoughts of Jennifer. He was failing miserably.

His stomach was in knots, his hands still ached to touch her, and he was annoyed he could no longer control his constant state of arousal. He felt like he was thirteen again!

Determined to regain control of his thoughts, he headed for his sweat lodge. Earlier, he'd started the fire necessary for his ritual; by now, only the needed coals would remain. Even though Jennifer had been out here, back of the cabin on several occasions, she had yet to spot the lodge. He doubted she ever would.

The slight mound of earth—no more than chest high—appeared to be a natural incline, blending well into the background. Unless you were practically on top of the lodge, it was hard to see the lines of it from a distance. There was no reason for Jennifer to be in this part of the yard, which is why he never told her about it.

He couldn't stop her from remaining on the mountain for two weeks, but he could keep her out of his lodge. It was his last bastion of privacy, and he needed it right now.

Bent over, he slid through the small slot like opening, covering it back up behind him. The door was nothing more than twigs and branches interwoven with grass and leaves. In place, it looked like the surrounding land. Only a small hole in the roof allowed the heat to escape. Earlier when the fire was at its fullest, a thin line of smoke escaped, now only the sharpest eye would detect the heat.

Already, he could feel the intense heat, and it warmed his skin. Able to stand to his full height in the lodge as the floor was several feet beneath the surface of the ground, he quickly peeled off his clothes, discarding them in a heap, then put on his loincloth. Instantly, he felt the magic of the steam, the earthy smell of the dirt lodge, the slight touch of leather around his waist and loins became one with him, until finally all time and space quietly transcended.

With his eyes closed, he eased down into a cross-legged position, his palms lightly touching his bent knees, his body facing the hot coals. He forced his mind to empty of all thoughts. For just a moment or two, he was successful, then Jennifer's image walked toward him.

She was wearing a white deerskin dress, beads as blue as her eyes, decorated in such a way it emphasized her trim waist, full breasts, and rounded hips. Fringe hung mid-calf and danced around her legs as she walked barefoot toward him. Her head slightly lowered, her eyes gazed sleepily at him, daring him to reject her.

His eyes popped open. Even here, the woman intruded! How could he get control of his body, if he couldn't control his mind!

Taking a deep breath, Hawk tried once again to regain the mindless thought that would allow his heartbeat to slow, his muscles to relax, to become one with nature again.

But, once again, thoughts of Jennifer filled his mind. His hands literally ached to cup her breasts, and he found himself clutching his knees.

Damn the woman! He refused to allow her to intrude in his ancestral sanctuary. He'd leave before he allowed her entrance here, even if her presence was only mental.

Disgusted with himself for being so weak of mind, he got up to leave.

***

Inside the cabin, Jennifer grabbed the poker, and stirred the coals, throwing a few pieces of kindling on them. In moments, she had a small fire going.

Glancing at the wood box, she saw that it was nearly empty. Since their return, Hawk had spent his time out back chopping wood. By this time, however, he should have finished and have brought some wood in. Listening for the sound of his ax, Jennifer frowned. Now that she thought about it, she hadn't heard anything resembling wood being chopped for some time.

She left the cabin and went around back. A few pieces of wood were stacked near the stump, but the majority of it lay strewn around the stump. And, there was no Hawk.

It wasn't like him to leave and not tell her. Bewildered, she glanced around. Not seeing any movement, panic seized her. Could the poachers have taken him?

No, that didn't make any sense. First of all, she didn't know they were poachers. She was letting Hawk's accusations get to her. Second, there weren't any signs of a struggle. Third, if someone or something had come for Hawk, wouldn't they have come to the cabin too?

Just then, she noticed the thinnest line of wavering heat floating toward the sky, just inside the tree line. *What in the world?* And then, just as she took a step, Hawk appeared, as if he had come out of thin air.

She blinked hard, then looked again.

Her mouth dropped open and instantly went dry. She thought she saw lightning behind Hawk, but she couldn't tell if it was real or imagined. He wore nothing but a breechcloth. Her imagination earlier of picturing him in such a garment was child's play to the real McCoy. He was beautiful. Magnificent. There was no other word that described him.

She tried to move, but found she was frozen in place. He'd seen her. She wanted to bolt, but her knees locked. The intensity of his gaze frightened her. He pressed on, looming larger and larger, each step silent, but determined.

She gulped. More lightning crackled the air. Thunder followed, quickly. She was mesmerized by the Indian who stalked her. It was as if the earth was in sync with his primal energy, the storm a perfect background to the intensity of desire shown on his face. She was powerless to do anything but admire the hard muscles of his thighs that flexed with each step.

When he stood next to her, she felt his heat, and she placed her hands on his hard chest, feeling the bronzed skin that glimmered in the fading light. She moaned at the sensation. With her fingers extended, she moved her hands with just her palms touching him, and slowly inched her way to his shoulders. At the same time, she closed the distance between them until they stood thigh to thigh, the tips of her breasts so aching close but not close enough. She melted against him, rubbing up against his thigh. Instantly, she felt a wetness between her legs. Pressing herself even closer, she felt his excitement, his hardness, and knew he was as ready for her as she was for him.

She moved her hands across his shoulders, toward his neck, wondering if this was what warmed steel felt like. He stood there like granite, looking down at her, his arms at his side. His eyes, flashing with fire, bore into her.

She tilted her head and rose on her toes, while pulling his head down. Greedily, she kissed him.

Ignoring the fact that his arms still remained at his side, she moved her hands down his chest, then skimmed his hips, then down his thighs. Hesitating just for a fraction of a second, she moved a hand under his breechcloth and cupped the leather triangle that was the only barrier between them.

Hawk gasped, and grabbed her, moving his hips into hers. Pulling her hand free, she clasped him around the neck, allowing him to pull her up until their bodies meshed perfectly. Slowly, he eased her back to the ground until she was standing again, letting her feel the full length of his desire. For just an instant, he loomed over her, and then their mouths fused. She curled her fingers in his hair, crushing the strands as she sought his tongue. His tongue dueled with hers. Though her lids were closed, she saw a blinding light. An earth shaking crack followed, and she jumped. Rain pelted them, soaking them.

In that split second, Hawk, towering over her, looked fierce and massive, looking every inch the Indian that he was. Had she not known him, she would have been inclined to scream. Instead, she lowered her arms and took a step back.

Oh God, how could she have gotten so carried away, caught in the moment after he had mystically appeared before her? He had given her no inclination, other than his arousal, that he wanted her, and he had already admitted to that weakness he had for her.

"Why did you stop?" he asked.

"I...I don't know."

"You're afraid of me."

"No...no. I told you I wasn't." It was true. She wasn't afraid of him. Instead she was drawn to him, wanting to feel his arms pressed around her, feel the strength and comfort in his arms. She wanted someone strong in her life. She knew now that she wouldn't settle for anything less. Once she left Hawk, he would always be the man everyone else would have to measure up to.

"Then you must be afraid of yourself."

Unable to breath, and feeling trapped, she did the only thing she could do.

She ran.

CHAPTER 10

Unmindful of the rain, Hawk stood rooted to the spot and watched Jennifer run away from him. How could he have been so stupid to think Jennifer could be here for two weeks without their engaging in any sexual behavior?

It was impossible. They had already admitted to each other they were attracted. Though he'd never admit it, he was just as scared as she was. She had the power to hurt him. Badly.

Not only had she crept into his life, but she'd snuck into his heart, as well. He didn't know if he could go back to a solitary life, not after living with her. Emotionally, he was a knotted ball of yarn and he couldn't find the strand that would allow him to untangle his feelings. She had the power to destroy his work, too. He was proud knowing the birds had a stronghold on the area, but at the same time, their existence was still so fragile, any major catastrophe to their numbers could set them back years in trying to regain their present population.

Hawk cursed and went back to the sweat lodge to get his clothes. Earlier, when he'd stepped from the entrance, he'd been surprised to see Jennifer. He'd spontaneously moved toward her and the closer he got, the more drawn he'd been. And then, the way she'd approached him, it was more than his control could take. He had snapped, crushing her to him, letting her feel the intensity of his desire. He wanted her so badly, he couldn't look at her anymore without seeing her welcoming him to her. For a moment, when he'd looked at her, he thought he saw her arms wide open, beseeching him to take her. And then, the storm struck. Reality won.

It wasn't her fault. It was his. Damn that Edwards! He jerked his clothes on over his wet skin, determined he wouldn't subject Jennifer to his nakedness again. It had been a mistake to come out here, but he had needed the solitude, was looking for a vision. He had received nothing. No vision. No nothing other than Jennifer. His frustration equaled that of his desire to bed the woman who filled his dreams.

His emotions had taken a beating earlier when he had grabbed her, trying to stop her from hitting him. He didn't mind so much that she had been beating on him physically—he welcomed it. It was bad enough that he felt like a heel, but it had stung that she was angry at him too, even though he had it coming. He just couldn't stop feeling like he'd violated her, treated her roughly. And yet, when he'd finally found the strength to push her away, he'd nearly dissolved seeing her lip swollen from his kiss, the dewy look in her eye, the way her heavy eyelids gave her a sleepy, sexy look.

All he wanted to do was forget Jennifer Frost, wishing she'd never entered his life.

Unfortunately, he could do no such thing. She'd come into his life and turned it upside down. The only thing he could do now was follow her lead. Heaven help him, he knew he didn't have the strength to resist her anymore.

Back out in the rain, Hawk gathered as much wood as he could carry into his arms.

Going into the cabin, he half expected Jennifer to come at him with her claws out.

Instead, she just stood in the middle of the room, wet, her blue eyes like saucers as she looked at him. His heart twisted. This was an impossible situation. He had no answers.

Not knowing the right thing to say, he unloaded the wood. Turning around, he was surprised to see her still standing there, watching him.

"Hawk—"

"Don't Jennifer. Nothing needs to be said. It's over." He walked past her and opened the door. Rain gusted in dampening the wooden floor.

"Where are you going?"

"Anywhere. I need to cool down. A dunking in the stream sounds good."

"But the water's got to be freezing."

"Exactly. But, know this. We will make love." He shut the door.

***

Jennifer stared at it, horrified that she'd driven him away, stunned at his last words. Sinking into the rocker, she bent her head, placing her forehead in the palms of her hands. *What have I done?*

All along she believed they had to keep their distance from each other or her work would be in jeopardy. Now, she wasn't so sure.

She knew, just as Hawk had spoken, that it was inevitable another incident like the one that had happened moments ago would happen again. The question was, did she want it to happen? Did she want to make love with Hawk?

She did. She couldn't deny it. Nearly every thought she had these days focused on Hawk in some way, if not his work, the way he looked, the way he moved, the things he did and said.

Jennifer groaned. She had it bad. She was in love with Hawk and there was nothing she could do about it. It hurt her that in trying to pretend, to deny her feelings, she had ended up hurting Hawk, too.

Gripping the rocker's arms and pushing herself out of the chair, she decided she wasn't going to hurt him again. He'd have to be the one to say no next time—she wouldn't or couldn't any longer. Although, from what he'd just said, it didn't sound like he was going to say no at all. Ever.

Hawk was right. She had been afraid of herself. If only Hawk would say how he felt in his heart, then she could be sure she was doing the right thing.

Needing something to do, Jennifer got out her tablet and started making notes about Hawk, his work, and the birds. It was better to record these things while fresh in her mind rather than wait until her return to New York.

Minutes after she was finished and had returned the notebook back in her suitcase, Hawk entered the cabin. He was soaking wet. The rain hadn't stopped.

He glanced at her, then headed for his wardrobe. Nervously, she stood, not knowing what to do or what to say. He pulled a pair of jeans, a shirt and underwear out, at the same time unbuttoning the shirt he wore. He glanced at her again.

She felt like she was caught staring. *Idiot. You were.* Unable to go outside, because of the pouring rain, she did the next best thing to give him privacy. She walked across the room, her back to him, pretending to get a drink of water.

By the time she'd pumped the water, however, she did need the drink. Her mouth had gone dry hearing his zipper, easily visualizing the movement. Then, she'd heard the scrap of his jeans as he pulled them off his body. Her nerves tingled and all she could do was gulp the water down. Hearing his clothes drop on the floor, she pumped more water, this time filling a pitcher. They'd need it for dinner anyway, and this way the added noise would deafen her ears to the sounds across the room.

No such luck. She easily heard him sliding on the clean, dry jeans, heard the zipper a second time. But, now, she gave a sigh, accepting that he had always tempted her senses beyond reason.

When Hawk announced he was ready to start dinner, she pasted a smile on her face. At least, he was speaking to her.

As had become their custom, they shared the chore of fixing their meal. While they worked, they commented on things they had seen that day and the pictures she had taken, hesitantly at first, but soon their usual camaraderie returned. Neither brought up the subject of the poachers. And, neither talked about the earlier incident. But, Jennifer knew it was still on his mind—just as it was on hers. His haunted look was all her fault, and several times she caught him staring at her when he thought she wasn't looking.

She noticed all right.

Soon, he was talking about the first year he settled here, how he raced to build the cabin singlehandedly before the first snow. And, how he was able to implant the eagles that first year, too.

She couldn't imagine why Hawk didn't want the public to know of his work now. Especially after all the eagles had fledged this year. He'd have five full solid years behind him, each year with more eagles nesting in the area successfully. In another six months or so, his book would be published, and the public would certainly be aware of his project then. Did he still not want her to do the article? Though he hadn't mentioned it, she didn't want to bring it to his attention, either. She didn't want to drive a wedge in their relationship, not at this point. She'd confront the issue when it was time to go, after she had all the pictures she wanted.

In her opinion, her pictures would help his concern. By having them published, the public could see what he was doing. He'd be surprised at the support he would garner, even the donations that would start pouring in. Not everyone was out to destroy the endangered birds.

After dinner, they sat in front of the fireplace, enjoying the radiating heat. A cold wind whistled around the corners of the cabin. The nights had gotten chillier, hinting at the freezing temperatures that would follow in the weeks to come and settle in for the winter.

Hawk tossed another log on the coals. "I told you about my childhood earlier. Tell me about yours. What were your favorite games as a child?"

Jennifer thought for a moment, fingering a chestnut. They had filled their pockets with them earlier when they were out hiking, intending to add them to the fire. Hers was the last one left. As she thought, she rocked in the chair, her coveted seat every evening. Hawk never disputed her right to it, always leaving it for her. He usually sat in one of the chairs, either sprawled out with his legs crossed at the ankles like he was doing now, or had it turned backwards, his chin resting on his forearms. The squeak of the rocker was accompanied by the wail of the wind and an occasional pop from the fire. Strangely, the sounds all comforted her, but she knew the true source of her feeling of security. She sat across from him. "I can't say I had any one particular favorite game." Then she chuckled.

Hawk glanced at her. "Except for...?" he said, waiting for her to fill in the blank.

"My mother claims I purposely tried my best to aggravate her." She smiled. "And according to her, I succeeded fairly well and quite often. Playing spy was a favorite pastime whenever mother had company. I'll never forget the time I spied on her and her bridge club. I hid in the palms and ferns with my little notebook and pen, thinking I was invisible. No one paid any attention to me, so I thought I was doing a good job of hiding. It wasn't until the ladies were all leaving that I realized they knew I was there all the time."

"How'd you find out?"

"They all said goodbye to the plants where I was hidden when they left. Mother was livid. Claimed I had embarrassed her and that she'd never hear the end of it."

"And did she?"

"Whenever I talk to any of those ladies today, they still say it was one of the more titillating bridge games they'd ever had. They enjoyed leading me on, giving me juicy tidbits to write down."

"One thing hasn't changed," Hawk commented.

"What's that."

"You're still a pest." He ducked as the chestnut sailed past his head. "With a temper, too," he added with a chuckle.

***

It was mid-afternoon the next day when they heard the shots. They'd just come from a nest site area that had two young eagles nearby. The sound stopped both of them, immediately.

"What was that?" she asked.

"It's got to be the poachers. I'd stake my mountain on it," he answered grimly.

It *was* his mountain, she thought. In the last few days, she'd come to realize that.

Before they had left the cabin, Hawk had radioed the ranger's station again. When he asked if any hunters had received special permission to be in this area, he was told no. He informed them about the men they kept seeing, and the rangers told him to keep his eye on them. Then Hawk was asked if he'd seen Andrews.

"Ranger Andrews? The old codger that lives on a neighboring mountain. Over."

"Yeah, that's the one. Over"

"No, I haven't. Why?"

"We haven't been able to get him on the radio. Smitty's going to be delivering supplies tomorrow."

"Let me know what you find out," Hawk told him. "Over and out."

Hawk hadn't said anything to her, but his look had spoken volumes. He believed the poachers and Andrews' disappearance were tied together. She had asked if the shots could have been fired by Andrews, and Hawk had told her that if Andrews were in trouble, the man would have sent up flares.

"What are we going to do?"

Hawk appeared to be weighing something in his mind. He looked at her speculatively. "Whoever it is, I want to try and track them, but I have to have your assurance you'll do as I tell you. I mean complete obedience."

Jennifer looked at him with pretended hurt, her eyes wide. "I'm serious," he said. "One of these days I won't be there to save your skin. I've been the one keeping you out of trouble."

Jennifer gazed back at him, and felt the familiar flutter in her stomach. Never again would she be able to see a stand of pines or anything remotely connected to a rugged countryside without remembering Hawk.

Her eyes slid down to his mouth. His lips were slightly parted. The kisses they'd shared filtered through her mind.

"You're trouble, Jennifer. You need someone to take care of you. Someone stronger than yourself."

She laughed, nervously. She knew exactly who she needed and she needed him for every reason that a woman needed a man. She needed him physically and she wanted him to need her emotionally, to love her just as she loved him.

"You don't believe me?"

She couldn't answer. He was too close. Her nerves acted like wires that had been crossed. And the fact that he looked like he was ready to kiss her if she gave him the least little provocation or invitation didn't help.

"You know I'm right," he said softly. "Are you ready?" he asked.

More than she wanted to be and more than he knew.

After all her effort during the past few years to rise above her vulnerability, Hawk in less than one week had completely destroyed her defenses. Oh, she might appear strong on the outside, but inside where it counted, she was like a bowl of Jello, quivering at the littlest disturbance. And, oh, how he disturbed her.

At every turn, Hawk managed to surprise her. He was unlike anyone she'd ever met. It saddened her to think in another week she'd be leaving.

She shifted the weight of her bags. "Let's go."

***

Many hours later, they trudged into the cabin. As they both pulled out chairs and sank into them, Jennifer noticed their muddy boots; it would take several days for the ground to dry from last night's rain storm. "Why couldn't we find them?"

"Damned, if I know," he said grimly. "When we're not looking for them, we're stumbling over them. Then, when we want to find them, it's like looking for a fawn in the forest. They're probably tracking fast-moving animals." His boots landed on the floor with a thud. He leaned back in the chair and gave a tired sigh. "If we're going to eat, the fire needs tending, but right now I haven't even the energy to get out of this chair."

"Same here. I'd just as soon open a can of beans."

"We can finish the corn bread left from last night."

"That takes care of the menu," she said. "Unfortunately, that doesn't take care of the poachers."

Despite his statement about being weary, Hawk jumped up and threw some logs on the fire. Jennifer could tell by his jerky motions, the way he stabbed the wood with unnecessary force with the poker, that he was upset.

She couldn't blame him. She was upset, too. Every day since she'd been here, except for her first day, they had seen the three men. Why was it so impossible to find them today? It frustrated her that they hadn't been able to even get a glimpse of the men, let alone find a trail. She knew Hawk had expected to find them, but luck had been with the men—more rain had covered their tracks.

The poker was dropped heavily into its stand. Jennifer jumped. Hawk darted a glance in her direction. "Sorry. Didn't mean to startle you like that."

Not knowing what to say, she just sighed. She wished she could help him.

He verbalized what she had been thinking. "I just can't understand how we missed them. Expert trackers that we are."

"We'll find them sooner or later."

"We must have walked twenty-five miles."

"You look like you could walk another twenty-five," she said.

At that Hawk gave her a slight smile. "Not today, Sweetie." He dropped back into his chair, stretching so the back of his head lay on the chair and his body was a flat plane. His toes rubbed up against hers. He closed his eyes and wiggled his feet. She wondered if he knew that he was playing footsie with her, and she considered moving her feet out of his way, then reconsidered. It felt cozy, comforting, and though they were only touching toes, she felt they were exchanging much more than just a touch. She didn't want to be the one to break the mood.

Hawk opened his eyes and looked at her. "You really enjoy all this, don't you?" He asked, with sincerity. "The hiking, tracking, the outdoors?"

"I told you I did." It was so easy to see that they both cared about the wildlife, and they both loved the remote environment. Did he still doubt her interest in his eagles' welfare?

"Seeing is believing, and I believe you now. What's more, you're good. What physical training have you had?"

"Nothing more than jogging and working out in the gym. It keeps my body tuned."

His gaze started at her hair and traveled down. "I'll say." Tremors skated under her skin, and she detected heat curling at the juncture of her thighs.

"Where did you really learn to track? I can't believe you learned at camp. You've been taught by a professional. Where did you get your training?"

Any other man would have had difficulty admitting she was as good. Though she knew Hawk had his pride, by now she also knew him well enough to know it wasn't like him to hold back the truth. It made her feel even more guilty that she was still holding out on him.

How could she possibly ever tell him of the second assignment now? To do so would to be suicide. To their relationship. Though she had thought and thought about the problem over the last few days, she had yet to come up with a viable solution. "I told you, I had some good teachers at camp when I was kid. They taught me how to trust my instinct."

CHAPTER 11

The bittersweet knowledge that she'd be leaving him soon made her weak with emotion. Her instinct told her to love this man unconditionally. She felt as if she'd been drugged and had stepped off the edge of a cliff, spiraling down into a yawning chasm that had no bottom. Never had she felt such an intense feeling, a longing, and there was nothing she could do to shed herself of this feeling. If she ever had any doubts before, she didn't now. She loved him.

Hawk had become more than a friend; he was a mentor, a playmate. Someone who was her equal, just as she was his. She'd never been this close to anyone. She could count on one hand those few times she'd been with a man. So far, she hadn't been lucky in love.

A fear unknown to her swallowed her soul. She ached to utter her new-found feelings to Hawk, but because she wasn't sure how he'd respond, she kept silent. How did he feel about her? Beyond his physical attraction?

For the first time in her life, she wondered if her instinct was failing her.

Sure they talked about the birds, the environment. They talked about concrete things. They had talked not only about their pasts but of their goals. But, not once had either of them mentioned the other being in their future.

Hawk picked up his boots and they scraped against the floor before being lifted into the air. "Mind if I use your shower? I feel dirtier than a bear in a wallow, and somehow, a sponge bath seems inadequate right now—plus, I'm too tired to hike half a mile to the stream."

"Be my guest," Jennifer said. She bent to remove her boots. "I'm after you. Don't use all the hot water."

"I won't." He reached for the necessary equipment. "Wait a minute—there is no hot water."

Jennifer dropped her last boot on the floor and looked up at him with amusement in her eyes. "Gotcha."

Minutes later, doused with water, Hawk scrubbed at his skin, attempting to rid himself of the day's dirt. He tried to hurry. It was cold enough as it was. There was another hour of daylight left and once the sun set, it would turn colder. Jennifer was waiting her turn.

As he rubbed the washcloth against his chest, his thoughts turned to her. With each passing hour he spent with her, his desire increased. At times, he felt like a furnace heating up with no way to control the thermostat. She'd been here a week, but it seemed much longer than that, and yet, at the same time, it was as if she'd just arrived.

Whenever he got close to Jennifer, he found himself sniffing the air. He likened himself to a buck smelling for the doe that was in heat. The more he touched her, the more he wanted her. He couldn't satisfy the hunger that drove him to her. She was driving him insane!

He knew her work consumed her. Even though she didn't hold anything back, Hawk sensed a wariness whenever their talk turned personal. Though they talked about her background and his, she was holding something back. But what? Would he ever know? And about his work? Wasn't he forgetting it? He moved the washcloth down his stomach to his thigh. He groaned, feeling his blood thickening.

Would he never stop reacting to this woman? Disgusted with his own weakness for her flesh, he grabbed the nozzle of the sprayer and pumped, gasping as the cold water hit his too hot skin. Minutes later, he resigned himself to the fact that a few cold squirts of water weren't going to wash away the depth of desire he was feeling. Right now, only a tub full of ice cubes set in the middle of a deep freezer had that potential.

Still wet, he reached for his jeans, yanked them on over his nude body, slid his bare feet into his boots and grabbed the container. Jennifer would want it refilled for her shower.

As he walked up to the cabin, he saw her through the window, arranging a few wildflowers in a cup. Quickly, he noticed the wildflowers that had been growing by the door were greatly diminished in number. His gaze returned to Jennifer, just in time to see her set them on the table, then step back to admire her work. She cocked her head to one side, then rearranged a couple of sprigs before stepping back again. Behind her, on the wall, hung the small pine cone wreath she'd finished yesterday. She had started collecting the cones every time they went out, filling her pockets. At first he had teased her, comparing her to a chipmunk storing seeds in its cheeks. Anytime she had the chance, she added her feminine touch to the decorating of his cabin. Hawk grinned. Despite her original denial, she hadn't been able to resist that natural nesting instinct common to all women.

Feeling desire pour into his veins one again, Hawk gritted his teeth. He had no pride left when it came to Jennifer Frost. He wanted her. Again and again.

Other than Annette's quick one-time visit—no woman had ever set foot on the mountain. Jennifer had yet to show signs that she was tired of the lifestyle. Maybe sometime in the coming week she would; no woman could enjoy this way of life as much as he did.

In a week's time, she'd be gone for good. In the meantime, he was the one that was like the chipmunk—collecting memories and storing them away for the long lonely winter that would come after she left.

***

For two days, Hawk felt confined. During the last two nights, he'd gotten virtually no sleep. How could he sleep when he heard every breath Jennifer took, watching her turn in her sleep? He wanted to howl at the moon. He wanted to scratch the trees like the bears, marking his territory. And, he wanted to make Jennifer Frost his, exhaust her with his love until neither of them could move.

Instead, all he could do was sit here, pretending to concentrate on the scenery around him, while next to him, Jennifer dug around in her bag. It was mid-morning and they'd been to several sites already—a good day in his estimation, despite the clawing hunger he felt, needing

150

to satisfy his sexual appetite that had gnawed at him all day. This morning, both of them were awake long before dawn. By the time the first threads of light filtered across the sky, they were out the door.

"I know it was here somewhere," Jennifer mumbled. He turned to watch. Her hair veiled her face, but he could see the pale nape of her neck. He ached to kiss her there, softly, teasingly. Her head straightened and she held up a bag of trail mix, apples and carrot sticks much like a trophy.

Hawk laughed. "Is there ever a time that you're without food?"

She thought for a moment. "No." She noticed Hawk didn't refuse when she offered him some.

Finished with her snack, Jennifer felt some of her energy returning. She grabbed her camera and shot three pictures of Hawk before he realized what she was doing and lunged for her. Laughing, Jennifer escaped his clutches and snapped another two pictures in quick succession.

The next time he grabbed for her, however, she wasn't quite so lucky.

He pinned her to the ground, using his body to keep her legs and torso under control, then grabbed a feather and tickled her with it. She twisted her head from side to side, gasping for air in-between her bursts of giggles at the feather's touch. Hawk grabbed her camera with one hand and held her hands at the wrists with his other hand. He arched his back so his upper torso was up in the air as he snapped Jennifer's picture. She stuck out her tongue, then laughed, realizing how ridiculous she must look.

Suddenly, she was aware of their position. Tortured by the feel of his body on hers, Jennifer twisted, trying to escape. As Hawk's hips fit snugly against her, she stilled. The feel of him was so right.

Jennifer gazed at Hawk and watched as the smile froze on his face.

Slowly, he bent toward her, and her eyes drifted closed as their lips met. Hawk's hand slipped beneath her head, cradling it in his palm, his fingers stroking her hair.

His tongue slipped between her teeth, exploring the corners of her mouth. Her hands slid around his back, and she reveled in the feel of his strength as her hands caressed his hard muscles.

He drew a lazy circle around her lips with his tongue, and she sighed tremulously, returning his kiss fully and with passion unleashed. Oh, how she loved this man! Her heart swelled at the thought, and filled her with a resignation that no matter how the week ended, she would always love this man.

The lone cry of an eagle rent through the air. Hawk raised his head, and she opened her eyes. His dark eyes mesmerized her. What was he thinking? She wanted to talk about her feelings, but what could she say? I want to stay with you. Do you love me as I love you?

Hawk's mouth reclaimed hers, his lips moving slowly and sensuously back and forth before settling for the full pleasure she offered and he took. His labored breaths told Jennifer that he was fully aroused. And if that wasn't enough evidence that he was aroused, the hard length of him that pressed against her belly was.

When she felt his hand upon her breast and his fingertips rub against her nipple, her back arched automatically. A sweet pain radiated from her breast to the pleasure point between her thighs, and she squeezed her thighs together gasping at the intensity of desire that gripped her.

With a strangled moan, Hawk rolled off her.

With Hawk's body no longer warming hers, the air suddenly felt cold. Twisting her head toward Hawk, she saw he lay with his forearm across his head, his eyes covered, and his chest heaved like her own.

"You make me forget everything, Jennifer."

She sat up, her fingers combing the leaves and other debris from her hair. "Is that so wrong?"

He jumped to his feet and batted away a low hanging branch, moving out of its way as it came back. "Yes."

His anger perplexed her. He'd been upset about the poachers all week but not this intensely. Instinctively, she knew she was the reason for his frustration. Hadn't he just said as much, that he forgot everything else when he was with her? Hawk was a passionate man, and she had experienced it in more ways than one. Beyond the intense fiery desire he had for her was the passion he felt for his eagles and their safety and everything else living in the area that the poachers were destroying.

She wasn't about to throw herself at him, professing her love to him—she'd never be a sacrificial lamb to anyone. Considering what he'd said before that he might not be able to stop if they made love, it certainly didn't appear he had any trouble stopping himself this time. Had he tired of her already?

Or was it something else? Though every day she waited for Hawk to say something—anything—about the film he expected her to leave behind, he didn't. At times, she felt as if she was on pins and needles waiting, wanting to know how he felt now. But, she didn't pursue it because she was afraid of the answer. Afraid that nothing had changed. Afraid he didn't care for her.

Despite everything she knew, Hawk wouldn't use her, no matter how long he'd been without a woman. It wasn't his style. If she knew nothing else, she did know that Hawk had integrity. He lived by a code that few men lived by these days: honor. In fact, now that she had thought about it, Hawk encouraged her photography skills, helping her get the best shots she could.

She was no closer to knowing why he had rolled off her or how he felt about her.

Maybe she was wrong to think consummating their relationship would be the right thing to do. Their separation at the end of the week was going to be hard enough as it was. It saddened her to think that by next week, her time here would be only a memory. It was obvious that Hawk wasn't going to ask her to stay with him. So why did she keep torturing herself, thinking that he might? It was pure fantasy.

More frustrated than ever, Jennifer gazed at the clouds slowly drifting overhead.

Unaware of how much time had passed, she heard an animal call out. "What was that?" she asked.

Hawk didn't answer.

Leaning against a pine, his back supported by the trunk, he stared across the mountains, deep in thought.

Hungrily, she gazed upon him, from his booted feet crossed at the ankles, to the dark hairs of his eyebrows above his eyes, and the lashes that framed his cocoa colored eyes.

Though he stood still, much like a statue, she knew a strange sound would have him spinning on his heel in a crouched position, prepared for whatever faced him. She'd seen it before. It was his nature—instinctive and ingrained.

Her gaze skimmed below his belt, totally aware his masculine form showed definite form and promise. An image of the two of them naked, tangled in the sheets, tugged at her imagination, sending a rush of excitement flow through her veins as it did every time she pictured them together.

The slight breeze ruffled his hair. A lock fell on his forehead.

She went and stood in front of him until he finally looked at her.

"I need some time to myself. I'm going for a short walk. I won't be far away."

He gave her a simple nod, and she felt more depressed than ever. Now he didn't even want to talk to her.

Grabbing her camera bag, she went a few yards, then looked back. He still stood by the tree. He hadn't moved at all. She took his picture, then quietly left the grassy knoll. Further frustrated that she couldn't say the words she wanted to say sent her into the immediate forest. She needed the cover it gave her. Except for that first day, she hadn't had an opportunity to be alone. Now she needed it, craved it. Despite Hawk's warning that they always remain together, Jennifer felt safe. She wasn't going to wander too far away—she'd remain within shouting distance.

The shrill cry of a Steller's Jay had her searching among the branches, trying to spot the lyricist. The sun filtered through the trees, creating a scene that reminded her of stain-glassed windows. The forest was ethereal, and the muted sounds of the forest charmed her. Water bubbled over rocks in the distance, and she headed in that direction. A mouse crossed her path, scattering the leaves as it scurried out of her way. She watched its hurried movement and then heard it no more.

A short distance away, she spotted a large cluster of white violets with a multitude of butterflies flitting from flower to flower, gathering nourishment. Entertained by the butterflies' motions, Jennifer exchanged the camera's lens for a macro lens, then lay belly-down on the soft ground and propped her elbows on the ground to form a tripod. Focusing on one particular group of flowers nearby, she waited for a butterfly to land. In minutes, she had her quarry. She held her breath as its wings stilled, and squeezed the shutter. Just as fast as it had arrived, the butterfly left. Jennifer waited for another.

After several frames of film had been exposed, she was ready for something different, another challenge. Jennifer rose, gathering her equipment and continued on, still following the sound of water. Moments later, she stood at the bank of a small pond surrounded by grass and boulders. The pond was fed by water cascading down a drop of about twenty feet from sheer rock that had been eroded with time. She saw by the blackened sides of the rock on either side of the waterfall that during spring, the water literally poured over the edge of the rock. Now, water merely trickled down the cliff. But, the effect as the water broadened as it dropped closer to the pond, in front of the concaved rock base was that of a shower.

Jennifer grinned. It was too hard to resist. She sat and removed her shoes and socks. Her shirt, shorts, and underwear quickly followed.

The cold water made her inhale sharply, and she felt her stomach muscles tightened so much it felt as if her belly button was touching her backbone. Unable to stand the torturous slow movement forward, feeling the cold water over and over as more of her skin disappeared beneath the crystal clear water, she chose for a quick freeze and dove headfirst. The shock sent her quickly back up to the surface, gasping for air. Then suddenly, it wasn't nearly so cold. She floated on her back, kicking the water, looking around at her surroundings. It was such an idyllic place, she wondered if Hawk knew about it.

He must, she thought, as she headed for the wall of water, wanting to experience nature's shower. Minutes later she stood beneath the cascading liquid, gasping at the stinging cold as it pelted her skin. She loved it! Standing here naked like this, she felt naughty and wondered what Hawk would think of her now if he could see her like this. She laughed with delight. Even the chilling temperature of the water couldn't douse the heat that flamed within her. Or make her forget the man who ignited the fiery heat.

***

His emotions finally under control, Hawk went looking for Jennifer.

He was feeling the same way about her as he once had for Annette. No, that wasn't true. He had lusted after Annette. He didn't think he had ever loved the woman; he had been too young to know what love was really all about.

Love! Was it possible? He knew he cared about Jennifer. And, he knew he didn't like thinking about the time that was approaching all too soon, that time when she'd be leaving. So what had he done? Snapped and snarled at her like a badger. At this point, he wasn't sure how he was going to resolve either problem.

First, however, he had to find her. She couldn't have wandered off too far, not after the discussion they'd had earlier. Hawk scanned the ground for her tracks. It was clear she'd gone in the direction of the waterfall.

When he came to the small cropping of flowers, he found plants crushed and could piece together her movements. She'd lain down to film her subject. Seeing a variety of butterflies and moths filling the air, he didn't have to wonder what her subjects had been.

A splash in the distance caught his attention. It had to be her. Stealthily, he walked to the clearing surrounding the waterfall. He intended to surprise her; what he saw surprised him, instead.

She rose out of the water, naked as the day she was born. His feet were rooted more deeply to the spot than the trees that circled the area.

He couldn't move.

Water dripped from the tips of her breasts and ran in small rivulets down over her flat belly, gathering into the dark V that covered her feminine secrets. His lungs filled with air, and his stomach muscles tightened. Blood coursed through his veins and sounded loudly in his ears, like the beat of the tom-tom he'd heard on the reservation when he was young.

Hawk's eyes followed the movement of Jennifer's hands as she reached up and gathered her hair, squeezing the excess water from the strands. Fully aroused, he continued to watch as more water ran between her full breasts, and over her belly to disappear between her legs. He wanted her.

He couldn't deny his savage desire, anymore, to have those long legs wrapped around his waist, to tighten as she crested over the edge of pleasure. He wanted to taste her lips again, lips she now licked and moistened. Wanted to hear her moan with the ecstasy of fulfillment that only he could give her.

But instead of approaching her, lowering her to the ground and fulfilling the desire he ached to quench, all he could do was stand there and stare. Suddenly, he realized it was more than a physical fulfillment he wanted. He wanted to mate with her soul, to discover what it was that enticed him so.

Jennifer had spirit, determination, and spunk. More than any woman he'd ever met before, and he wanted her for his own.

Unaware of his presence, she shook her head and smiled. She felt alive, clean, and oh, so wicked. No, wicked wasn't the right word. Sensual. She'd never done anything like this before—nothing that brought all her senses to such keen appreciation.

Closing her eyes, she stood still for a moment, her feet buried in the soft sand, the water up to her ankles. She stretched her arms out, soaking up the warmth of the sun.

Looking down at the ground, she opened her eyes, and continued walking out of the pool, shaking her hair letting the last of the water droplets escape to the ground. Noticing a feather at the edge of the water, she knelt to pick it up. Twirling it in her fingers, and recognizing it as an eagle feather. With one hand, she reached up and stuck it in her hair.

A groan sounded.

She jerked her head up and gasped seeing Hawk standing ten feet in front of her. How long had he been there, she didn't know. Her mind raced. Where were her clothes? She couldn't remember where she'd placed them, nor could she tear her gaze from his to look for them. She'd been nude in front of him before, but suddenly, she felt vulnerable. Naked. Really naked.

Hawk didn't move. He wasn't looking at her body, he was looking at her, his gaze searching hers, his soul asking of hers. Silently, she answered. Yes, she wanted him. She didn't care what the future held. All she could consider was now, the place they were at. Even if they were to part and she were never to see him again, she wanted this memory of him.

The sounds of the forest drifted away. All she saw was Hawk. He started toward her, his hands traveling down the length of his shirt, tugging it out of his pants, unbuttoning it, shedding it from his body.

She couldn't breathe. Air, trapped within her lungs, ached for release. Her gazed lingered upon his chest, and her fingers curled with a need to touch him. His gaze moved to her breasts then back to her face, again. She could feel her breasts swelling, tingling, aching for his touch.

Two last steps and he stood in front of her. Not once did she look away. She knew the longing in his eyes merely reflected the same desire she felt. Never had a moment felt as right as this one did.

She lifted her arms to his shoulders, and slowly ran her fingertips along his collarbone, then down the middle of his chest, across pectoral muscles that swelled beneath her touch. Oh, he felt so right, so good. When her fingers crossed his nipples, she lowered her eyes to watch what her hands were doing. She felt him shudder. She heard him struggle to catch his breath, and she smiled at the realization that he was having as much trouble breathing as she was.

She raised her gaze to his, and floundered in the depth of desire that shone brightly in his. Hawk's stomach muscles contracted when Jennifer's fingers unsnapped his jeans. With a smile on her face, she lowered the zipper, slowly.

Fire seared within. With his hands on her shoulders, he rubbed her skin in slow circles, sliding his hands slowly down her chest. She watched him as he watched her breasts rise. She closed eyes close and tilted her head back. He rubbed both nipples with his thumbs and she felt them harden.

The sensation in her breasts traveled down her belly until muscles that ached for Hawk's touch tightened with desire. Her hands on either side of his hips, Jennifer opened her eyes and pushed down his jeans, along with his underwear. She looked down when the material met resistance. It was stuck against his erection. Gently, she pulled the material free, then she continued the downward motion of his clothing slowly...ever so slowly.

He was magnificent.

Impatient, Hawk finally kicked the offending clothing off his feet. On tiptoes, Jennifer leaned into him, letting the tips of her breasts brush against his bare torso, the tip of his hard length brushing against her womanhood.

Hawk groaned. He kissed her throat over and over, each time in a different place.

Slowly, Jennifer ran her hands down the length of his arms, and took his hands in hers. She placed his hands on her hips, but they didn't stay there. His hands slid until they rested on the curve of her buttocks, then he grasped her tightly, pulling her up against him.

Soft met hard.

Femininity met masculinity.

Hips moved together, her breasts flattened against his chest.

Her hands went to his temples, and she ran her fingers through hair she'd so longed to touch earlier. The air suddenly stilled, the wind ceased to move.

Only the warmth of his breath touched her lips. It was a kiss neither could deny any longer. A kiss that burned deeply, touching their souls as they twined their arms around each other.

His tongue licked at the corners of her mouth, then he nipped lightly at her lower lip, before his mouth recaptured hers fully.

When he finally pulled his mouth from hers, they both gasped for air. Her body felt as tight as a coiled spring. She rested her head against his chest, wanting release and fulfillment at the same time.

If she wasn't sure before, she knew it now—she loved this man. She wanted him to father her children, to share his life with her. A lifetime of loving and living with Hawk would be far too short.

They kissed again, and he folded his legs, pulling them both down to the grassy bank. On their knees, his hand cradled her head, the other supporting the middle of her back as he lowered her to the ground. Heat spread throughout her body like lava sliding down a hillside. Through half-closed eyes, Jennifer watched Hawk. His eyes darkened with passion as his hands gathered her closer.

Hawk's mouth found hers again, trailing kisses down her neck and across the upper portion of her chest. Her breasts rose, and she ached for his mouth to take a nipple and suck.

When he did, Jennifer cried out, her hips tilting upward. The intensity of the heat licking at the entrance of her womanhood inflamed her. His mouth sought out her other breast, his hand caressing the breast his lips had just abandoned, his thumb rubbing across the nipple, turning it into a harder pebble.

When his lips trailed across her stomach, she inhaled sharply, holding her breath. His warm breath fanned across her thighs, and his tongue flicked at the center of her being. Moaning his name, she thrust her hips into the air, her head moving from side to side as he took her into his mouth. Pinpoints of light exploded behind her closed eyelids. Her heart beat faster than a hummingbird's wings, and she cried out.

As her body shuddered from the wondrous sensation, Hawk kissed her belly, then her breasts again. His hands followed, caressing every inch of skin his lips had missed. Opening her eyes, she saw Hawk poised above her, and felt his throbbing member teasing her with its touch at the apex of her thighs.

Unable to stand the waiting, she grabbed his hips and pulled him into her until she sheathed him. He moaned. Her hips rose to meet him more fully.

"You feel so good," Jennifer said.

"And you're so hot."

He clutched her, wrapping his arms around her, pulled his hips back, then sunk deep within her. She fastened her legs around him and matched his thrust with the motion of her hips.

He moaned again, the sound of his voice lost in her hair. Their rhythmic movements, as old as the mountain, consumed them. Then every muscle in his body tightened as he came to a climax, and before he finished, she climaxed again, too.

Exhausted, she lay still, smiling, holding him close to her, relishing in his weight that pressed against her. This was how lovemaking ought to be. Soul to soul. Intense, like a crackling hot fire. She rubbed his back with her hands, but before she could express what she felt, she sensed a change overcome Hawk. He tensed.

"What is it?" Jennifer asked, puzzled. She could feel him pulling away—not only physically, but emotionally—and it frightened her.

With his hands on either side of her head, his fingers threaded in her hair. "I'll remember this afternoon for the rest of my life," he said.

Jennifer smiled nervously, her stomach sinking with every second that ticked by. From the serious look in his eyes and the soft tone of voice, she wasn't sure she wanted to hear the rest.

"You're so special."

"But..."

"Being together like this only complicates matters," he said.

"It doesn't have to."

"Does that mean you're giving up your assignment?"

CHAPTER 12

Shock ran through her, and she pushed him away. "What do you mean?"

"You know what I mean." Hawk leapt to his feet, grabbed his jeans, and tugged them on.

She reached for the only piece of clothing close by—his shirt—and pulled it on. She didn't have the patience to wait to button it, nor did she think she had the ability to perform the simple task. Hugging the shirt tightly around her, she steeled herself for his answer. "What are you saying?"

"If you forget about your assignment, we have no problem."

"In other words, there is no *us* if I continue with my work. Is that it?"

"It's not what I want."

"Are you sorry we made our love?"

Too much time passed. The silence stretched uncomfortably, but Jennifer remained still, waiting for his answer. Was he weighing his answer against her probable reaction? Hoping she'd quit if he told her what he thought she wanted to hear?

His expression told her nothing. But, his eyes searched her face relentlessly.

Finally he spoke. "No."

Joy leapt through Jennifer's heart, then resignation filled it again. Hawk was right. Despite her own feelings, this was an impossible situation. They were at an impasse, and from where she stood, it appeared they both were about to lose.

"I'm glad," Jennifer said. "But, that doesn't change why I'm here.

If I were to ask, would you be willing to stop your project early?"

"No."

"Then I guess there's nothing more to say."

Hawk studied her for a moment, then turned, retreating down the trail that had led her to the pond, leaving her standing alone at the water's edge.

Jennifer had never felt such rejection. He hadn't rejected her personally—just the work she was doing, this particular assignment. So why did it feel like he was rejecting her?

She swallowed the large lump in her throat. She'd loved and she'd lost, all within the space of an hour. Forfeiting her work to gain love wouldn't work—not for either of them. If Hawk wouldn't quit his work for her, how could he expect her to do so? There had to be another answer.

Feeling the threat of tears, Jennifer looked up at the trees. She wouldn't cry. The last few hours were hours to treasure, and regardless of what happened, she would always remember the pond and the afternoon that she and Hawk had made love. Some people had a lifetime together; they'd had only minutes.

Jennifer moved to her clothes, dressed, then followed the path back to where Hawk and her stuff were. As she approached the clearing, she saw that Hawk stood with his back to her. He threw pebbles at a lone rock at the fringes of the grassy knoll. He was an excellent marksman; the thud of each pebble hitting the rock echoed through the air.

By the way Hawk's arm jerked with each movement, Jennifer knew he was still upset.

She ran a hand through her nearly dried hair. What a mess. The intensity of her feelings scared her. If only Hawk loved her, then she was sure they could work something out...

Maybe Hawk had done the right thing by bringing up her assignment. She was tired of pussyfooting around the subject. At least now, he knew she hadn't given one thought to discontinuing the reason she was brought here in the first place. He'd been honest and she could leave with her pride intact. The sun disappeared. Shivering, Jennifer looked up. Rain clouds obscured the sun. The day, like her mood, had darkened considerably.

Hawk, having run out of pebbles, turned, and saw her standing there. Taking a deep breath, she pasted a bright smile on her face, walked up to him and held out the shirt she'd donned at the pond. "Here's your shirt." It bothered her more than she wanted to admit seeing his naked torso, so she turned away from him as he put it on and went to their discarded supplies to gather them up. "Do you think it'll rain before we get back?"

"Possibly. Probably. We need to head back."

"We're not going to any other sites today?"

"No, the eagles have to wait. I've got something more important to take care of. When we get back to the cabin, I'm going to radio Smitty and tell him to come get you."

Stunned, she spun around and stared at him. "What for?"

"I think it'd be best." He jammed the shirttails into his pants.

"You're doing this because we made love."

"No, I'm not."

"You are. You're afraid it's going to happen again."

"Isn't it?"

"It doesn't have to, not if you don't want it to."

"That's just it. I do. Over and over and over."

"Well, I've got news for you, Hawk Who Flies Alone. So do I."

"I still want you off this mountain."

"I'm not leaving until my two weeks are up."

"I could make you go."

"You could try."

But, he wouldn't. It was going to be hard enough when she did leave. He wasn't ready to face that day yet—it'd be here soon enough. Hell, he hadn't set out to make love to Jennifer even though he wanted to undress her and take her again, here, right now.

Instead, he turned, grabbing his things, and in a gruff voice said, "Let's go."

As she walked behind him, she remembered the film in her camera and rewound it. Taking it out, she fished in a pocket for a pencil and label, attached the label to the film, then stopped. Blinking rapidly, she wrote "Fuss and Feathers." Then she placed the film into the camera bag next to the feather she had worn in her hair just before they had made love.

***

By mid-afternoon, they had hiked to an area she hadn't seen before. Just above the tree line they sat and observed the countryside.

Hawk's binoculars were pointed towards the sky.

"What are we looking for besides eagles?" she asked.

"Just eagles," he said, peering through them. He fastened his gaze on one area of the sky, down near the opposite mountain. "Welcome to Circus In The Sky."

"Circus in the sky?"

"The thermals are plentiful here and the young birds like to test their wings. You'll see. The wait won't be long."

Jennifer aimed her camera with the telephoto lens in the same direction Hawk searched. She scanned the sky, unable to find anything. "I don't see anything."

"You're looking in the wrong direction. Look up there, about two o'clock. There's a new eagle."

She lowered her camera and peered at the sky. "Where?"

Hawk dropped his binoculars and saw Jennifer peering into the sky, squinting. He put his head next to hers, then lifted his arm, pointing a finger, so she could follow the line. Jennifer felt the heat that radiated from his body, her nose picking up the smell of musky pine she'd come to love.

"There."

Refocusing her thoughts, she peered at the sky. "I see it." Again, she raised her camera and caught the bird in her viewfinder. She watched as the eagle rose and dived, gliding out of the fall smoothly. "How can you tell it's a new eagle? It's so far away."

"At first, they all look alike. But, after a while, small differences become distinguishable. This one's a stranger to the territory. I think he's a young male looking for a mate."

For about five minutes, they watched the bird circle around and around, slowly descending until finally, it settled on the tip of one particularly large lodgepole pine.

"Aren't eagles territorial? I know, for instance, the great-horned owl needs about four square miles from which to hunt."

"In that way, eagles are identical. But, when it comes to feeding and nesting, with food centrally located, the boundaries overlap. Same with bears. For instance, the salmon run is the only time you'll find them clustered together in one small area, tolerating such closeness."

Eyes tired, Jennifer lowered her camera. Without the camera, she could barely make out the bird. She looked around, then spotted another one. "Look," she said, nudging Hawk. She pointed to the second eagle that took off from another tree, some distance away from the first eagle.

Hawk looked at it through his binoculars. "That's Beauty. She's about three, just coming into maturity." He, too, lowered his glasses. "I wonder if that's her future mate up there." he said, indicating the other bird.

"They mate for life?"

"Usually, like Canadian geese and less than fifty percent of the human population."

"Sad, isn't it?" Jennifer commented.

"What?"

"That animals seem to do it better than we do—mating for life," she added, seeing Hawk's baffled expression.

Hawk agreed. "How come you're not married?"

"Haven't found the right person."

"Why not?"

"Maybe I'm too fussy."

"Are you?"

"I don't think so. I just want a mate with a sense of humor, someone who'll let me work and not feel threatened by it. Beyond that,

I have an open mind." She put down her binoculars and looked at him. "What about you? Why haven't you remarried?"

Hawk laughed. "Up here, where am I going to meet anyone?"

"You've got a point," she acknowledged. "But then, if you gave more interviews, you could eliminate that problem."

"But then, I'd have other problems."

"Like what?"

"Having to share my cabin more often. Giving up my bed, having to sleep on the floor."

"I thought you gave up your bed quite easily. I offered to be the one sleeping on the floor." She knew what he meant. He had said it often enough in the beginning—he didn't want anyone disturbing his solidarity, his environment.

She brought the camera up to her eye. The male flew closer to the female, then together they perched in the same tree, this time several yards from each other. She started shooting. Unable to talk and shoot at the same time without jiggling the camera, she focused on the birds. After she finished the roll, she set about reloading the camera, and labeled the film Pairing Off. She swallowed the forlorn feeling that threatened to overwhelm her and fought the urge to succumb to the feeling.

She knew from the beginning, from that first time they made love, what she was getting into. Just because she loved him, that didn't mean he was expected to return her feelings. *Idiot*, she thought. *So you're unlucky in love again. What else is new?* If it had been any other man, she might have been concerned her feelings weren't reciprocated, but this man was an entirely different species. Now, if she hadn't fallen for him—like every other woman—then, she should be worrying.

The sun, high in sky, warmed Jennifer's bare legs as she stretched them out in front of her. The day had turned out unseasonably warm and today she'd chosen to wear shorts. She knew by the time the sun started setting, they'd be back at the cabin. For now, she wanted to enjoy the sun. She turned her legs a bit, observing the golden tan she'd acquired so far. Not a sun worshipper like other women, she obtained her coloring while working outdoors.

The heat felt good, making her lazy. She yawned. This late in August, this could easily be one of the last warm, summery days—at least, at this elevation.

Earlier, she'd discarded her sweatshirt, leaving only her purple T-shirt. Two days after the bear attack, Hawk had deemed her healthy enough to return to her own clothes. He had told her he didn't mind her wearing his shirts—but she did. Wearing his clothing had only increased her awareness of him. His scent was with her every second of the day and while wearing his shirt, she felt as if Hawk himself was wrapped around her body. It wasn't an image easily forgotten. Even now, just thinking about it, she felt her pulse quicken and bit her lip to stop the returning sensations.

She raised her face to the sun, letting the rays strike her face. Minutes later, she turned her head from one side to the other, canvassing the area.

Down in the valley, a moose drank from the river's edge. "Moose Landing" Hawk called that particular embankment. She could see why. A sound in the nearby trees attracted her attention. A rabbit bounded away. For a moment she followed its path, then her gaze focused on Hawk's profile.

The lines around his eyes crinkled as he squinted through the binoculars. His hair, gently lifted by the breeze that swirled around them, shone black like the feathers of a raven in the sun. His jaw, firm and square, showed signs of needing a shave. The corners of his mouth were turned up in obvious pleasure that he'd found a new pair of eagles settling in the area. His large hands held the glasses steady, his fingers and hands brown from the sun. She remembered how his hands had caressed her and how he'd lovingly stroked the injured fawn. And yet, the same hands could grip an ax, splinting a good-size piece of wood in one downward stroke.

Silently, she wished he'd remove the binoculars and look at her instead of the eagles. But, he didn't.

From out of the corner of her eye, a flash of light in the trees halfway up the mountain opposite them caught her attention. She studied the area where she thought she'd seen the light. There it was, again. Moving through the trees.

She raised her camera with the long lens and searched the landscape. Unable to find the source of light, she lowered the camera. A few minutes later, she was about to give up when she saw it again. There. Across the valley and halfway up the next mountain.

Again, she raised the camera to her eyes. Suddenly, she found what she was looking for. Three men entered a small clearing, the same three men they'd seen before. The poachers they had been looking for and couldn't find. She remembered the scruffy gray beard on one of the men. This time they had guns. She twisted the focusing ring until the image she wanted was sharp. Automatically, she squeezed the shutter release. She'd taken only half a dozen pictures when Hawk jerked her arm and pulled her down.

She shrugged off his arm and started to rise, agitated that he'd stopped her.

"Stay down!"

"Those men are over on the far side of the valley—they've got guns!"

Hawk yanked her back down. "They saw you!"

"They couldn't have."

"Something made them look this way." Hawk looked her over. "Could have been your lens, my binoculars—anything that reflected the sun." He raised his binoculars to his eyes and quickly lowered them, still studying the area Jennifer knew the men to be in. "Great, now all three of them are searching with their binoculars. If we move, they're sure to spot us. Out here in the open we're as visible as elephants in a football stadium." He glanced at her. "Your fluorescent shirt doesn't help."

Hawk brought his binoculars up to his eyes again. She saw his jaw tense.

"Well?"

He cursed. "They've got guns that could kill a bull."

She moved, accidentally knocking her canteen.

He grabbed for it, stilling it, then quickly brought the binoculars up. He continued gazing through the glasses. "Can't you ever stay still?"

"I'm sorry. Maybe they didn't see us."

"Don't bet on it."

She wouldn't know until the pictures were developed if she had gotten any good clear shots. If she did, at least, they'd have something to show the authorities if Hawk's suspicions were correct. But, what would happen in the meantime?

As soon as Hawk felt it was safe, they left the ridge, and the immediate area. He didn't want to take any chances.

A few hours later, and several miles from where they had been spotted, Hawk and Jennifer came to a clearing plush with grass. They stopped for a rest.

"Are we safe?" she asked.

"Right now, here, we are. I'm not sure about later. If you were those guys what would you do?"

"Try to find us, I guess. Especially, if I thought my picture had been taken."

Hawk nodded. "The thing is, we don't know if they saw the camera or not. They don't know who we are."

"If it were me, I'd be leaving the area."

"But, that's you. They're meaner, they're not afraid of anything, and they've got a lot to lose."

"So what do we do?"

"We stay together. Stay alert. Keep our distance from them."

"Do you think they'll find the cabin?"

"I was just wondering the same thing." He wanted her safe, away from any danger. "Jennifer, you need to call Smitty and tell him to come get you."

"Now, wait just a minute—"

"We found the poachers, and they spotted us. It's not safe here— not for you anyway."

"But what about you?" Apprehension filled her with a new terror.

"You want to go after them, don't you? You can't! You're only one man!"

"And they're three men destroying everything in their path."

"There's nothing you can do about it. Call the rangers and let them take care of it. You're forgetting about Andrews."

"Not for a minute. He's still missing. That's why I want you off the mountain. As long as those poachers know we're here, you're in danger."

"You're in as much danger as I am."

"I know how to take care of myself."

With tight control, she said, "Yes, you most certainly do." She turned back to her work, irritated that she let him get to her.

Her arm was grabbed and she was suddenly hauled to her feet, held against his chest, much like the first time they met, she thought. She arched an eyebrow at him, refusing to respond angrily even though she wanted to desperately.

As the seconds ticked by, and he waited for her reaction, he realized she wasn't going to respond like he wanted her to. He'd expected her to come at him spitting and clawing. Instead, cool silence greeted him.

***

Until the poachers were taken care of, he couldn't promise her safety. Right now, he felt like a new jigsaw puzzle still in its box—rattled and mixed-up. Only time would allow him to straighten out his feelings, put into proper place the pieces of his emotions.

He had to get her off the mountain. Nothing else was as important, and he would do anything to see that she left. Even if it meant risking her wrath.

***

As Hawk searched her face, she saw something in his eyes she hadn't seen before. It wasn't desire, nor was it anger. She couldn't determine what it was, but she sensed that Hawk was at war with himself right now.

She bit her tongue, unwilling to let him provoke her. She was staying until she'd completed her assignment, and he wasn't setting her off this mountain one minute sooner. She'd go along with notifying Smitty and contacting the rangers again, but she wasn't leaving.

Hawk's hold on her softened until finally she realized his hands were no longer touching her.

"Get your gear." He turned away from her, grabbed his own stuff, and started back to the cabin.

She had no recourse but to follow. Was it her imagination or had she seen a hunger in his eyes just before he let her go? She could only hope that his need was as raw as her own. It was so tempting to say yes, yes she'd forget her project, and do as he asked, but what good would it do her? The memory of his rejection she'd felt earlier still stung. And all because of her assignment. It wasn't fair that she had to make this kind of decision—to put her career over her feelings for Hawk. But, wasn't he doing the same thing?

What choice did she have?

None.

Somehow, come hell or high mountain, she would get her pictures published.

Hawk was right. She'd made a choice, and it sickened her to think that to save herself she had to destroy him. No, that wasn't true. Destroy was too harsh. What he had accomplished here could never be destroyed.

***

The sun was in its final descent when they finally arrived back at the cabin. She frowned when Hawk stopped mid-way across the clearing.

"What's wrong?" she asked.

"You were the last one out of the cabin. Did you forget to shut the door when we left?"

Her gaze darted to the door, and she saw it stood open. "No, I shut it. I know I did."

"Wait here."

She didn't want to wait, nor did she want him entering the

structure alone. Frightened at what he'd find and even more frightened for his safety, Jennifer watched Hawk peek into the cabin through a window. He stepped into the cabin and then disappeared from view. She knew only seconds had passed, but it seemed much longer than that.

"Hawk?"

He didn't answer. She didn't know whether to follow or turn and run. She followed. Cautiously. The sun disappeared behind the trees. When she peered into the cabin, it was dark. Slowly, she stepped inside. "Hawk?" she whispered.

"Don't move."

She jumped hearing the sound of his voice, felt her toe catch on something, and was pitched forward in the blackness. "Oh," she cried.

Hawk grunted as she fell against him. He fumbled for her, trying to grab her around the waist. Failing miserably, they crashed to the floor.

She moved hands through empty air. "Hawk! Where are you?"

"Here. Are you hurt?" he asked.

She grabbed toward the voice, this time feeling his arm that was extended to her. She clutched at him and scooted to him. "No. Are you?"

"No. Don't move."

"Why not?"

"Because the furniture isn't in the right place. I told you to stay outside. One of these days you'll follow my advice."

"Don't bank your birds on it."

His hand brushed her thigh, then she felt him lean back. She heard the rustle of his jeans and felt further movement against her thigh as he dug into his pocket. She heard the scratch of a match, and then the match flared.

Jennifer gasped.

Even though the light was dim and didn't extend into the whole cabin, Jennifer was shocked at the utter destruction of the cabin. It had been ransacked thoroughly.

Flour dusted everything, broken dishes were scattered on the floor, furniture had been tossed around, and there were paw prints in the flour.

"Raccoons," she said, pointing to the telltale foot tracks.

"If you had latched the door, this wouldn't have happened." The match went out. "Have you got your flashlight handy? I dropped my knapsack when you crashed into me."

Blindly, Jennifer unzipped her bag and fished for the light. Seconds later, her fingers felt the familiar cylinder. She pulled it out and turned it on. Hawk took it from her, searching the room with it until he found his knapsack. Taking out his own flashlight, he handed hers back to her. "Let's find the lantern first. We can't do much of anything with these."

"What a mess," she said.

Hawk found the lantern, picked it up, and set in on the table. "We're lucky this didn't break. The cabin could have gone up in flames."

Jennifer shuddered at the image of the cabin afire. In seconds, he had the lantern lit and the room was adequately illuminated. She turned off her flashlight and took a closer look at the shambled interior. She was so sure she had closed the door securely that morning, but obviously she hadn't. "Hawk, I'm sorry. I could have sworn I shut the door. This is my fault. I'll clean it up."

"Don't be ridiculous. I'll help you. It'll take us hours to straighten this up, and don't feel responsible. If you say you latched the door, then I believe you. Maybe a critter finally outsmarted me. Guess I'll have to put a regular knob with a lock on the door."

She saw him frown. His gaze was centered on his desk, and quickly he went to it. Papers were scattered everywhere. Then she saw the radio was on the floor the same time he did.

"Is it okay?" she asked.

He picked it up and set back on the table. He turned a knob. Nothing. "No."

Suddenly, he was moving around at the rest of the cabin, pulling up blankets and clothing.

"What is it?"

"Something's not right."

Fear coiled in her stomach. "What do you mean?"

Hawk stopped what he was doing, looked at her, then seemed to reconsider what he was about to say. "Nothing. Let's just get this stuff picked up."

"If the radio isn't working—"

"I've got some spare parts out in the refrigerator for safe keeping. I'll get them right now."

"I'll take care of these while you're doing that," she said, indicating the blankets.

***

Taking a flashlight with him, Hawk went outside and shut the door behind him. He didn't turn on the light right away. He didn't want to frighten Jennifer unnecessarily, but this whole business left him uneasy. Since spotting the poachers earlier, he assumed this was their doing. Until he was sure of it, he would remain cautious. And until he was sure, he'd wait before saying anything to Jennifer.

His eyes searched the landscape, but he couldn't detect anything unusual. Birds were settling down for the night, and he heard an occasional howl, most likely a wolf. If anything was out there in the darkness that shouldn't have been, the animals would have told him as much by their silence.

So far, they were safe enough, but he wasn't about to let Jennifer out of his sight. Quickly, he went and retrieved the box of parts. By the time he returned, Jennifer had set the chairs they had stumbled over upright again and was trying to fold a blanket that seemed to be getting away from her.

"Let me help," he offered, setting down the box.

"Thanks. I suddenly seem to have two left hands." He didn't blame her for feeling like she had two left hands. So did he. Though she hadn't questioned him, he knew she sensed his fear. He admired the way she was holding up. As they searched for the four corners to fold it up, a glove dropped to the floor. Picking it up, she looked at it, then held it out to him. "It's not mine."

"It's not mine either."

Jennifer dropped it. The glove landed with a soft thud on the floor. "Then, whose is it?" she croaked.

CHAPTER 13

She didn't have to ask. She knew.

Hawk tossed the blanket down. "We're getting out of here."

"And going where?"

"To the cave. Take anything you'll need for the next few days. We're not coming back, at least not tonight, and I don't know how long it's going to take me to fix the radio. I'll have to come here to repair it. It's too bulky to carry to the cave. I can't operate it from there anyway. The antenna is built into the cabin. The poachers didn't discover the antenna and aren't likely to. In the meantime, I'm going to hide the radio out in the refrigerator."

"Why don't you fix it now?"

"Even if I could get a hold of anybody, it's too risky for Smitty to come this time of night. The winds get gusty and the air is unstable. Besides, we don't know how long ago the poachers were here or if they're planning to come back. I don't want them finding us fixing it. It can wait until tomorrow." Grabbing the bulky box-like radio and stacking the box of parts he'd just brought in, he lifted them both. "Get the door, then bolt it after I leave. Don't open it until you hear my voice. Got it?"

"Yes." She rushed ahead of him to the door, then did as he told her once he disappeared into the dark.

A cold panic washed over her, and she swallowed the nausea that filled her throat. She wouldn't panic now. Later maybe, but not now.

Spotting the smaller of her two suitcases that held her clothing, she leaped for it. Her fingers shook when she realized someone had been searching through it. Willing herself to concentrate on her task and not think about what had happened, she dumped it upside down, then took the empty case over to the cupboard, and started tossing canned goods and any other rations she thought they would need in the next day or two. Clean clothing they could do without—food they couldn't. That was when she discovered Hawk's bow, broken in two, hidden under the debris by the cupboard.

"Jennifer!"

She jumped hearing Hawk's voice.

"Let me in."

She did and stepped back seeing a rifle in his arms and a gun tucked into his belt.

"I had these stored away. They took the weapons I had in here."

"I found your bow. They broke it." The full implication that their lives were at stake hit her. Suddenly, she felt violated. Before she had a chance to dwell on the thought, Hawk turned her around and pushed her toward the pump.

"Fill the canteens. We won't be able to get any other water tonight. If we can't come back to the cabin, we can refill them from a stream or pond."

Five minutes later they were out the door.

Hawk had filled the rest of the suitcase with blankets. He carried that now, along with her duffle bag filled with other emergency supplies. The two canteen straps were crisscrossed around his chest and with his free hand, he carried the rifle and flashlight. Following him, Jennifer carried a bag that held as much wood as she could carry—since it was pitch black they wouldn't be able to find much wood in the dark and already the temperature hovered near freezing. Under her other arm, she carried a box of cooking utensils they'd need for the most basic of meals. And despite their weight, she carried her camera bags around her neck and shoulders. No way was she going to leave that equipment behind. She had told Hawk she didn't expect him to carry it, that she would. Now, as he followed Hawk through the tangled brush, she refused to think about how heavy the cameras were and that maybe she should have left them behind.

Loaded as they were, it took them only a few minutes to complete the five-minute hike. While Hawk went into the cave first with the flashlight to make sure no one, or anything else had taken up residence, she leaned against the outer stone wall to catch her breath. She'd managed to keep up with his punishing pace, but just barely.

She saw the light before she saw Hawk.

"All clear," he told her. "Here, I'll take the wood."

Minutes later, he had a small fire going. By then, her eyes had adjusted to the dim light. Her nose twitched at the dank, musty smell. "Are you sure we can't be detected in here?"

"I'm sure. We can't have a roaring fire, but we're deep enough inside, plus that little twist of the walls just before we reached this back wall will hide the light. No one will ever know we're here as long as we're careful."

She scooted closer to the fire, holding out her hands to warm them. The cave was humid, thus colder inside than it was outside for the moment. She knew, however, once the fire continued, it would warm up. Not much, but a bit more. "Do you think you can fix the radio?"

"I hope so."

"I don't think we should be down at the cabin any more than we have to be."

"I agree. That's why tomorrow we'll get everything else we need until we can get help." Taking the flashlight with him, he rose and started toward the cave entrance.

"Where are you going?"

"To cover up our trail. With all that weight we were carrying, our footsteps will be easy to follow."

While he was gone, Jennifer retrieved the plastic from her supply bag. Usually she used it for a tent or a raincoat. For one person, it was quite adequate. Now, however, it would have to serve as a barrier between the cold cave floor and their blankets. It was the only protection they had to keep their bedding dry.

Spreading the blankets on top of the plastic, she wished they had brought her sleeping bag out of her other box. Tonight, they'd have to make do with what they brought with them; tomorrow, they could plan better. Tomorrow, she hoped, they'd at least be able to notify the authorities of their predicament. Her two weeks here was turning out to be one heck of a story. Despite the turn of events, she was glad that she'd had the opportunity to photograph it.

Hearing footsteps, Jennifer froze. A shadow moved toward her, then Hawk was in the firelight. She breathed a sigh of relief. She hadn't realized how nervous she was until he'd reappeared just now.

"Can we throw more wood on the fire?" she asked.

"No, not yet. We've got to keep it smokeless. It's not going to warm us up, not as we'd like it to. It's basically to keep the critters away."

Jennifer shivered knowing a cougar or bear wouldn't come into the cave, not with the human scent in the air. But, a snake could easily slither into the cave. In fact, at this time of year, they were usually looking for a den to hole up in for the winter.

Determined not to think about it, she resumed her task. Suddenly, she realized they'd be sharing a bed tonight. They had no choice. The plastic wasn't any bigger than a double bed—if that. And they'd only brought three blankets, hardly enough considering the temperature outside, let alone in the cave. The only way they'd stay warm would be to share body heat.

After what had happened before, she wasn't sure Hawk wanted to share a bed with her. With anxious eyes, she glanced at Hawk.

Hawk was busy stowing their belongs away, finding ledges for most of their supplies, rather than taking a chance on leaving anything on the cave floor for any creature that might wander in. She couldn't tell anything by his expression. Ever since they'd discovered it was the poachers who'd ransacked the cabin, he'd been all business, and during much of the time, wearing a scowl. At least now, the scowl was gone. He looked tired. The corners of his mouth drooped. She wanted to wrap her arms around him and tell him that it was all right—they were safe, and they were together. That's all that mattered.

But, she held back. She wasn't sure whether he'd welcome the gesture or not.

Seeing Hawk open a can of fruit cocktail, she moved to the small fire and sat down next to him. "Need any help?" Now he was opening a can of pork and beans.

"Sure. Get out the silverware. We're dining out of the can tonight."

"Ah..."

"Let me guess. No silverware."

"That's right. Wait a minute. I think I've got something here," she said, digging into her duffel bag. "Ta-da," she said merrily, holding up two plastic spoons still individually wrapped in cellophane. "Anytime I eat fast-food I grab a couple extra utensils and throw them in here. They don't weigh much or take up room. I forget I've got them sometimes. And, they come in handy. I've used them for digging earthworms—in soft soil of course—when I've had to fish for my supper unexpectedly. I had to move a hummingbird egg back into its nest one time. I knew if I picked it up with my fingers, I'd break it. And, I've stuck them in the ground to use as trail markers before." She stopped, feeling as if she was talking too much.

Hawk raised an eyebrow. "I can see I'm going to have to keep a supply of plastic spoons on hand in the future. I don't know how I've survived without them."

"Go ahead, make fun of me, but if I hadn't had them, we'd be eating with our fingers right now."

"You're right. This is so much better."

At least their spirits were lifted by their banter, if only by a little bit, she noticed. The tension was thick.

Jennifer opened two more cans of food. Since it was late, they didn't bother heating them up. Eating out of the cans, they switched them every few bites. Jennifer could have used her mess kit, but with the limited amount of water they had on hand, she didn't want to waste any water washing dishes tonight.

Afterward, while Hawk arranged loose, large branches near the cave's entrance to camouflage it better, Jennifer buried the cans in a shallow hole outside. Luckily, the ground was soft underneath the leaves, so she was able to scoop the dirt with one of the empty cans. It was important that any wildlife nearby not to be able to smell their food and come to investigate, although she wondered if she was burying them deep enough to escape an animals good sense of smell.

They'd have to go to the refrigerator for the more perishable groceries as they needed them. Then, again, they might have to survive with nothing more than what they already had.

They'd already decided that each time they visited the cabin, they'd approach it from a different route. Tomorrow, Hawk planned to make a new bow and they'd hunt for what little fresh meat they needed. That would eliminate some of the trips they might have made to the refrigerator.

She completed her task, replacing dead leaves and other debris over the buried cans. Rising to her feet, she dusted off her hands removing the dirt as best she could, then went and relieved Hawk of a few pieces of wood. They started back to the cave.

Inside, they dumped the wood near the fire. Their supply of fuel was meager, but it would have to do.

Inside, he took a stick with a rag on the end of it and dipped it into a can. It came out dripping and somewhat gooey.

Jennifer crinkled her nose at the smell. "What is that stuff?"

He smeared it around the shelf ledge where he had put the bulk of their food supply and other equipment. Seeing her scrunched-up face, he laughed. "Bear grease." Next, he dragged it on the ground at the entrance and various other spots in the cave.

"What are you doing?"

"Making it appear to other creatures that there's a bear living in here. I'll spread a bit around the ground outside too. It'll tell other bears—should they venture too close—that this apartment's already settled."

"Are we going to have to live with this awful smell?"

"No. Soon you won't even notice it. But, the animals will."

"How did you get that stuff?"

"The rangers gave me a dead bear."

"What for?"

"It was a rogue. The bear had killed two campers and had to be destroyed."

"I remember reading about that," she said. "How often does that happen?"

"Not too often. Usually a bear is tranquilized, then moved to a remote area where's there limited human habitation. But, this fellow had already been moved twice and kept returning to the scene of his crimes. So, I got his carcass. Gave me enough steaks for the whole winter."

"Are we still going to follow our usual routine, checking up on the birds? Or, do we have to stay cooped up in here all the time?"

"Tomorrow I'll repair the radio. We'll know more after that."

Jennifer stared at the fire, then felt a yawn coming. She tried to hold it back, but couldn't. Then Hawk yawned. Nervously, she glanced at him, then returned her gaze to the fire. She yawned, again.

The words she'd been dreading and yet waiting for came from Hawk. "I guess it's time we turned in. It's been a long day."

She mumbled her agreement and made her way to their bed. Her heart quickened and her stomach flip-flopped. She tried to reassure herself that all they were going to do was sleep. But, she didn't believe it. She wanted more. She ached to have Hawk's arms around her. For all she knew, this could be there last night together.

She pulled back two of the blankets and sat on the third, hearing the plastic crackle beneath it. She pulled off her boots and tried not to notice that Hawk was doing the same thing next to her.

But, notice him she did. She saw how he wiggled his socked toes, flexing them one way then another. When he unbuttoned the cuffs of his shirt, she saw how his knuckles rubbed up against the fabric, the sound just a mere whisper to her ears. The plastic crinkled loudly as he lay down with his arms behind his head, creating a pillow.

When she lay down, her head bumped his elbow. Quickly, he

moved his arms, turning on his side so he faced her.

She pulled the blankets up over them both and lay down again. Seconds later, she moved so she was on her side. The ground was just too hard to lay on her back.

They faced each other.

Her eyes were level with his mouth. She saw one corner move. She tilted her head back just enough so she could look at his eyes. He was staring at her.

"Goodnight, Hawk."

"Goodnight, Jennifer."

She started to lower her gaze, then glanced back up at him again. He continued to stare at her.

First, she bit her lip, then she swallowed heavily. She cursed the sound she made doing it. Without realizing what she was doing, she sighed heavily. Why couldn't she just close her eyes and go to sleep?

Because your heart is racing like a wild mare on the open prairie, she thought. She heard the hoot of an owl and then something running through the underbrush just outside the cave. A squeal of fear—from a mouse or some other small creature—echoed through the cave. She shivered at the sound, wondering if the animal had escaped or became someone's meal.

She licked her lips. Despite the cave's humidity, they felt dry.

"Don't do that."

Startled hearing Hawk's voice, she looked at him. "Do what?" She licked her lips, again.

"That."

"Oh."

"Damn!" Instantly, his arms were around her and he pulled her closer to him.

"What are you doing?"

"I can't be next you all night and not touch you."

"But nothing's changed," she reminded him.

"Yes it has."

She started to protest and he pressed a finger to her lips to quiet her. "Tonight we're just two people who care about each other."

Her heart filled with tenderness. His breath caressed her skin, and she kissed his chin. Then his mouth. He tasted sweet like syrup. Eager to taste more, she slipped her tongue into his mouth.

Hawk groaned and clutched her tightly against him. Through their clothing, she felt his hardness against her thigh, and moved her hips until he was cupped against the juncture of her thighs.

He groaned again.

She felt his fingers at her belt, then his knuckles dragged against her lower abdomen as he pulled the zipper down. Her sweatshirt was raised, and then the hem of her T-shirt was tugged up. When his fingers touched her belly, her muscles contracted. It gave him the entrance he sought, and he slid his hand, palm-down on her belly into her panties. He inched his way down until he could curl his fingertips against the sensitive tip of her womanhood.

She moaned and arched, wanting more, her muscles contracting around his fingers. "Oh, Hawk."

"Tell me what you want."

"I want you."

"You're wet." He moved his fingers in and out making her aware how slick she was.

"Don't do this to me."

His movements ceased. "You want me to stop?" he breathed in her ear.

"No, no. Don't stop." Cupping her hand, she rubbed it up against his arousal several times. She grinned, hearing him moan. Fumbling for his belt, she finally got it undone. With his help, they pulled down his jeans, then hers. Before he could touch her, she had her hand wrapped around him that had him moaning.

"Oh, baby," he whispered, before capturing her mouth with a kiss.

He rolled her on her back, then placed his hands beneath her buttocks to cushion her softer skin against the hard floor. She guided him into her pocket of warmth.

She clutched the rounded flesh of his bottom and pulled him

against her, rotating her hips. Faster and faster they gyrated together until the darkness behind her eyelids exploded into a convulsion of color.

Her body quivered as his did, and then they both went slack. She welcomed his weight upon her.

"That was great," he said.

"We do well together, don't we?"

Hawk laughed. "Amazingly well."

She glowed. How she loved him so. If only he would tell her that he loved her. Then, she'd feel they had half a chance. They could work anything out.

But he didn't, and she felt as though they had no chance at all. She would never regret sleeping with Hawk. Never. These past few days had been the best of her life. Even, if she never found another love again, at least, she had this.

Contented, she sighed. Hawk rolled off her and she tried to right her clothing. She had no energy to do the task, but she made the attempt. Blankets were tucked around her, and she felt his lips against her cheek, then he tucked her under his shoulder and held her tight.

She knew the contentment she felt right now wouldn't last, but while the emotion was hers, she was going to wallow in it. With that thought, she fell asleep.

***

By degrees, consciousness returned to Jennifer. At first, she thought it was a swarm of hummingbirds that hovered nearby, their wings beating simultaneously. Then she realized, she'd been dreaming that the little birds were the source of the noise.

Louder this time, the noise was next to her ear. She opened her eyes and found her gaze level at Hawk's throat. His Adam's apple stuck out. He was snoring in her ear.

She moved slightly, just enough so she could see his face. Seeing his mouth open, she smiled. Then unable to resist, she pressed her lips against his.

Slowly, she felt him come awake, and quickly his lips returned her pressure.

"I like the way you wake me up," he said huskily, with sleep still in his voice.

"Too bad you couldn't return the favor. You snore."

"I do not."

"You do too."

"You have no way to prove it."

He had her there.

***

A short time later, they arrived at the edge of the cabin's clearing. They waited five minutes, making sure the area was deserted, before leaving their hiding place in the bushes. Staying in the fringes of the forest, they circled around until they came to the refrigerator. Only then did they come out into the open.

"I think it'd be safer if I repair the radio in the refrigerator. It'll be cold, but we won't be exposed, out in the open."

Later, Jennifer brought her hands up, cupped them to her mouth and blew. Stomping her feet, she paced the length of the small icebox one more time, watching him. He wasn't shivering at all. "You're not affected by the cold, are you?"

"I keep thinking about being in the city in August."

"New York?"

"Any city. Miami. L.A."

Jennifer smiled. His control was amazing.

"Let's go give it a try," he said, tucking the radio under his arm. He checked the clearing before leading the way out of the refrigerator.

In the cabin, Hawk handed her his rifle and had her stand guard at the window; she was to alert him to any movement. As she stood there, her eyes constantly searching the clearing, she heard Hawk mutter to himself, prodding the appliance to work at the first try.

He flipped a lever and gave the call signal. The sweet sound of static filled the room, then seconds later Ranger Tom Brown answered. She remembered meeting Tom when she'd arrived at Smitty's office, located at the ranger's station.

"We've got a serious problem up here," Hawk said. "Poachers ransacked my cabin. Over."

"Are you in any immediate danger? Over".

"I don't think so. Tell Smitty to come get us. Over."

There was a moment of silence. Hawk looked at Jennifer, she stared back. The line crackled then went silent. Then it crackled again.

"Lair's Den, I understand the situation, but we can't help you right now. Flu cut our staff in half and we're battling a fire about a hundred miles north of you, trying to remove the tourists. Right now, you're safe—these folks aren't. Over."

Hawk looked up at the ceiling.

Now what would they do? Jennifer thought.

Hawk lowered his head, speaking into the microphone. "Let me talk to Smitty."

"He's not here. He's in Boise getting medical supplies and is grounded tonight due to high winds. He'll be back tomorrow, late, providing the weather improves."

"Any other transportation available?"

"None. Over."

Hawk's hand holding the microphone dropped to his side. "They can't come get us," he said to Jennifer. He jerked the microphone back up to his mouth. "Any word on Andrews?"

"None. Still missing."

"We'll call each morning by nine," Hawk said. "Over and out."

"Now what?" she asked.

"You heard him."

"But..."

"But what?"

"I'm surprised you're not thinking about us hiking down."

"Like I said, it's too rough for an inexperienced climber."

"Like me."

"Let's get the radio back out in the refrigerator."

"Will it be safe there?"

"I don't want to risk damaging it by taking it back and forth to the cave. We'll cover our tracks to the refrigerator and put some limbs in front of the door."

Hours later, they were halfway to one of the older nesting sites when they heard shots.

Jennifer glanced at Hawk. By the way his jaw muscles were clenched, she knew he was gritting his teeth.

"No proof," he muttered.

"What about my pictures?"

"They just show three men with rifles. Even though they're in prohibited territory, there's no way I could ever prove they were here."

Jennifer wished she'd been lucky enough yesterday to get more on film than just their faces. Maybe today, just maybe, she'd be more fortunate. That is, if Hawk would let her take the pictures. He hadn't let her out of his sight all morning. And after yesterday's travesty, she doubted he'd let her photograph anything within five miles of those men.

"Do we go on?"

"To the west."

"But the shots sounded like they came from the east."

"Exactly."

Soon, they reached their destination, but Hawk stopped before they got to the edge of the ridge. "You stay here." Even though they'd gone the opposite direction of the sound of gunfire, Hawk was being careful.

Jennifer watched Hawk move silently toward their usual lookout spot, then disappear from view. She settled against a tree, feeling the rough bark at her back.

High in the sky she saw an eagle circling, riding the thermals, flapping its wings only once or twice as it continued to glide through the air. A noise from the right caught her attention.

She looked, but didn't see anything. Then, she heard the sound again. This time, she saw something move. It had white and dark markings. She moved away from the tree, straightened, and took a few steps towards the activity. There was a flutter of movement. As she got closer, she saw it was a bird. An eagle. And it was injured—it could only raise one wing.

Cautiously, so as not to scare the animal, she moved closer. It tried flapping it wings again and cried out in pain. Suddenly, she saw the blood on its side and realized in horror that the other wing was gone.

"Oh, no," she cried, dropping to the ground. Five feet from the bird now, it didn't move, only stared at her. She crept closer, untying the bandanna from around her neck. The bird remained still as she crept next to it. Carefully, she stroked its head. It tried to peck at her hand. Moving her hand away from its sharp beak, she stroked its back. "What happened to you?" she crooned.

Feeling a stickiness on her hand, Jennifer raised it and saw blood. With shaky hands, she examined its back and saw another wound, a gaping hole. "Oh, Lord. How could they do this to you?" Another hole, a bit smaller, was on the opposite side of its body. A bullet wound. A monstrous, steely anger consumed her.

Here was the proof they needed! No, it wasn't. It was only proof that someone—it could have been anyone—had shot the bird. With tears in her eyes, she continually crooned at the animal while she tied the bandanna around the bird, covering both wounds as best as she could. The animal didn't react. Then, it started to convulse uncontrollably under her hands. It was in shock. She blinked, rapidly. Shrugging out of her jacket, she wrapped it around the eagle, then gathered the bundle in her arms, holding it to her own body for added warmth.

Her efforts failed. With a last shudder, the bird died in her arms. "No," she moaned. "No!" She hugged the bird to her body. Nothing would bring it back to life. Nothing.

She stroked the majestic bird, and the feathers that were sleek and smooth beneath her fingers. How could someone destroy such a beautiful bird? She looked down at the broken body. What kind of man ignored the law, taking delight in extinguishing the life of an animal that harmed no one, a bird that so rightly represented their symbol of freedom? What freedom did these birds have if driven to the edge of extinction?

She clutched the bird tighter to her chest, wishing life back into its still body. She sat there, rocking back and forth, angry that such precious life had been destroyed, wishing she could do something more.

There is something I can do, she thought looking down at the eyes that stared blankly into space. *I can see that your pictures are used for the right purpose—to move the public.* There had to be more people like Hawk who were willing to do something to ensure this kind of thing didn't continue to happen. The poachers—every blast one of them—had to be stopped and publicity was the only way it would happen.

As she stroked the still warm body, she vowed no one would stop her. She'd see those pictures got published one way or another. Granted, she understood Hawk's project and his wanting more time. But, he didn't *need* the extra time; he wanted it. This poor creature needed its life back but wouldn't get it.

No one, not even Hawk, would stop her. She'd use every one of her photos if she had to. Edwards would be pleased with that, she thought grimly. Hang Edwards—she wasn't doing it to please him. She was doing it for the birds. She was doing it for this one bird, a bird she had come to know, a bird that'd had a beautiful future. Now, it had none.

***

Satisfied the area was free from danger, Hawk retreated off the ledge. Other than the one lone eagle in the sky, he hadn't seen any other bird. Usually, there were three or four in this large, fertile valley. The Snake River below was a common feeding ground. Something had scared them away. In fact, he couldn't spot wildlife of any kind in the vicinity. In all likelihood, the shots they'd heard earlier were responsible.

He and Jennifer could safely stay in this area for the day. With no wildlife around, it wouldn't be profitable for the poachers to stick around if they'd, indeed, been responsible for the animals disappearing. But, Hawk knew, in a couple hours the wildlife would return and continue with their search for food. The poachers were probably gone, too, now that there was no wildlife.

When he came into view of the area where he'd left Jennifer, he couldn't see her. He swallowed the panic he felt. If she'd left after he told her to stay, he'd wring her neck! The area wasn't disturbed, so obviously, she'd left on her own. He'd still wring her neck! How could she be so careless, after everything that had happened?

It was then he heard the soft crooning sound. He twisted and saw her rocking back and forth, stroking something in her arms.

Then, he saw her hands looked red. Blood. Thinking she was hurt, he raced to her. She didn't even hear him until he touched her. "What happened?"

She looked up at him and he saw tears filling her eyes, spiking her lashes as they spilled out, running down her cheeks. It tore him up inside seeing her like this. He couldn't even begin to imagine what had happened to cause her this much suffering.

"Look what they did," she said, moving her jacket aside. Shock ran through him, when he saw the familiar feathers. The bird was the mate to the male that'd been circling overhead moments ago. "Beauty." The two birds would have produced their first clutch next year.

"What? Oh, God. This is Beauty?"

He knelt down to Jennifer's side, stroking her back in comfort. It hurt him more to see her in such pain than to see the dead bird.

"They killed this beautiful, beautiful bird. How can you not want me to publish any photographs after this? How can you ask that I wait?" She thrust the bird into his arms, then rose. "I don't care what you say anymore. For the last five years, you've done it your way. Well, you're not going to do it alone anymore. I'm going to work hard on my story and when I get back, people are going to know what's going on out here. I don't care if it upsets your time schedule. Stopping this kind of thing from happening again is more important. Your project is nearly finished and you should be proud—you've succeeded—but I'm going to succeed too."

CHAPTER 14

She walked away from him, taking huge angry steps.

He felt as if she'd pulled the carpet of grass he was standing on out from under him. What did she want him to do? He couldn't tell her not to be angry. Hell, he was angry too. "Where are you going?" he asked.

"To get my camera. That bird," she said pointing to the eagle in his arms, "is going to be part of my story. After I get my pictures, I'll bury her."

He wanted to stop her, but he couldn't. Her anger right now ran deeper than his own water well back at the cabin, and the best medicine for her was to take the pictures. If he tried to stop her, she'd never forgive him.

And, he didn't think he could forgive himself if he did try to stop her. She'd fight him every step of the way to get her work published.

As much as he wanted her to publish Beauty's tragedy, he couldn't permit her to go back East with the film, either. He had to delay her project. It went beyond the poachers. The birds needed the extra time. This unnecessary killing angered him, too. He wanted the public to know what a few of their own could do. But, the timing was all wrong.

Yes, he'd let her take the pictures, but he'd also find a way to keep the film here in Idaho when she returned to New York. In about six months, he'd mail it all to her. She could do whatever she wanted with it then. But, not until then. Not until he was ready. He wanted it done right. If it was just Jennifer alone putting together this feature, he'd have no problem—he'd let her do it. But, he wasn't satisfied that

Edwards wasn't involved. Until he was satisfied, no film would leave the mountain.

When Jennifer returned with her cameras, he saw an expression on her face he'd never seen before. Her actions were stiff, but she took the pictures with precise experience. If he had any doubts about her professionalism before, he had none now. As much as he wanted to talk with her, he knew it would do no good. Already, she was tuning him out; all her concentration was upon the bird.

He waited patiently while she burned three rolls of film, before picking up the bird. "It's time to bury her."

Jennifer nodded stiffly. They buried her at the edge of the ridge, out in the sun where she'd once thrived. Hawk noticed the hardness in her eyes. She had locked her feelings safely away, for now. He knew exactly how she felt. He'd been there before, and he had no idea how long it would be before he would be able to talk with her.

The rest of the day, she worked diligently, exhausting every possible angle she could achieve with her camera. She wasn't content to travel to their usual two or three nesting sites that day. She said she wanted to see as many sites as possible. She wanted to be sure the other birds were unharmed.

This wasn't the Jennifer he knew and was used to. This Jennifer was a professional, through and through, someone who was truly involved in her work. She was on automatic pilot. Even in that mode, her work was brilliant. As far as he was concerned, she was already the best in her field.

Hawk stayed with her. In her present frame of mind, he couldn't leave her alone in the wilderness. Not for a single second. Despite her tough exterior and her grim determination, she was too vulnerable right now. And the fact that they hadn't spotted the men all day worried him. Where were they?

When they arrived at the cave at dusk, Jennifer knew the true meaning of exhaustion. She'd driven both of them today, and yet, not once did Hawk complain or tell her to slow down.

"Let me check the cave first," Hawk told her as she started the slight upgrade to the entrance. She stopped, letting him pass. "The area doesn't look disturbed, but I don't think we should take any chances."

Jennifer nodded. Tired, she couldn't even speak. But, she wasn't so tired she couldn't appreciate watching Hawk's long, muscular legs carry him towards the cave. She saw his wide shoulders braced for any possibility, his arm raising the rifle he'd carried all day. He disappeared into the cave, then returned an instant later, the weapon against his relaxed shoulders. He gave her the thumbs up signal, indicating that it was safe.

She climbed up to where he stood waiting. How safe was she from him? Already, he had gained entrance to her heart. It just a matter of time before he broke it. What difference did it make? Her heart was already broken having witnessed Beauty's death.

Hawk studied Jennifer's pale face. There were shadows beneath her eyes, and every step she took seemed an achievement. She was near exhaustion. He wanted the other Jennifer back, the one who joked and could work him into a frenzy. This cool woman frightened him.

When she walked past him, he'd grabbed her arm to stop her. She looked at his hand, then at him. Her face showed no emotion. "Are you all right?" he asked. He knew she wasn't—she was sickened at what had happened this afternoon just as he was.

***

She couldn't look at him. "I'm fine," she muttered. "Just tired."

Hawk dropped his hand, and Jennifer continued on into the cave. Dropping onto the blankets, she reached for her camera bags, then put her equipment away properly. The humidity in the cave could easily damage her equipment if she wasn't careful. No matter how tired she felt, her equipment came first.

That done, she lay back on the blankets, her feet resting on the cave floor, her knees in the air. Lord, but she was tired. Now that she wasn't moving, she noticed the chilly air. Had it been cold all day, or had it just turned that way?

She refused to think about the night to come, the time when they'd be together under the blankets. She didn't know if she could handle a repeat of last night. Right now, she didn't want to be comforted.

She loved Hawk, but she loved her work too. As angry as she was at the poachers for killing Beauty, she felt alive when handling her cameras. Her work gave direction to her life. She wanted to be respected for the great photos she took. Nothing else mattered.

Nothing but Hawk, that is. Now she had to wonder if she had chased him away. But, how could she chase him away if he was never hers to start with? She'd seen the concern in his eyes, the way he'd held back today giving her space. She was grateful to him for that. She knew he cared for her, but did he care enough to let her to do her job?

She sat up, running a hand through her hair in frustration. Would she ever get what she wanted?

But what is it you really want? she thought.

Heaven help her, she just didn't know any more. One minute she knew quite clearly what she wanted—to be a great photographer. The best in her field. The next minute everything was fuzzy around the edges or turned upside-down. And, Hawk was in the middle of it all.

She noticed he had started a fire.

"Hungry?" he asked.

She shrugged. "Should be starved considering the pace I set." She paused, picking up a twig and dug into the cave floor with it. "Hawk, I'm sorry for...everything."

"You don't have to apologize. I understand."

Jennifer chewed her lower lip. She felt the need to explain. She knew he had been relieved too, finding the rest of the eagles safe and unharmed.

Hawk extended a hand to her. She glanced up, hesitant to touch him, but feeling the need to connect with another human being. She loved Hawk. She didn't want to push him away. She accepted his hand, and he pulled her up. They stood close, just a hair's breadth away from each other, their hands still linked. She saw his jaw tightened, then he swallowed heavily.

He smelled like fire, earth and pine—all mixed into a musky scent that was his alone. Shadows in the cave enveloped the upper portion of his face. She wanted to run her finger along his jawline, over his lower lip. And, taste his lips. He stood tall, so very tall, next to her. Just having him wrap his arms around her would feel good right now. "Please," she mumbled. "Just hold me."

He did. Long moments passed. Finally, she sighed. "I've got a rabbit to clean," he told her.

She nodded. She wanted to cry. She wanted to make love. She wanted to stay angry at the senseless killing of the eagle. She wanted to know how he could hold to his schedule.

While the rabbit Hawk had snared earlier cooked, Jennifer sat by the fire, mesmerized by the flames. As she stared at the flickering waves of heat, she kept seeing the images of eagles soaring in the air and Hawk's face interchanging with them.

She couldn't separate the man from the birds any more. As much as she wanted to forge ahead with her assignment, she didn't want to hurt him either. But, she couldn't tell him what he wanted to hear—that she would walk away from her project. She hated the position she'd been put in—if she got what she wanted, Hawk lost. If Hawk got what he wanted then she lost.

The rabbit smelled delicious, but she wasn't hungry. She took a few small bites but couldn't continue.

Setting her food down, she excused herself on the pretense of answering nature's call. Just outside the cave, she leaned against the wall, and stared at the heavenly sky. Stars winked at her, but she couldn't appreciate their beauty. Not tonight. Her heart was too heavy.

She wasn't being fair to Hawk. He'd done everything in his power to ensure her safety, making sure she was fed. Weren't people more important than wildlife? And yet, after what had happened to Beauty, she had an obligation to help the bird's tragic demise from happening to other birds. Who was right here? She, for wanting her goal met, giving the information to the public now? Or, Hawk from wanting to sit on that information for a while longer?

The stone behind her back felt cold, and she shivered. With a tired sigh, she pushed herself away from the rock and returned to the cave. She walked past Hawk and crawled into the bedding. Though the blankets felt clammy even through the layers of her clothing, the cold didn't bother her tonight. She felt as if her emotions were on auto pilot and that she was incapable of feeling anything, anymore. Earlier, when she had asked Hawk to hold her, she had hoped the action would help sort out her feelings. Though she'd felt comforted, she was left feeling equally confused. Now, she felt numb. Even the thought of a tub full of hot water and bubbles when she returned to civilization didn't appeal to her anymore. And, she loved bubble baths.

Minutes later, Hawk joined her. A sadness crept over her as he tucked the blankets around her. Hawk's arm went around her waist. She wanted so much to talk, to make him understand how she felt, but she knew it wouldn't do any good. She knew him well enough now to know he wasn't going to budge from his position.

***

The next morning, Jennifer woke, feeling warm and toasty despite the cold air circulating through the cave. Hawk hadn't moved much during the night. He was still holding her, but she had turned around, so now she faced him, an arm wrapped around his waist, their legs intertwined. Jennifer sighed. She wished she could always wake up like this, next to the man she loved.

She lay still, listening to the sounds of morning outside the cave, feeling Hawk's slow even breaths against her cheek. Unabashed, she studied his features. He looked so peaceful in sleep, the facial muscles relaxed, his mouth lifted just enough to let her think he was smiling as he dreamed. She wondered what he dreamed about. Her eyes drifted closed again. She'd wait a few more minutes before getting up.

When Jennifer opened her eyes again, she was alone. Glancing towards the cave's entrance, she saw by the shadows that she'd slept for another hour.

A shadow fell on the wall opposite the entrance. Immediately, Hawk's figure came into view as he made the turn into the back part of the "L" of the cave. He saw she was awake. "As soon as you're ready, we're going to the cabin."

Jennifer threw back the covers and jumped up. "I'm ready. We need to bring up more blankets," she told him.

"Didn't I keep you warm enough?"

"You know you did."

"If we hadn't been so tired, we could have warmed the whole cave up."

Jennifer didn't say anything. Truthfully, she was glad they hadn't made love last night. But, today was a new day, and she was eager to avoid yesterday's maudlin mood.

"The fire felt hot at my back, small as it was," she said.

Hawk brought her around until she faced him, lifting her so that only her toes reached the ground. He moved his hands to her behind and tilted her pelvis so that her thighs fit snugly against his. He growled at her and nipped at her neck. "I was talking about the fire we make, our bodies rubbing together." He moved her against him, tilting his pelvis against hers. The heat he spoke about licked at her nerves. Slowly, she felt it whisper through her veins, curling around each nerve until she throbbed, until the heat finally consumed her totally.

She kissed his jaw line, then the edge of his mouth. She was his and he knew it. Turning his head, his mouth captured hers. Hungrily, he kissed her until she felt her knees buckle. He held her tight, not letting her drop. Finally, he moved his lips from hers.

"You're right," he said. "We do need even more blankets. It gets cold sleeping with a blanket hog."

Jennifer laughed, the sound echoing through the cave. He had the ability to turn her into pool of pudding, where she lost her thoughts, her direction, her ability to say no. But, she also knew just as fast as the sun could disappear behind a cloud turning a warm sunny day into one that chilled the skin, her heart now filled with joyous love could flip-flop into a sour mood if she tried to resolve the problem of her assignment.

Well, she wasn't about to let her problems spoil her day. What use was there in brooding over something she couldn't change? The cards had been stacked against them from the beginning. If this were a poker game that she was going to lose, then at least she would have finished playing the game. If nothing else, she wasn't a quitter when the going got tough. Either way she looked at it, she would lose. Her career. Or Hawk. No way was she going to get to keep both. Only her career was the sure bet; not once had Hawk said he loved her.

At the cabin, Jennifer went immediately to the outhouse, then joined Hawk in the cabin at the pump, filling a pan with water. They took turns washing their face and hands while the other stood guard. "Much better," she said patting her face dry with a towel. "I feel human again."

Hawk had several blankets, a bulky jacket, and a sweater stacked on the bed already. She added another jacket and sweatshirt of hers to the stack.

He went to retrieve the radio from the refrigerator. So far, the poachers hadn't returned to the cabin, but she didn't believe for a minute that they intended on staying away forever. By the time Hawk reached the door of the cabin, she was there holding it open for him. In minutes, he had the radio set up and was talking with the rangers. Nothing had changed. In fact, the fire had turned direction and the winds were picking up.

***

As Hawk followed Jennifer back up to the cave, he wondered how soon before she'd be leaving. As much as he loved her, he wanted her safe. Besides, in reality, they were two different people; two comets passing in the galaxy. They weren't destined for anything more than what they'd already shared.

But if that were true, why did he want more? Why couldn't he keep his hands off her? *Because she's got your hormones revved up, that's why. She feels good in your arms. Face it, you've been up here so long, anyone would feel good in your arms.* Hawk tried to tell himself the relationship was temporary, but deep down he knew he was lying to himself. He also knew he wanted something beyond temporary. He wanted to spend the rest of his life with this woman. She did more than excite him; she made him laugh, she teased, she was interesting to talk to, and she challenged him. In his mind, that alone made her special.

In the short time they'd been together, he could almost believe they'd become best friends. And, she certainly felt the same way he did about the wildlife. He'd never seen anyone so upset about a dying eagle before. To Jennifer, it had been as if a close friend had died. And, there had been nothing he could do but comfort her.

Yes, he wanted her. Forever.

But, she didn't belong to him. She belonged to her career and that damnable magazine that employed her. In that way, she belonged to Edwards and it was killing him. Suddenly, he felt vulnerable. Never in his entire life, not even having his cabin ransacked and his personal belongings scattered about, had he ever felt this way. It shook him to his soles.

***

The following morning, after another call to the rangers told them nothing had changed, Hawk and Jennifer were making their usual rounds, checking on the birds, when once again they heard gunfire.

Jennifer paused. "That sounded close."

Hawk's steps stopped as well. "It was. They're in Billy Goat Pass."

Thirty minutes later, Hawk and Jennifer were on their bellies, peering over the edge of a ridge.

"My God!" Jennifer hissed.

Below them two men were bent over an assortment of dead mountain goats and sheep, examining their bodies. She heard their laughter. A faint growl drew her attention to a third man, tying a bear cub to a tree. Beyond them lay the body of the cub's mother.

Jennifer gasped. She grabbed Hawk's arm, shook him, then pointed in the direction of the dead bear. "Look!"

When Hawk didn't say anything, she glanced over at him. He wore a murderous scowl.

Her heart went out to him. She had the sensation that Hawk was seeing members of his own family murdered. If given the opportunity, she knew if Hawk could get his hands on these men, he would show them no mercy.

Jennifer twisted so she lay on one hip, and pulled her camera bag forward so she could get at her equipment. Unzipping the bag, she dragged out the camera with the telephoto lens.

Hawk glanced at her, started to say something, then clamped his jaw shut. He was going to let her shoot. He wanted the proof as badly as she did.

She hooked the camera strap around her head, then in quick succession snapped half a dozen shots of the two men examining their kill. She got a couple of pictures of the third man, with the bear cub, before the man rose to join his buddies, but she couldn't get the dead black bear into the camera frame. The bushes, rising out of the cliff just below them obscured her view. To compensate, she got up on her knees, but still kept down by hunching up in a ball. Then, she extended her body out beyond the ridge just a little bit.

There, that was better. Just a little bit more...and she'd have the picture she wanted. She edged out just an inch.

Suddenly, the earth moved under her. The ground gave way under her knees.

Jennifer gasped, dropping the camera, letting it bang against her chest as she grabbed for something to cling to. There was nothing but air.

She heard shots. In minutes, she'd be at the feet of the poachers!

More shots rang out. Bits of dirt flew around her.

Frantic, she tried to clutch the ground but kept sliding.

A hand grabbed her leg. A hard yank and she was away from the edge, pulled back with a force that knocked her teeth together. She felt the camera strap move over her head. Immediately, the strap was gone. She swallowed, realizing she wasn't going to fall after all. Her camera lay on the ground next to her. Hawk was on his feet and started to drop back down out of range.

Another shot rang out.

Hawk jerked and fell to the ground, his right hand grabbing his right thigh.

She saw blood between his fingers.

"Let's go," he growled, struggling to move away from the ledge. "Stay down," he urged.

Jennifer grabbed his left arm and pulled him along with her. Hawk pushed against the ground with his left leg, his right leg dragging, helping her.

As soon as Jennifer thought they were out of the poachers' vision, she rose to her feet and helped Hawk to his. With his left arm draped across her back and shoulders, Jennifer moved, accommodating her walk to Hawk's. Suddenly, she remembered her equipment. "My bag." She twisted her head and looked over her shoulder. Her camera and bag lay on the ground near the edge of the cliff.

"Never mind."

She tightened her grip around Hawk's waist. He was more important right now. She had to get him to safety. It was obvious he was in pain. She started forward, but he said, "Go get it."

"No, Hawk. Let's go. You're more important."

"I said, go get it. You've got the evidence we need. You want them to find us here arguing? Move!"

Jennifer hesitated, but only for a minute. He wasn't going to move until she complied. She dashed back to the precipice.

"STAY DOWN!" he hissed.

She dropped to the ground and grabbed the bag and camera. Quickly, she popped her head up, took a quick look, lowered her head, then crawled back to Hawk's side.

She stuffed the camera into the bag and slung the bag over her head and shoulder, then positioned herself under Hawk's left arm again, circling his waist with one arm and grabbing his arm that lay across her shoulders with her free hand. "They're gone."

"Damn."

They struggled for about ten feet before Hawk moaned.

"Hold it," Jennifer said.

"We've got to keep moving."

"Not at this pace."

Jennifer took a look at his leg, then unhooked her belt and pulled it out. She wrapped it around his leg just above his wound, then threaded the belt through the buckle. She pulled the belt tight. Then, pulled again.

Hawk sucked in air, then exhaled it, shakily.

"I'm sorry, Hawk. Tourniquets are a last resort, but you're not going to make it to the cave unless—"

"Let's go. Wait. I need something to soak up the blood."

He was right. The last thing they needed was a trail of blood. She imagined the men would first go to the cabin, then up here to this spot, trying to find a lead to follow.

She tore a sleeve from her shirt, then wondered how to best use the material without undoing the belt.

Hawk groped for his own belt, fumbling with it. "Stuff it down my pants," he breath heavily.

Quickly, Jennifer unzipped his pants, then pushed the material down his pant leg, undoing the belt to get the material on the wound, and then, refastening the tourniquet, quickly.

"I have a woman with her hand in my pants and I can't do anything about it," he joked.

"How does it feel?" she asked.

"Like fire."

"Can you make it?"

"Do we have a choice? I'm woozy, but I'll make it."

She rezipped his pants and they began to snake their way down the mountain, to the cave. Fear pulsed through Jennifer's veins. They were moving too slowly. At this rate, the poachers would find them. Another cold front had passed through a couple of hours earlier. At the time, they'd thought nothing of it; now, the weather threatened his survival. Though it was the middle of the day, the temperature had changed dramatically from this morning. Hawk needed shelter now or he'd go into shock.

She struggled to remember what they'd brought to the cave. She knew her duffle bag held a few first aid supplies, but would it be enough? Lord, she hoped so. If not, she'd have to go to the cabin.

Finally, she spotted the cave. "Just a few more steps, Hawk."

"Easy for you say," he breathed heavily.

Wet with perspiration, Hawk looked pale to her. Through her own clothing, she felt his wet garments. His hand felt clammy, too. She couldn't imagine how he'd managed to stay conscious and help her get him to the cave. If he'd passed out anywhere on the trail, she could have dragged him, but they'd have left a long visible trail to follow.

In the cave, she bent her knees, trying to lower him gently onto the bed, but with his weight nearly double her own, he dropped heavily, and groaned in pain.

She rolled him onto his back, found a knife and cut his jeans at the cuff. She tore the jeans up to the tourniquet, unfastened and removed the belt, then tore the pants even further, allowing adequate exposure to the wound. She had to clean the area, to see what they faced.

She threw a blanket over the rest of his body and his uninjured leg, then went to the fire. It had burned out long ago, but she looked in the can they had used to heat water. There were several inches of water left. A hand placed on the outside of the can told her the water was still warm—barely. The stones making up the fire circle were warm too.

Jennifer dipped a cloth into the can, soaking it, then wrung it wet. She felt her knuckles scrape the sharp edge of the can but ignored the pain when she cut her hand. With her lower lip caught between her teeth, she wiped at the outer edges of the wound on his leg.

Hawk moaned.

She paused, then continued, now ignoring the sounds of his pain. She had to get it cleaned. Finished, she saw his skin was already red and swollen. The bullet was still in his leg.

He needed help and fast.

She looked around for the first aid kit. Finding the box, she opened it and swore. "Damn, Hawk. Now what do I do?" There weren't many bandages, and nothing she could give him for pain. She knew she had aspirin, and more first aid supplies in her big box, but everything was back at the cabin.

She looked down at his face. Perspiration beaded on his forehead. She wiped it away with her hand. His eyes opened.

"How bad is it?"

She shook her head. "Hawk, you need help. I've got to get some supplies and get you off this mountain. I've got to radio for help."

His hand shot out, grabbing her arm. "No! Don't leave this cave."

Her eyes widened. "If you don't get help immediately, you'll die."

"You're not going. We stay here. Maybe tomorrow."

Jennifer removed his hand, then stood. "You won't last that long." She grabbed the belt and refastened it around his leg to slow the bleeding again. Then she tied a shirt around the wound, securing the bandages that covered it. She couldn't trust him to hold the bandages in place. If he lost consciousness,,,

She wouldn't think like that. He was going to be okay.

She emptied her camera bag—she'd need something to carry everything in. Hawk watched her through glazed eyes. "Jennifer, don't go."

"I'll be careful. If there's anything suspicious, I'll come right back."

Hawk leaned back into the blankets with an exhausted sigh. "Take my rifle."

"It'll slow me down. Don't worry, I won't take any risks."

She left the cave, hearing him call after her.

"Jennifer..."

CHAPTER 15

As Jennifer approached the fringes of the cabin's clearing, she slowed down, then stopped. Everything looked peaceful. Birds chattered in the trees, squirrels chased each other, circling around the trunks of the tall pines. It appeared safe.

She ran for the cabin. Still cautious, however, she ducked when she got close and peered through the window.

It was empty. She gave a sigh of relief.

Confronting the poachers was the last thing she wanted to do.

Quickly, she went to the refrigerator and grabbed the radio. By the time she was at the cabin door, she was breathing heavily.

She pushed the door open, latched it, then picked out what she needed to tend to Hawk's wound.

Every few seconds her gaze swept the windows, insuring there was still no unusual movement outside. Finished gathering everything she needed, she hooked up the radio and called, thankful when she heard Smitty's voice.

A couple moments later, she signed off, satisfied that help was on the way. Her job was to keep Hawk alive until then. Not bothering to return the radio—Hawk was more important right now—she left the cabin at a run.

Just before she reached the woods, she heard, "Get her! I want her alive!"

Not stopping, she glanced over her shoulder. The poachers—all three of them—had arrived from the far side of the clearing and had spotted her! She could only hope she'd be faster than they were.

The only question was, could she make it back to the cave without them seeing her entering it? She had to try. If it looked like they'd be able to find Hawk, then she'd have to head them away from the cave. She had no choice.

She threw the camera bag's handle over her head and shoulder as she ran.

She needed both hands to push the branches from her face.

Scrambling up the incline, she used anything she could get her hands on to help pull her along.

Huge thorns dug into her hands, but she didn't let go.

Her calf muscles screamed in agony and her lungs threatened to quit, but she continued to climb and run.

The snapping of branches and the grunts of exertion told her the men were closing in behind her.

It was imperative she gain some ground. Halfway to the cave, she knew she had to make a decision and fast. She couldn't let them get close enough to spot any trail she and Hawk might have left. Nor could she take the chance they might see her, especially in the last seconds when she entered the cave.

"I see her!"

Jennifer's heart lurched at the sound of the voice.

She knew then that she couldn't go back to the cave. But, would Hawk survive the night if she didn't return?

Not concentrating on her footing and handholds, Jennifer grabbed a branch and pulled with all her might. The branch in her hand snapped, and horrified, she felt her feet slide.

She dropped to the ground and clawed her way up, digging her feet into the hard, dry earth.

They were gaining on her!

She could hear the panting of one man directly behind her. She didn't dare look back to see where he was.

She had to keep going.

She couldn't make her directional change here.

She'd have to go right on past the cave, and hope they didn't see it or spot the path to its entrance.

She and Hawk had been so careful not to walk in the same spot each time they left the cave or returned.

Would it work?

Run girl, just keep running, she told herself. Finally up the incline, she straightened to run.

Whoever was behind her was pulling himself up the incline now. She'd never lose them.

But she had to. Hawk's survival—and hers—depended on it.

Stiff legs demanded she stop, but she continued not caring that branches slapped her in the face and tore at her clothes.

The turnoff to the cave was only twenty yards in front of her. She had to keep going.

The movements behind her told her she'd never make it. Not only could she hear the one man getting closer to her, but now she heard the other two not far behind him.

"GET DOWN!!!!!" Hawk's voice rang out sharp and clear.

She dropped immediately.

The blast of a gunshot deafened her ears.

The ear-splitting sound came again. Then it was quiet.

She twisted around and saw two of the men on the ground. They'd dropped their rifles; one clutched his skinny leg, the other his shoulder. Both were bleeding. The third man, the one with the beard, disappeared into the brush, retreating fast.

Jennifer scrambled to her feet, and ran back toward the two injured men, and grabbed the two dropped rifles. Out of the corner of her eye, she saw Hawk sink to the ground, his rifle still in his hand.

Quickly, she cocked a rifle and aimed it at the two men. She glanced at Hawk, then returned her focus to her captives. "Hawk? Are you all right?"

"I'm surprised you dropped," he gritted out between clenched teeth. "You haven't done anything I've told you to do since you've arrived."

"Till now, you haven't told me anything worth doing. What about the third guy? He's getting away."

"I heard helicopters just before you appeared. He's running right toward them."

"I don't hear anything."

"Listen."

Jennifer concentrated, listening for the familiar sound. Finally, she heard it, faintly. "You've got good ears."

"Among other things," Hawk replied cockily, then grinned.

***

Fifteen minutes later, Smitty and four rangers crashed through the underbrush. With the captured men no longer her responsibility, Jennifer lowered the rifle. Smitty, bent over and hands on his knees, gasped for breath.

Hawk laughed weakly. "First exercise you've had in years."

Smitty stood back up, his face a rosy color. He pointed to Hawk's leg. "The lady take a pot-shot at you?"

Three rangers attended to the two poachers, while the fourth went to Hawk and inspected his leg. "We'll need a litter for this one," he informed his co-workers.

"I can walk to the helicopters."

"You'll ride," Jennifer told him, handing Hawk's rifle to a ranger. "What about the third man? Did you get him?"

"We got him," one of the rangers said, his face sooty, and his jacket smelling like smoke. "We were on our way home from the fire when we heard your call. You got the whole cavalry. There's two more rangers headed back to the helicopters with him now."

Jennifer stood aside while Smitty and a ranger lifted Hawk onto a stretcher.

"I can walk," Hawk insisted.

"Enjoy the ride for once, will ya'?" Smitty turned his head back and spoke over his shoulder to Jennifer. "He's never satisfied with my driving. It's always hurry up and get me to Boise. Hurry up and get me home. Hurry up—"

"Shut up and drive, Smitty."

Smitty chuckled. "And, make you happy? No way."

Three other helicopters holding the rangers and poachers were already in the air. At Smitty's smaller helicopter, Smitty and the remaining ranger strapped Hawk and his stretcher to the outside. The interior could only hold two people and oxygen tanks and other equipment was strapped onto the other stretcher on the other side. There was no room for her. Hawk motioned for her to come to him.

Bent down, she tried to hear Hawk above the whirling blades. She stared at his mouth, so she could read his lips as he spoke, but it didn't matter what he said. She couldn't think beyond getting him immediate help.

Hawk grabbed her arm. "Promise me you'll stay until I return," he shouted.

Jennifer didn't know what to say. How could she make a promise she wasn't sure she'd keep?

Hawk squeezed her arm. "Promise."

She looked up and saw Smitty indicate he was ready to leave. She nodded at Smitty then looked back down at Hawk. Nothing was more important than getting him to the hospital. He needed medical attention, and she knew he wouldn't let Smitty leave until he had gotten her to promise. Hating herself for what she was about to do, she said, "I promise."

Hawk's eyes bore into hers. She forced herself to maintain eye contact with him. She didn't want him to doubt her for a minute. He had to believe her.

Finally he nodded, lying back on the stretcher, closed his eyes, then let her go.

She moved back, away from the helicopter and waved as Smitty gave her the thumbs up signal. Dust and sand tore through the air as the mechanical bird lifted into the sky. Jennifer squinted and turned her head away from the maelstrom. Instantly, the earth settled back down, and soon the helicopter became a dot in the sky. In a minute, they were gone from view, and then, silence returned to the mountain. It was a deafening sound to her ears.

He was gone.

Jennifer pursed her lips and stared at the horizon. She stuffed her hands into her jean pockets and stared at the ground. Digging her toe into the hard earth, she managed to loosen a stone. She leaned over, picked it up and rolled it around in her palm. Then she drew her hand back over her shoulder and threw it as far as she could. The sound of it hitting a tree reverberated in her ears and a jay screamed loudly as it flew from its perch nearby.

Now what?

It'd be a while before she could call Smitty to see how Hawk was doing. She imagined the doctors would keep him at least a week. Edwards expected her back in the office the day after tomorrow.

Why had Hawk demanded she stay? He never spoke of a future where they'd be together. If anything, he'd said he couldn't wait until she was gone. At least, he had said as much in the beginning. How he felt now was a complete mystery to her. She knew they were good together, they were companionable, and the sex was great. But, so what? Without a commitment from Hawk, what future did she have with him?

She decided to gather her equipment and other supplies from the cave and return to the cabin.

At the cave, thinking about her project, she picked up the camera and suddenly remembered what Hawk had said the first day she arrived and several times since then. The film wasn't going to leave the mountain, he'd told her. That was why he'd made her promise not to leave until he returned. He wanted to be here to make sure the film remained behind.

What other reason could there be?

Never once had he told her he loved her. To expect him to suddenly announce that he loved her now was ridiculous. She'd made a promise to Hawk, but she'd also made a promise to Beauty. She'd vowed she'd get her pictures printed.

Back at the cabin, with the first load, Jennifer noted the time and figured she'd have to wait a minimum of four hours before Smitty would be back at his office. In the meantime, she'd restore order to the cabin and make the other trips to the cave getting the rest of their supplies.

Hours later, back at the cabin, she was putting the broom away when the radio crackled.

"Whirlybird calling Lair's Den. Over."

In two steps she stood at the radio, responding to Smitty's call.

"He's had surgery to remove the bullet and is stable, but he'll be there for several days. I imagine the nurses will be celebrating when he leaves. Over."

Jennifer grinned. Easily, she pictured Hawk, aggravated and feeling helpless, which would only irritate him more. She pitied the poor nurses having to attend to him.

"That bad? Over."

"Worse. Over."

"Smitty, come and get me. Can you do it yet tonight? Over."

"Sure, but you won't be able to see him until tomorrow. Over."

"I want to leave here tonight. Over and out."

Smitty had made it all the easier for her to leave by assuming she wanted to go to the hospital. Now that she thought about it, she did want to go to the hospital. She wanted to tell Hawk she was going back to New York. She'd leave it up to him to tell her whether she was welcome to return. Hawk would be upset with her, but he'd get over it. Question was, would she ever get over him?

Quickly, she set about packing her belongings. It didn't take long as she'd never truly unpacked, living, instead, out of her suitcase. When it came to packing her shower, she hesitated. Hawk got such pleasure out of it, she decided to leave it behind. Finished, she sat down and repacked her camera bags for the trip. To lighten the load on the damaged camera bag, she removed all the film, used and unused, and put it in another bag. She checked them over, reading the labels she'd attached, making sure she had all the film. She rolled the tube of film in her hand, then froze. It read "Fuss & Feathers."

That was the day they'd picnicked, snapping pictures of each other. The day Hawk found her at the pond. The day they'd made love.

The same day Hawk asked her if she was giving up her assignment.

She loved him so much it hurt. And, what she was about to do would guarantee his hatred for her.

Why couldn't things be different?

"Dammit!" She threw the film across the room. It bounced on the table, then onto the floor, then disappeared from sight.

Whirling blades, cutting through the air, caught her attention. Smitty was here. She grabbed her packed belongings.

When the helicopter landed, she was outside, ready and waiting.

Smitty jumped from the pilot's seat, his face wearing a puzzled expression. "I thought you were going to the hospital."

"I'm going back to New York. I've got business to take care of."

"Does Hawk know?"

"Not yet."

Smitty just shrugged his shoulders. "It's not for me to interfere."

Relieved she didn't have to explain, Jennifer handed him her bags and watched as he stowed them away. Finished they climbed into their seats. "Let's go," she said.

Fastening her seat belt, Jennifer took one last look at the cabin. Then, they were in the air, moving away from the place where she'd lived—and loved—for almost two weeks.

***

The stark white halls of the hospital were silent. Visiting hours were over. As she approached the nurses' station, she walked noiselessly. The nurses were in the back room, seated around a small desk, apparently in the process of a shift change, going over the charts. She walked past the station without being detected.

Her eyes scanned the numbers on the doors as she moved silently past them. Smitty had told her Hawk's room number. 212. She found it.

The door was partially open, only a faint light coming from inside the room. Slowly, she opened the door. There were two beds in the room, Hawk was in the furthest one. The light came from the bathroom, its door only opened a crack. She stepped into the room, sliding the door back to its previous position. She didn't want anyone seeing her.

Moving slowly, she approached Hawk's bed. His eyes were closed. She noticed an IV bottle hung on the corner, its contents dripping steadily into the tube that was connected to the back of his hand, and that it was taped in place. A blood pressure cuff lay on the bedside table next to him, as did a thermometer.

Her gaze went back to Hawk. He looked pale. His chest rose up and down slowly, steadily. She wanted to touch him, but she dared not. She didn't want to wake him.

Softly, ever so softly, she spoke. "I'm leaving, Hawk. I'm going to be coming back—if you'll let me. I don't know when, but I will. I love you."

She gazed at him lovingly, longingly. He continued to sleep.

It was just as well. Maybe, by the time he was released from the hospital, she would have found a solution. She could only hope.

Just as quietly as she had arrived, she left. It wasn't until she walked through the front door that she realized there were tears on her face.

At a run, she went to the rented car that would take her to the airport, not once looking back.

***

At first, Hawk thought Jennifer was out with her camera, shooting, but minutes after he'd arrived home, he realized it wasn't so. Everything she owned, except the shower, was gone. So was she. He kicked the umbrella. It slid halfway across the room.

So much for promises made.

Angry, he limped out of the cabin, ignoring the pain both in his stitched leg and in his heart, not caring whether the door shut behind him or not. Any animal that wandered inside was welcome to anything he owned.

He slowed down, stopped, then turned around and saw the door wide open. That wasn't true. He did care. He went back, filled his canteen, gathered his usual supplies, then left the cabin again, only this time making sure the door was latched tight.

He'd been gone from the cabin only two days, and despite the doctor's warning that he shouldn't be leaving the hospital for fear of his doing further muscle damage, he'd left anyway. He was eager to see Jennifer and he wanted to check on his birds. All he had left now were the birds. Jennifer was gone. So what if it took him two hours to walk a distance that normally took half an hour.

Who was he fooling? he thought and stopped. *The birds are doing fine. It's you who needs looking after.*

Jennifer's disappearance explained why Smitty had been unusually quiet on the trip up the mountain. Smitty hadn't volunteered any information and Hawk hadn't asked. But, then, that was normal behavior for the two of them.

Why had she done it? Why had Jennifer promised she'd stay and then fled?

It had to be her project, he thought. She'd told him all along she'd get her story and pictures whether he wanted it published now or not. Well, she'd done exactly what she'd set out to do. She'd come to get pictures, she took them, and she left with them. Hadn't she told him, she would? He had thought he could outsmart her. He wondered how much information he'd told her off the record would appear in *Personality.*

He should have known better. She was just like Edwards. Deceptive and conniving. Not once had he been able to get the best of her. She'd fought him every step of the way.

No, that wasn't true. She'd fought him at first, and then they had found a peaceful compromise, even though he'd still planned to keep the film and she'd obviously planned he wouldn't take it.

Jennifer disgusted him. She'd taken advantage of him. Using his injury to her benefit. And, he'd thought she had integrity. She had lied to him. She had no intention of staying at the cabin after she'd promised him that she would.

When it came down to it, if he hadn't been injured, would he have been able to keep her from taking the film with her?

He didn't know. All he knew at this point was that she'd lied to him.

Pain ripped through his leg as he tried to climb the slight incline. "Hell," he muttered. "I can't even do my work."

Knowing the doctors were right, and that he had to let time heal his leg, Hawk turned around and retraced his steps back to the cabin. Though his leg throbbed, he refused to take a pill for the pain. He wasn't going to dull his senses, but he'd stay off his leg for a couple of days. In the process, he would become a prisoner in his home.

Isn't that what you've been all along? he questioned, as he sat down in the rocking chair. He glanced around the cabin. His self-imposed prison.

He had thought he didn't need anybody. He knew differently now. He had needed the rangers to help him with his project. He had needed Smitty to bring him his supplies. Though he hated to admit it, he wasn't as independent as he thought.

He leaned back, resting his head against the chair, and stared at the wall. What now? Despite everything, he missed Jennifer.

Telling himself he could forget her wouldn't work. He'd tried that once before with Annette. It wasn't until Jennifer's arrival that he'd finally been able to put Annette out of his mind. But, memories have a way of returning, he mused.

Memories of Jennifer would haunt him for a long time to come— like the way her hair glowed in the sunlight, the look of surprise on her face as she watched the eaglet leave its nest for the first time. The pain and sadness that she'd suffered when the injured eagle died in her arms. The way she felt beneath him when they'd made love—warm, welcoming, and soft like silk. He could hear her soft moans now as he brought her to ecstasy and—

"Enough!" Hawk leaned forward, his elbows on his knees, his head lowered. He rubbed his hands across the crown of his head, down to the back of his neck. *Enough.*

He sat back up, his eyes roaming around the room. Everywhere he looked, he saw Jennifer. The flowers—weeds actually—that she'd picked the day before they had to camp out in the cave were dead, the petals scattered on the table. She'd hung pans on the wall, next to the cupboard. It gave him more space, she claimed, plus it gave the place a homey look.

And as usual, she'd left the cabin neat and tidy. Jennifer's nesting instincts had amused him. That's why he found it unusual she'd leave something on the floor by the cupboard, underneath it actually, next to one of the legs. He frowned, recognizing the shape.

It was a roll of film. He got up, limping across the room. Picking it up, he straightened, his frown deepening as he rolled it in his palm. Did she know she left it?

He turned it around, so he could read the label. "Fuss and Feathers."

He squeezed his fingers tight around the film, holding it in his fist. He remembered their discussion about this particular roll. She was such a stickler, immediately labeling her film, so she wouldn't forget the contents.

How did this particular roll get left behind? Didn't she want it? Did it mean nothing to her now? Did he mean nothing to her?

Wasn't it obvious?

Cursing aloud, he told himself that he didn't want to know the answer.

Settling back into the rocker, he stared at the fire. He couldn't leave it alone. He'd be damned if Jennifer was going to have the last word. He'd find her, confront her, tell her what he thought, and then *he'd* be the one to say their relationship—such as it was—was over. Then and only then would he be able to return and get his life back to normal.

CHAPTER 16

Edwards laughed at her. "Honestly, Jennifer. You've got so much to learn."

Jennifer gritted her teeth. It'd done her no good to accuse Edwards of setting her up. He hadn't denied anything. And then, he told her she wasn't the first and in all likelihood she wouldn't be the last.

"I'm asking you to be reasonable," she said.

She should have known better than to reason with Edwards. He didn't know the meaning of the word. Instead of answering her, he leaned back in his chair, raised his arms and linked his fingers together placing them behind his balding head. Then he grinned at her, his thin lips appearing like a too-bright, fleshy red, angry line across his face.

"I don't have to be reasonable. Those are my photographs."

Angry, more at herself than anything, Jennifer crossed her arms under her breasts. The minute she did that, she was sorry. It drew Edwards' attention to them.

When she'd arrived in New York she had learned Edwards would be out of town for two days. It gave her time to make prints and formulate her plan.

This morning she'd been in his office for better than a quarter of an hour, trying to convince him it would be in the magazine's best interest to publish a story on the eagles, nothing more.

He had turned her down. No matter what she said, he wouldn't accommodate her.

She asked again. "What do I have to do to get you to change your mind?"

Edwards smiled at her. She noticed the smile didn't go up to his eyes. "What are you offering?"

Repulsed, she stepped back.

Edwards' eyes swept past her. He stood up, the chair crashing into the wall behind him. Jennifer noticed fear cross his face but for only a moment. Then, a lecherous smile appeared. "Well, well, well. Looks like the mighty mountain has returned to the city. We're not looking for models today, Hunter."

Jennifer spun around. Hawk's figure filled the doorway. Liquid sunshine filled her heart, and then just as quickly, dread filled her veins. He didn't look at her. Instead, he glared at Edwards. Hawk looked like a dark storm ready to spew its thunder and lightning. He'd heard their conversation.

Why had he come to New York?

Hawk came into the room, limping slightly, his eyes focused on Edwards, holding him in place much like a deer caught in the headlights of a car. It satisfied her to see Edwards' smile disappear and the look of fear reappear in his eyes. Then, as if he remembered where he was, Edwards threw out his chest and returned Hawk's stare.

Hawk continued to advance, walking around Edwards' desk, until he stood squarely in front of Edwards. Jennifer held her breath. The air, charged with electricity, frightened her. She wasn't about to get between them, but she didn't want either of them hurt. If a fight evolved, Edwards would call the authorities. She'd seen him do it before. Jennifer feared for Hawk. When it came to his eagles, he'd let nothing stand in his way.

The scene in front of her reminded her of the bighorn sheep during rutting season. Their heads bent down, they stared at one another, jockeying for an advantageous position. Finally, Hawk moved forward, forcing Edwards into his chair awkwardly. "I want those pictures," he said.

"Go to hell," Edwards sputtered.

Hawk grabbed the front of Edward's shirt, pulling him to his feet. "No, Hawk!" Jennifer cried out. "I have the pictures." For long seconds Hawk stared at Edwards, then dropped him back into his chair.

Edwards jumped to his feet, his face red. "Those photographs are company property, Jennifer."

Jennifer looked at Edwards, then at Hawk, then back to Edwards again. "No, they aren't."

"Those pictures are mine! If they leave the premises, I'll sue."

"Then you'll have to sue, because they're not here."

"If you publish those pictures, I'll be the one suing," Hawk said.

"You're a public figure, you can't sue."

"I *was* a public figure. I'm not Hawk Hunter anymore. I haven't used that name since I left New York. You're threatening to endanger an important environment project funded by the United States government. Shall we call the Secretary of the Interior?"

Edwards fumed. He turned to Jennifer. "You're fired!"

"You can't fire me because I quit." Pivoting, she walked past Hawk without looking at him and walked out the door.

Her spine was stiff, her heart raced like buffalos crossing the prairie at a run, and her skin went hot to cold, to hot again. Hawk had been following her, and she wanted him to follow her into her office.

He didn't.

What had she expected? She couldn't dwell on Hawk now; she had to get out of the building. No doubt Edwards had called security by now.

Minutes later, Jennifer was crossing the lobby and left the building, her few belongings in the briefcase she carried.

Her arm was grabbed. Immediately, she tried pulling away, expecting to see a security guard.

It was Hawk instead.

He pulled her out of the way of foot traffic, then before she could say anything, his lips were locked on hers, and she was held tight within his embrace.

"I missed you," he said.

This was the last thing she expected him to say. "I...I don't understand."

"I love you Jennifer. I didn't know how much until after you were gone."

"But my assignment—"

"Edwards is history."

"No, with *Wildlife and Wilderness.*"

"I saw Sam Wilkerson this morning. He said you and he arranged the article's publication to coincide with the publication of my book. Why did you do that?"

"When I learned that Edwards had no control over Sam, and that Sam was excited about my work—and wants more—it was the only thing I could do. I never wanted to hurt your project, only enhance it."

"It will. I love you Jennifer. His mouth covered hers, caressing her lips from side to side. Slowly, Jennifer felt the tense coil that'd been curled tightly within her stomach ease.

She'd missed him so much.

Her hands snaked around Hawk's neck, one hand going up to his head, her fingers entangling in his dark hair. His mouth followed an invisible path from the corner of her mouth to her ear, where he nibbled on her lobe. "I missed you, Jennifer. Don't ever leave me."

"I won't. Ever again."

EPILOGUE

A diver splashed water onto the heated cement surrounding the pool. Huge red-and-white striped tents canopied the table and chairs where many of the guests sat, watching the younger generation frolic in the sun. The entire back yard was decorated in red, white, and blue balloons. Miniature flags, serving as centerpieces, fluttered in the mild breeze. Later that night fireworks would put the finishing touches on the day's celebration of the Fourth of July.

"Jennifer!"

Feeling awkward with her rounded shape, Jennifer speared a meatball, then looked around for the woman who'd called her name. An elderly woman waved and approached. Jennifer smiled. "Mrs. Washington," she said, embracing the woman.

"Jennifer, it's wonderful seeing you again. It's been two years since your marriage. Seems the holidays are the only time you come home anymore."

"Mother wouldn't have it any other way," Jennifer said, smiling when her mother's friend laughed.

"Where are you living now?"

"Hawk and I built a house in Connecticut. Hawk has his office where he writes and I have my darkroom."

"Your book on mountain goats was wonderful. And the piece you did on poachers was extremely powerful. Especially the pictures of that poor dead eagle."

"Thank you. I think Hawk did a wonderful job on the article."

"He most certainly did. I understand you were instrumental in sending those awful men to prison. How dreadful that poor ranger was killed. At any rate, you look wonderful. You're positively glowing."

"I love what I'm doing. Hawk and I travel, do our own research, then go home and put the books together. Of course, we still try to spend a month or more at the cabin in Idaho during the summer."

"How are his eagles?"

"Thriving, I'm happy to say."

Mrs. Washington admired Jennifer's not-so-trim figure. "And when's the baby due?"

"Early September."

"And, that handsome husband of yours, did you bring him along?"

"She most certainly did," Hawk said, from behind Jennifer, surprising both women.

Jennifer twisted her head around and accepted his kiss on the cheek.

"Excuse me, ma'am, but I need to kidnap my wife for a few minutes. It's regarding our new book."

"Certainly," Mrs. Washington said.

Jennifer excused herself, then allowed Hawk to lead her away. "Where are you taking me?"

Hawk moved through the crowded house, working his way to the conservatory. "Remember how you've always said it'd be a cold day when your mother would accept the fact you were serious about your work?"

Jennifer rolled her eyes. "Yes. She nearly fainted when I told her I was pregnant and intended to stick to our elephant safari."

Hands on Jennifer's shoulders, Hawk pushed her ahead of him through the doorway, then into the palm trees, nearby.

Jennifer looked at him with a puzzled expression. "So?"

His voice lowered, he said, "I think that cold day has arrived even if it's only ninety degrees in the shade." He pointed through the palms.

Peering through the greenery, she saw a circle of people. Only one woman spoke. Her mother. "Jennifer's an accomplished photographer. She's always had that wonderful gift to capture animals on film. I'm so proud of her work. And—"

Hawk whispered in her ear. "And you said she'd never accept your work."

"Oh, it wasn't my publishing books that won her—it was you. You have this way about you," she whispered back. "Did I ever tell you about your aura?"

Hawk nuzzled her neck, his arms wrapped around her girth, his hands sensually rubbing her swollen belly.

"I'd like to have my way with you now, aura or not."

"Now?" Jennifer croaked. "Here? In the palms?"

Hawk chuckled. "All right. Later."

Jennifer smiled and heard her mother say, "Jennifer tells me the next project is going to be baby animals." Everyone listening murmured their approval. "So appropriate, I think," her mother continued.

"I agree," he murmured softly against her ear. "Happy Fourth of July."

She covered his hands with hers, turned in his arms, and kissed him soundly.

ABOUT THE AUTHOR

Diana Stout, MFA, Ph.D. is an award-winning screenwriter, author, and former English professor, whose writing led her into academic teaching. Her students would say, "She smiles when she talks about writing." Published in multiple genres, Stout has written three romance novels, published magazine articles and short stories, is a former magazine and newspaper columnist, optioned a Hollywood screenplay, and had several short plays produced in New York city. She is a contest judge for screenwriting organizations and enjoys helping other writers learn the craft. When not writing, she enjoys reading, watching movies, jigsaw puzzles, and visiting family and friends.

OTHER TITLES

Grendel's Mother

Tomorrow's Wishes

New Beginnings

Shattered Dreams #1 Laurel Ridge novella series

Maggie's Story

The Super Simple Easy Basic Cookbook

FOLLOW DIANA STOUT

Sharpened Pencils Productions:

http://sharpenedpencilsproductions.com

Only for the Brave – about writing: http://wryterinwonderland.com

Behind the Scenes – of the life of a writer: http://dianastout.net

Into the Core – paranormal experiences: http://dianastout.com

Facebook author page: www.facebook.com/writerDianaStout

Twitter: ScreenWryter13